Road to the Sea

Road to the Sea

Tim Schell

Serving House Books

Road to the Sea

ISBN: 978-0-9971010-8-9

Serving House Books logo by Barry Lereng Wilmont

Cover photo: PhotoSky © 123RF Stock Photo

Author photo by Sachiko Schell

Published by Serving House Books, LLC
Copenhagen, Denmark and Florham Park, NJ

www.servinghousebooks.com

Member of the Independant Book Publishers Association

First Serving House Books Edition 2016

A section of this book previously appeared in *Ploughshares*.

For Sachiko

Novels by Tim Schell

The Drums of Africa
The Memoir of Jake Weedsong

Textbook by Tim Schell and Jeff Knorr

Mooring Against the Tide: Writing Fiction and Poetry

Anthology edited by Tim Schell and Jeff Knorr

A Writer's Country

PART ONE

It was a long road which he walked, and as it was the end of the dry season it was hot and dusty, and the heat rose from the orange laterite soil in simmered waves. Along the road to Boda there were palm trees and ebony and mango and papaya trees, and sometimes, near a small village, there were orange and grapefruit trees, but mostly it was just thick, green jungle wherein the pygmies hunted for antelope and boar and sometimes the forest elephant.

He walked because his motorcycle had broken down again and this time he could not fix it and it would not start. He was tired of trying to repair the old Yamaha and in anger he pushed it in the ditch and removed the leather bag strapped to the seat, and he carried the bag in his right hand and walked, and then in his left hand and he walked, ever moving toward the village of Boda that was far away but not so far away as he thought.

Passing through the small villages that did not have names, he ignored the black children who shouted *moonju* at him, small children and big children, all with distended stomachs protruding like the drunken bellies of mirth that belied an apparent satiety. He stopped and rested at the side of the road where an old woman sat in the shade of a mango tree before a ten-liter jug of milky palm wine, and he bought a tin cupful for ten francs and drank the bitter juice quickly, wiped his mouth with the back of his hand, and he thanked her before walking on as the naked children watched in his wake.

The village of Boda was more than a village but less than a town. It was at a junction two hundred kilometers south of Bangui, the capital of the central African nation, and he walked to Boda now because there was a young African woman there in jail. He had known her in Bangui when she worked as a whore and he knew the chief of police in Boda from his friend in Bangui who had been connected with the last government, and now he only wanted to help her out of jail; he at least owed her that.

Her name was Mari.

Mari was from Kisangani in Zaire, the Kisangani that was once Stanleyville, and she was a whore and so was her sister, and they were good and kind and pretty, and he once lived with them and the sister's two children, Roger and Mari. He used to send Roger, who was three years old, to the bar with a thousand-franc note and Roger would carry the two large bottles of Mocaf beer back to the house where he sat on the shaded veranda listening to the Lingala music of Zaire on the black Phillips portable radio, and little Roger always had the correct change.

But he had quit them as he had quit his last job and now he was working for the United Nations building schools out of concrete block, the cement coming only in the rainy season when the barges from Brazzaville could traverse the rocky Ubangui River after having plied the wide expanse of The Congo that was like a sinewy sea. Now it was the end of the dry season and there had been no cement for too long, and he had the time and the inclination to go to Boda to help Mari because he had once thought he loved her and that was when he thought it possible to love.

His name was Jack Burke and he was young and American. He had been in the country for three years by then, his first year with the Peace Corps before the Peace Corps pulled out because of Emperor Bokassa's massacre of several hundred students who had been on strike because they could not afford the school uniforms that the Emperor demanded they buy. When the French Foreign Legion came in with guns and trucks and helicopters, the old government was newly restored, and Jack stayed on because he liked Africa and its lack of obligations. To Jack, Africa was a floating continent apart from the rest of the world, a place in between where one could live day to day and it was wide open and there were no walls. It was a place of escape where an unrequited love could be forgotten. A hundred years before him, Africa was a continent to run away to, a land without a past, a land without a future, a land of final escape.

Jack was twenty-five and was tall and strong from basketball and running, and he had come to Africa young and looking for escape and adventure, but now, after only three years, he was much, much older than he should have been. He had heard that for each year one lived in the tropics a year of life was lost, but it was as if he had been in this tropical jungle all his life now: he had seen too much hunger, too much death, and he no longer had the reckless humor that should have been his by rite of youth, the humor that had once been his, a humor he had owned and flaunted until he was twenty-two when all his hopes and all his optimism had been dashed when he found Karen, with whom he was engaged, to be less than faithful. He had left the states for change and now a country had changed him. Or was it time that had done this to him? Physically, he was still tall and handsome with a chiseled chin, black hair always neatly cut above his ears, but his brown eyes had faded, the life of them bleached pale by the heat of the sun.

Jack could hear the truck before it was close enough for the driver to see him, and it pulled to a stop next to where he walked. The driver's helper, who stood on the back bumper of the old Mercedes diesel behind the bed crowded with passengers, asked Jack if he wanted a ride. *Dix francs per kilometre*, he said. Jack climbed up and the women moved over and the chickens and goats stank and there was the smell of sweat of the two dozen bodies riding in the back of the *voiture en occasion*. The boy on the back blew his whistle and the driver put the truck in gear.

The truck stopped in every little village between and passengers climbed off and unloaded boxes and bags, and passengers climbed on and loaded bags and boxes, and the driver was a ladies' man who spoke to every woman he encountered in the small, thatched adobe villages where chickens pecked the barren earth before the squalid huts of adobe and thatch that lined the road. The driver spoke to these women with a rich, catholic confidence, and the village women who talked to the driver did so in awe because here was a man who traveled and to travel by truck was a magical freedom that could not be readily understood. There was a world down that dusty road beyond the village border and because these women had not been there, it held all the secret promises that could never be taken away.

When the truck drove off from every little village, the naked children would run behind laughing and shouting until they could run no more, and then they would just stand in the swirl of dust scratching at the lice in their matted hair, watching as the truck disappeared in the distance that had no meaning to them because everything they knew was spread from one end of the village to the other; beyond that was only the trudge to the creek for water, the hike in the forest for firewood, and the trek to the fields to harvest the manioc roots that grew gnarled and twisted like tumors in the hard laterite soil. The road held distance and in distance were the dreams of every child and the dreams were as fevered as those of malaria when there was no quinine to rein them in. Something was better out there and that thing was as amorphous as the clouds that passed freely overhead. Still, whatever it was that was engulfed in distance, it had to be better than the proximity of hunger and disease, the death marked by the nocturnal beating of the funeral drums, a perennial pounding of darkness into night. If the drums were to never beat again, then that meant everyone had finally died.

It was noisy in the back of the truck with the whine of the engine and the squawk of the chickens and the bleat of the goats and the women shouting gossip, and only the men were quiet, eyes closed, huddled with heavy hangovers. The road was rough and pot-holed and the driver hit each bump with equanimity and constant speed, and the passengers jarred into each other and the wheel-well gnawed at Jack's back. The stench of human sweat and goat urine was strong, and Jack was nauseous as the goats shit pellets in measured intervals. Jack felt locked in and he could only close his eyes and imagine open space, pretending he was anywhere but where he was; he thought that if he could imagine time had stopped, he would only be confined in this truck for an instant and that when the truck stopped, time could resume and he would again be free, free to move on his own, to get drunk if he wished to, as drunk as he liked with no one to care because he was alone and the Africans would not judge him, especially if he bought them beer.

A truck approached from the other direction and the two drivers honked and refused to move out of the other's path until the last possible moment of decision when both drivers slightly veered on guard for individual machismo. The trucks came together with only a meter of air between, and then the passengers held handkerchiefs to their noses and mouths because the dust of the road hung suspended for several kilometers, sticking to their sweaty skin, but nobody complained because everyone was traveling to some place better from some place worse, places that the village children could not conceive of. Just to be traveling was hope. Physical motion was the ephemeral escape from despair.

Only Jack knew better. Hope itself was a falsehood; hope meant a future, and Jack had had a future planned with Karen and then Karen had taken it all away. No, hope was a lie. If you had to have hope, Jack thought, you were not now alive: you were living in a future that was only a dream like betting you'd draw to the inside straight, and even if you did, there would always be someone at the table who would flush out.

He had loved Karen. They were to be married in July three years before. In March, however, he learned of her affair with her professor, a pedantic Modernist scholar recently tenured, and when he confronted Karen at dinner during spring break, she admitted to everything saying she was sorry, but she thought she was in love, and that, oh, she was so very sorry, she hadn't wanted to hurt him, *Oh, Jack, I am so sorry, I never meant for this to happen, I never meant to hurt you...*

Jack had gone to his office when classes resumed. He found him, Dr. William Johnson, sitting at his desk. "You're Bill Johnson?" he had said as he walked into his office and stood across the desk from him where the professor looked up from a pile of papers in surprise.

"No. William. Dr. Johnson to you."

"Well, fuck you, Bill. Billy. You little motherfucker." Jack reached across the desk and grabbed his tie with his left hand, and with his right he swung and clocked him, his glasses broken, his face a mess of blood. He turned and walked out of his office, and at that moment he felt like he had accomplished something important, that this revenge had set matters straight. At the time, he didn't understand that such satisfaction was both otiose and ephemeral and that it in no way mitigated the pain of having been cuckolded by a woman he thought had loved him.

He was threatened with expulsion, but the professor's own dalliance with a student was Jack's hole card, and the matter was dropped and Jack finished the semester and graduated in despair.

When the truck finally stopped at the market in Boda, everyone climbed out of the bed, even the passengers who were continuing to Carnot where the diamonds were mined. Those who were staying paid the driver's helper and dragged their cloth bundles from the back of the truck and stacked them on the side of the road above the ditch where the water would rage during the *saison des pluies*, and those who were going on stood and stretched their legs and some of these passengers bought peanuts and *mischwee*—strips of barbecued beef in a peanut butter sauce—and sodas and beer and palm wine from the vendors of the market who were setting up their stalls again in the angled light of late afternoon after siesta. The light was burnt orange as the sun was setting down over the far reaches of jungle, and there was laughter in the market now as Jack climbed down and paid his fare.

This market was like every African market, a vortex of commerce that swirled twice each day with women dressed in blasts of colored saris as they sat before concrete slabs laden with their fruits and vegetables—oranges, papayas, lemons and limes, potatoes, okra, lettuce and manioc roots that reeked of the cyanide they contained—and eggs and live chickens that squawked in their baskets, and fish and eel and carcasses of wild game—monkey and antelope and snake—and amid this cacophony of commerce barefoot children ran through the crowd singing and laughing and shouting. Wood smoke from the coffee fires and from the metal drums on which the meat was cooked hung languidly in the air, reluctant to rise, and the smells of barbecued goat and boiling coffee mingled in the air with the chatter of gossip that itself was a commodity to be shared. Holding all this in, encircling this activity like a roughly hewn fence, were the Arab stalls, ramshackle huts of cardboard and wood with roofs of corrugated iron under which the Arabs in their white robes and white cotton hats sat behind the counters selling cloth by the yard and batteries and flashlights and radios and shirts and pants—anything that was not grown from the hard African ground.

Jack stopped at the bar across the street from the market. He ordered beer and sat at a rickety table on the dirt floor and drank the warm beer that tasted bitter of hops but that washed away the dust on the back of his throat. It was early and the bar was empty. The woman who sat behind the bar did not hide her staring and Jack ignored her and drank another beer until the sun disappeared over the border far to the west, sinking into the sea that lapped at the shores of Cameroon.

The market was in the center of town as the markets always were, and women were making fires to boil coffee for the second time that day as children gathered under the one street light in the center of town. There must have been diesel fuel in Boda because the street light was on and children were reading tattered school books under the white glow while others were gathering the termites that had been drawn to the light where they now flew as if the light were the source of their food.

Jack stopped under the light and asked a boy where the Catholic mission was. *Ou est la mission?* he said. The boy stood from where he sat on a stump and he was as tall as Jack and he smiled and said he would take him to the mission. The children giggled and a girl grabbed a termite out of the air and asked Jack if he were hungry and would he eat it. Jack smiled and took the termite from her hands and put it in his mouth. It fluttered and tickled the roof of his mouth until he bit it in half and he could taste the juice on his tongue, acrid, bitter, and he swallowed with sanctimonious pride. The children laughed and as the tall boy led Jack down a dusty dirt street that had not felt rain in six months, the children continued their gathering of termites, still talking about the funny face the white man had made when he had eaten the termite. They laughed and laughed and talked about that for some time, and then it was late and they went to their thatched homes to go to sleep on the dirt floors next to their brothers and sisters, sleeping children lined up like so many corpses on the cold concrete slabs of a morgue.

At the end of the gravel drive that led to the Catholic mission on the hill above a coffee plantation overlooking the town of Boda, Jack thanked the boy and offered him some money, but the boy refused it and told him it had been his pleasure to guide him to the mission. Jack stuffed a five-hundred franc note into the boy's pants' pocket and turned and walked up the drive and then up the stairs to the porch of the concrete house that stood like a mansion above the coffee fields that stretched down the hill like green carpets lit now by the white light of the moon. Standing on the porch, Jack could hear the hum of the generator that fueled the yellow light that shined through the opened shutters.

A young woman answered the door, and before Jack could speak, she looked him up and down and said in French, "Another young Frenchman who needs a bed?"

"*Mais non. Je suis American.*"

"I should have known from your dress," she replied in English. "But you still need a bed."

It turned out that this was not a Catholic mission at all, but a Baptist mission of Americans and Jack was disappointed because he didn't like the American Baptists, but it was late and he was tired and he needed a place to stay. The young woman who answered the door had an American southern accent when she spoke English, and with some knitting in her hands she appraised Jack as he stood in the light from the open door.

"Yes. Sorry to bother you. Do you have a place I could stay?"

"Yes."

"Thank you."

She frowned.

"All right, then. Come around the back."

She went back inside and closed the door behind her. Jack walked around the house and the girl was waiting on the back porch without the knitting and Jack thought that she was of an indeterminate age between that of a girl and that of a woman, a dubious time when the transition to womanhood could only be marked by the act of having had sex. She wore a blue cotton dress and held a kerosene lantern in her hand. Jack thought she looked pretty in the amber light, and he thought she must be the daughter of the missionaries because she was young and he felt a little sorry for her because he did not like Baptists and at her young age she did not have a choice.

She could not have been more than twenty.

"This way," she said.

Jack followed her to an outbuilding across the dirt yard behind the house. She handed him the lantern and unlocked the door. When she opened it, it was like opening an oven door, the heat wafting out into the relative cool of evening.

"There are beds inside. There is a spigot behind the church." She pointed toward another building across the yard and Jack could just make it out in the dark.

"Thank you." Jack nodded.

"Have you eaten?"

Jack looked at her eyes and could see they were earnest and matter of fact and wide open with nothing to hide because there were no questions that could not be answered, and to be as sure as she seemed, Jack felt, was due to her youth and religion and maybe, too, because she was in Africa where no one would question her conviction. Maybe it was Africa that had made her so cold, Jack thought, cold to a fellow American, cold because he was not a Baptist as was she. "No, but I don't want you to go to any trouble."

"You're hungry but you don't want to eat with Baptists."

"No, that's not true. I just don't want you to go to any trouble."

"Trouble? We've had trouble before."

"No, what I meant was..."

"I know and I already have gone to trouble. You interrupted my knitting. Wash up and come up to the house. I'll fix you something to eat." Without waiting for an answer, she turned and walked away.

Jack thanked her again but not so she could hear and he entered the outbuilding. It had a concrete floor and a corrugated iron roof, and four beds with metal frames were lined up like beds in a barracks and each had a mosquito net hanging above it. There was a neat pile of sheets and blankets at the foot of each bed. The beds themselves seemed eager for guests and Jack wondered if this was how the Baptists sucked you in: a warm bed, a hot meal, and then the hand down your throat groping for your soul. Jack set the lantern down next to the black Bible on the table, around which stood four chairs, and he set his duffle bag down at the foot of the bed nearest the door before opening the shutters to the cool evening air.

Outside he stripped down to his shorts and splashed water on his body from the spigot, and he soaped up and rinsed again. The water was cool and refreshing after the motorcycle ride and then the walk along the dusty road and then the cramped ride in the bed of the truck, and now the water rinsed away those memories, and he felt clean and no longer so tired and dirty.

He dressed in clean clothes, blue jeans and a plaid shirt of cotton. Back in the outbuilding, he took out a bottle of White Horse Scotch and he took a sip because he knew there would be no alcohol in the Baptist mission. That was one of the many reasons, or at least several reasons, he preferred the Catholic missionaries. He hated the Baptists because of his foster father who was a Baptist minister, a violent son of a bitch who had viciously abused him, an obese man clad in a wrinkled gray suit who on Sundays would preach of the sanctity of the church in its efforts to convert the heathen masses on distant continents, and on Mondays the abuse would resume once again. That man could be here in this mission,

17

Jack thought, and as long as he could convert lost souls, each conversion paving his own road to heaven, he would not give a good god damn if they were malnourished and hungry and sick with malaria or dysentery or gout.

Jack preferred the Catholic missionaries because they did practical and important work like drilling wells for clean water, but he admired them mostly because they had tricks to wash away guilt as if it were dirt on the skin, the magic of confession like a hot shower after being out in the mud all day long. That, Jack felt, was the best trick of all.

He took one more sip of the Scotch, a long one, spilling a little that dripped down his chin and onto his shirt, and the Scotch warmed the back of his throat and the inside of his chest, and he thought it sad that there were those who did not drink at all because they would never know the wonder of the first real drink of the day, especially the magical dash of whiskey.

He knocked on the back door and the young woman appeared wearing an apron embroidered with red apples. She seemed to be as out of place in Central Africa as the apples themselves; she seemed young and fresh and Jack wondered if it were religion that preserved her because Africa plucked the youth out of those just born. Africa could do that with its life-sucking dysentery, malaria, filariasis and gout, with the snakes that lurked everywhere there was anywhere to hide. Looking at her, Jack resented her youth. It was something that did not belong here, not if you were in Africa for long. In Africa, youth was like a flower plucked and placed in a vase of cold water: it would age as quickly as the water warmed.

Jack followed her into the kitchen where a young African woman was knitting at the table. She looked up at Jack and in French Jack said hello, and she returned the greeting before looking back down at her knitting.

The young missionary said something to her in Sango, and the woman gathered up her yarn and stood, saying good night before going out the door Jack had just come through.

"What was she making?" Jack asked, still standing next to the table as she stood with her back to him ladling stew into a bowl.

"Uniforms for the children."

"Uniforms?" Jack said, sitting down at the table without invitation.

"Yes, for our school. That's what we were doing when you arrived." She looked down the hall into the living room where her parents sat. "That's what we do every night, Felicite and I."

He could smell the warmth of food cooking on the gas stove and it made him hungry. The kitchen was light and she apologized that the outbuilding was not yet wired, and Jack could hear the generator humming outside.

She set a plate of stew before him and sat down across from him. Through the open door and down the hall into the living room, Jack could see a man reading the Bible and a woman knitting, and he knew they were her parents. He had mixed feelings about their hospitality as they did not come to greet him, but they were Baptists so he did not care.

"You've been drinking," she said.

"Just a sip of Scotch."

"I could smell it when you walked in."

"Sorry."

"If my father knew, he would make you dump it out if you were to stay here."

"Sorry. And you?"

"I don't care if you drink one way or the other. That's your business."

Taking a bite, Jack said, "It's good."

"It's fresh today. There's pie, too."

Jack ate and mopped the thick, brown sauce with a piece of white bread with a heavy brown crust, and she watched him eat and offered him more which he accepted.

"Oh, I'm sorry. I forgot. Would you like something to drink?" She seemed nervous now and this amused Jack and put him at ease—it was almost as if she were an actress and had forgotten she was supposed to be tough and cold.

"Please," Jack said, his mouth still full. "Thank you."

"Is water okay? We've run out of milk."

"Fine."

She paused as if thinking of her next line before saying, "The goats are not as regular as a milkman."

19

"No, I suppose not." Jack guessed that this was a well-practiced phrase, most likely that of her father's.

She brought him a glass of water and sat down across the table from him again. In the light of the kitchen, she looked even younger than before, maybe eighteen or nineteen, and had light brown hair cut off at the shoulders and she was slim. Jack thought she was pretty, but seeing her beauty made Jack feel sorry for her again because she was a Baptist missionary in Africa and he thought she would never have her beauty truly appreciated in love.

"I'm sorry," Jack said. "I haven't introduced myself. I'm Jack Burke."

"I'm Faith."

She reached her hand across the table and Jack wiped his hands with the napkin before shaking hers. Her wrist was thin and her hand was delicate and despite the heat it was cool to the touch, fresh like butter almost.

"Faith's a good name for a missionary, I guess," Jack said before taking another bite.

"*Doubt* might be better." She looked down the hall.

Jack looked up from his food. "Why do you say that?"

"Forget it. It was just a joke."

Jack looked at her and then resumed eating. He took big spoonfuls of the stew. "Why did you think I was French?"

"What?"

"When I knocked on the door."

"Oh. I don't know. Our last visitor was French."

"Not a missionary."

She laughed, but it was devoid of mirth. "No, no. He was not a missionary. He was a journalist with *Jeune Afrique*."

"Doing a story on young American missionaries."

"He could now."

"What?"

"No. A story on deforestation. And what about you? What are you doing in Boda?"

Jack picked up the tall glass of water and took a long drink and set it down and the generator hiccuped some bad diesel and the lights dimmed before coming back on bright.

"I'm here to help a friend."

"An American?"

"No. An African."

"Is he in some kind of trouble?"

"She."

"She, then."

"Well, it's a long story, but she's in jail and it's really no fault of her own."

"People get into trouble through no fault of their own all the time."

"Well, that's what happened to her."

Faith stood and went to the refrigerator next to the sink and Jack could see a faint blue wave of heat emanate from the glass chimney of the refrigerator as the kerosene burned. Faith took out some pie and Jack thought this was just like being out in eastern Oregon on the ranch where they hunted pheasant and chukar and quail. She set a piece of apple pie before him, and the kitchen was homey and nice, and somehow it seemed sad to Jack that this American girl, young and pretty, was in this kitchen so far away from everywhere where time mattered. It seemed to Jack that not only Faith, but this entire house and family was in the wrong place, that it should have been set outside some little town in rural America. But it did not belong here in Africa, Jack thought. Besides, Africa had its own Gods and Jack resented this family for bringing theirs here, for their knitting uniforms the children would have to wear, for their thinking that if you dressed up the children their God would fit in here as neatly as it fit in back in the south, and he thought that was just like Americans to travel to new countries and paint them with faint hues of red, white and blue, hoping the colors would take hold and that the people would be thankful. No, Jack thought, these people were anachronisms.

After taking a bite, he said, "It's good. Thanks."

"Where're you from?"

"You mean in the states?"

"No, here."

"Bangui."

"What do you do?"

"Build schools. With the U.N." He took another bite of the pie and wiped his mouth with the cloth napkin. He took a drink of water.

"You like it?" Faith had her elbows on the table, her hands clasped, her chin resting on her hands.

"Some. It's okay. It's a job." He drank the water and wished he could have a cigarette.

"And in the states?"

"Oregon."

"I'm from Alabama."

"Crimson Tide. Never been down there. How long have you been here?"

She told him that she had been in Boda all her life except for the first year after she was born, and Jack thought it curious that she had the Alabama drawl growing up here in Africa, but she said she went to Alabama every year for two months where they stayed with her mother's sister, but that her work and her parents' work was here in Africa and always had been.

"So you like the missionary work, I suppose."

She thought about that for a moment. "Sometimes. I'd like to travel some, though."

Jack looked through the door down the hall to the living room where her parents sat, but they didn't seem to hear, and Jack wondered about them.

"I imagine it could get pretty boring here."

"No, not at all." She looked down the hall, then looked back at Jack and smiled. "Well, sometimes. I read a lot, though. The classics, mostly. I read Proust in French."

"I didn't mean anything. I just mean being young and pretty, you probably miss social events. Parties and stuff. There's more to life than books." He forked the last bite of pie.

She blushed and reached for his plate and took it to the sink and with her back to him, ran water over the plate.

"You're not that much older than me," she said.

"No. Twenty-five."

She washed the dishes and placed them in a rack by the sink, and Jack watched her from behind.

22

"I suppose you're a Catholic?" she said.

Jack laughed at that and she turned around and looked at him.

"What's so funny about that?"

"Nothing at all, really. It's just that nobody I know has ever asked me if I were a Catholic."

"If they knew you, they wouldn't have to ask."

Jack laughed again. "Yes, you're right. Anyway, I'm not a Catholic. I'm not much of anything at all, really."

She came back to the table and sat down across from him where she had been sitting before and she sat straight up and her posture was perfect like she had taken a lesson on how to sit in a chair. "You mean you're not any religion? What were you raised as?"

"For a while a Lutheran and for another while a Baptist."

"And you're no longer a Baptist?"

"Nope. Call me a secular, non-sectarian humanist, I guess is the best description I can come up with."

"And what is that?" She furled her eyebrows, leaned forward, put her elbows on the table and cradled her chin in her hands.

"You got me. When I was in college, I thought I was an existentialist, but I don't know what that is either."

She laughed, a short, light laugh like a whisper. "You and Jean-Paul Sartre. A dubious pair."

"What?"

"Just another confused existentialist. People search and search for meaning when it's usually right before them."

"Right. Right before them."

She cradled her chin in her hands. "How is it you were raised in two religions?"

"Different foster homes. The first was Lutheran. The second, Baptist. The father was a minister." He frowned. "A terrible man."

"How terrible?"

He thought about this and then said that "he was just terrible. That's all."

He wiped his mouth with a napkin, and then he looked down the hall at her mother and her father.

23

"Say, you wouldn't have any books I could borrow, would you?"

"No, not with me."

"Oh. I just thought you might. It's so hard to get good books here. My relatives send them, but they're not always what I like to read."

"What do you like?"

"Oh, I like everything."

"Except for what your relatives send you."

"Well, they send books mostly on religion and we have plenty of those."

"I see."

"I like adventures and romances, and as I said, the classics. I just finished *The Guermantes Way*."

"The what?"

"*The Guermantes Way*. Proust. In French. The Frenchman, our last visitor, left it for me. It's the third section of *Remembrances of Things Past*."

"Maybe when I'm back in Bangui I could send you some books."

"I'd appreciate that very much."

Jack stood and pushing the chair back to the table, thanked her for the dinner, turned down her offer of more pie, said good night and walked out into the dark. She stood in the open doorway and watched him cross the dark yard to the outbuilding, a young silhouette against the outpouring of yellow light behind her.

He sat on the porch of the outbuilding and lit a cigarette, and he looked up at the stars and smoked. The funeral drums were beating on the night, a steady hollow sound echoing the darkness, and he thought about just how he could help Mari when he knew she hadn't killed the Frenchman in Bangui, but that he had done it and would do it again, but there was no way he was going to go to jail for killing a man who deserved to die, a son of a bitch who had raped both Mari and her sister one night three weeks before, a *patron* of a coffee plantation near Boda. Jack could still feel the push of the knife into the man's fat belly, he could still hear his guttural cries, he could still feel the sticky warm blood on his hand and wrist and arm as the man struggled. In a red rage as he jabbed with the

24

knife, he was stabbing two men, this French rapist and his former foster father, killing them both at the same time.

Lying back now on the concrete, blowing smoke at the black sky of night interrupted by a myriad of stars, Jack thought of how he had pulled the knife back out and in a rage, jabbed him again and again and again and again, until the cries stopped and there was blood all over the concrete floor of Mari's house and how Roger and the little girl Mari, named after her aunt, huddled in the corner with their arms around each other, quiet as two terrified children could be.

Three weeks later Mari had gone to Carnot on a *voiture en occasion* to visit a Monsieur Duvalier, and when the truck stopped at the barrier before Boda and the passengers got down from the truck to show their papers to the gendarme in the hut by the barrier, Mari had shown hers and she was arrested. Mari wired her sister and her sister found Jack and told him of the arrest and how three children found the body of the fat white man with a dozen vents in his chest and belly, found him with the vultures competing for his flesh in the dump at *Kilometre Cinq* in Bangui, and Jack thought himself stupid for having disposed of the body there. It had been a mistake, he thought, the last one he would make.

Later that night, he woke from a dream when it was still dark and he could not go back to sleep. He heard the call of the roosters and he rolled over in bed and tried to forget the dream and go back to sleep, but he could do neither. He dreamed that he had been arrested and that the judge was Emperor Bokassa and that Bokassa had laughed at him when Jack said it was in self-defense that he had killed the Frenchman. Then Bokassa stood and shook his ebony cane at Jack and said that he would be imprisoned in Ngaragba Central Prison for life because no one would murder Frenchmen in his country. Jack woke up when he was being escorted in chains from the court room.

No one was up at the mission when Jack walked down the hill to the market square in the darkness of false dawn. The market was still waking up and Jack sat down on a bench by a fire and had a cup of bitter coffee sweetened by sugared canned milk, and he sat there in the cool of the morning, the fire warm on his legs, and he smoked and drank three tin cups of the coffee, and he ate a couple of the greasy doughnuts the old woman sizzled in the yellow palm oil on the fire. The sun rose above the horizon, and the shadows of the palm trees surrounding the market were long and stretched west toward Cameroon. Jack worked on making up his mind on how he had to do what he had to do, and he thought that by now he'd at least have a plan, but he didn't. He only knew that Mari had not told the police that he had been the killer and that made him smile; he thought that if he had still been living with her this never would have happened, but instead he had moved out of her house and on that Sunday night had gone to see her and he had heard the screams inside and now there was no going back, but he would have to get Mari out of jail because she had done nothing wrong. She had been raped.

He paid for the coffee and the doughnuts and stopped at an Arab stall and bought a pack of Siats, and he lit one and walked to the police station, a white stucco building with tall palm trees growing beside it and a mango tree where children were throwing rocks in an effort to knock down some of the fruit that wasn't yet ripe.

As Jack walked up the stairs to the porch, the children saw him and stopped their work and they yelled *moonju*, white man, and he passed them and went inside. He asked the sergeant if he could speak to the chief and the sergeant said he was away on business and would not be back for two days. Jack asked if he could visit with the prisoner Mari, and the sergeant raised his eyebrows in surprise.

"*Porquois?*"

"She is a friend."

The sergeant smiled. "Yes, I see. She is a *poopalingi*. She is beautiful. And young. She cannot be eighteen." He used the Sango word for butterfly and Jack ignored him and the sergeant stood and said, "Why not," and led him through a door and down a hall that was lined with three cells. In the last cell he saw Mari in an orange and black sari sleeping on a cot and the sergeant unlocked the iron door and it creaked when he opened it. Jack went in and the sergeant locked it behind him and said through the bars, "Yell for me when you are done."

Jack sat down on a stool next to the cot and stroked her arm and said, "Mari, *C'est moi.* Jack," and she opened her eyes, smiled and sat up.

"Jack."

"*Comment va tu?*"

She frowned. "I am in jail. How do you expect me to be?" And then she smiled. "I am fine. They are sending me to Bangui in two days." She spoke in an admixture of French, Sango and Lingala and Jack understood because he had known her as a lover for two years and her peculiar syntax had at first confused him yet it had always amused him.

"What did you tell them?" Jack spoke in French.

"That he raped me and that I stabbed him with a knife."

"Mari, you'll go to prison."

"Why? It was self-defense." She stretched her arms.

"No. Because you're black. And he was white."

"So? He raped us."

"I know, I know, but it is France that sends all the money to Bangui, and anyway you know what they will say, what the jury will say."

"That I am a whore?"

"Yes."

Jack stood and walked to the barred window and he looked out at the children throwing rocks at the mangoes and he kept his back to her. He hadn't wanted to say this and was glad she had so he could know for sure that she knew just what was at stake because the jury would ask how a man could rape a whore, and then they would convict her and hang her at Ngaragba Central Prison because she was just a black African and she had killed a white Frenchman, and Jack now could see her beautiful body swing from a rope and he was glad he had killed the Frenchman. He wished he could kill him again.

"Then what am I supposed to do?"

Jack turned and looked at her from the window. "Mari," and Jack's eyes were on the edge of spilling tears, "there is no one in the world like you. You know that? No one. I wish, I wish…"

"What?"

He turned back to the window. "I wish things were different, that's all."

"And the baby? If he had lived, I would have named him Jack and when you were gone back to America I would have had your souvenir."

"I know." He came to the cot and sat down next to her and he put his arm around her shoulders.

27

"He would have been as handsome as you."

"Mari..."

"But it is too late for that. How is my sister?"

"She is fine, but she is worried."

"And the children?"

"They are fine."

"Good."

"Mari, I know the Chief of Police here. I met him in Bangui. He's a friend of Jean-Paul's, the manager of the San Sylvestre. I will talk to him when he returns in two days. He is a reasonable man."

"Why? They will send me to Bangui in two days."

"But you did nothing. It was I who killed the man. Dieudonne, he is the Chief of Police, is a fair man. I will talk to him. I will tell him that it was I who killed the man. I will tell him the whole story."

"But you will go to jail. I know you, you cannot be in jail even for an hour. You would go crazy. What is the word?"

"*Claustrophobie.* No. They will see the truth. They won't convict me."

"But before the trial. They will keep you locked up like me. You told me about that man when you were a boy."

"Mari..."

"About the closet, how he locked you in it."

"Mari..."

"That you could never be locked up again. You said..."

"No. That is why I am waiting for the Chief of Police. He will understand that I am not guilty and that I will not run. I will cooperate and go to Bangui and they won't keep me in jail."

"Are you sure?"

"Yes."

She smiled. "Thank you."

"There is nothing to thank me for. It is I who should be thanking you. Can you manage here two more days?"

"Of course."

"I will bring you some food."

Jack called for the sergeant and in the front office of the police station, the sergeant winked at Jack and said, "Was she good?"

Jack ignored him and told him he would be back with food.

In the market, Jack bought two saris from an Arab and then he bought *mongbelli* and *mischwee* and orange soda and the sugared peanuts that Mari liked so much, and after having delivered this to Mari he went to a bar and he drank warm beer because there was none cold and he thought of the miscarriage and how he had left Mari because he had thought that she had aborted the child; he had been angry and slapped her, and he had packed his things and moved out, and a week later her sister Francoise had come to him to tell him that he was mistaken, but he had not wanted to believe her because it was easier this way. Yet he knew he had not wanted a child for the burden it would be, but neither would he admit to his willingness to abort a child of his own so as to avoid such a burden, and when he discovered Mari to have been pregnant and then not, he was sure she had aborted the child and it was with relief that he could feign anger that she had aborted the baby, relief because he had not wanted a child, relief until he discovered he was wrong.

Three months later on that Sunday night just three weeks before he had gone to her house to apologize and he had heard her screams. He kicked in the door and he found the flabby Frenchman astride her, his fat white ass bobbing up and down, and the children in the corner and Francoise unconscious on the floor of her room. With a fist full of hair, Jack pulled the man off her from behind and he threw him to the floor and took his Buck knife from the sheath on his belt and opened the knife and the man sat up and pushed himself backwards to the wall. Jack walked toward him in the orange glow of lantern light, his own shadow diminishing on the wall as he stepped toward the Frenchman and away from the lantern behind him, the Frenchman in his dark shadow, and Mari had screamed no, but Jack walked to the man slowly and with measured steps, the knife tight in his hand, and he kicked the man in the face and it was the first noise he made when he screamed from the brunt of the steel-toed Red Wing boot hard against his nose, and he was the Baptist minister, his foster father in Estacada, Oregon, and now he was here in Bangui and he was raping his girlfriend. As the man put his hands on his face, blood seeping through his fingers, he slid toward the door with his back against

29

the wall and Jack lunged at him and stuck the knife in his belly, and the knife went in more easily than Jack could have imagined. When the man slid down, Jack bent down with him still holding the knife, and when the man was lying down groaning with blood spreading across his shirt, the only garment he wore, Jack pulled out the knife and jabbed it into the man again and again and again and again, and he was unsure as to whom he was killing—this French rapist or his foster father rapist—hard steel into the soft flesh of the man, no end to the blood that was sticky and warm, and now, sitting in the bar, he swore to himself that he would do it again and he did not have a single regret except that he wished the man could have lived longer to die more slowly with more pain.

He ate lunch at the bar—manioc leaves sauteed in a peanut butter sauce with small chunks of river snake, and *mongbelli*, long sticks of boiled manioc root—and then he drank more beer and the sun was hot when he finally walked back to the mission. He took a siesta and he dreamed of Mari and the dream was strange as all his dreams now were, and in the dream Mari was in a baby buggy and Jack pushed it along a dusty road in Oregon and Mari was no baby.

When he had first come to Africa, and before he had met Mari on the veranda of the New Palace Bar, he had dreamed of Karen whom he had met his Freshman year in college. He dreamed of her and of how in love they were and he dreamed they were married and that they celebrated communion together, both on their knees, the Eucharist, and then he dreamed that he killed her by slitting her throat and he caught her blood in a chalice, but he didn't dream of her anymore after he had met Mari.

When he awoke he was sweating. He pulled back the mosquito net and opened the shutters and went out and washed at the spigot. It was late afternoon and the sun was at an angle and the outside was now orange instead of white light.

He sat on the concrete porch of the outbuilding in the shade of an orange tree and this late in the dry season it was still laden with wasted fruit. He was smoking a cigarette when Faith came down from the house in jeans and a western shirt as if she were a cowgirl, and she carried two bottles of orange soda. She sat down next to him and handed him a bottle.

"How is your friend?"

"Okay. You want a cigarette?"

She frowned. "No, I don't smoke."

He smiled. "Of course not. But you don't mind one way or the other if I do?"

She caught herself smiling at his mimicry and she frowned again at her own betrayal. "No, not one way or another. That's your business."

He laughed.

"What's so funny?"

"Nothing. It's just that you said the same thing about drinking, that it was my business."

"So?"

"Nothing."

He sat with his back against the wall of the outbuilding, his legs stretched out before him, crossed at the ankle. He rubbed out the cigarette on the porch and tossed the butt into the dirt at the foot of the stairs and she watched it fall onto the ground. He took a sip of the soda and it was cold and tasted good to him because his tongue was dry from the alcohol he had drunk that morning and afternoon. She took a drink of her own.

"Why is your friend in jail?"

"Because the police think she killed a man who raped her."

"And she didn't?"

"No." Jack stared out at the empty yard.

"How can you be so sure?" And then: "Anyway, he would deserve it."

Jack turned and looked at her now and into her blue eyes that were big and clear, and he could see her youth and how fresh she was and clean, a girl who was naive and who believed in the goodness of mankind maybe, and for a moment he wished he were like that, wished he could be as pure as she seemed, pure and clean as cold water from a spring. Her skin was smooth and clean and when she smiled he saw her teeth gleam and he felt her life could not possibly be real for there was no sign of hardship on her body, no wrinkles, no scars, and even her voice was like clear water. She was smooth like a new candle that had never been burned.

"I just know, that's all."

"What will they do?"

"They're sending her to Bangui in two days."

"And then you'll go to Bangui?"

"Yes. If you don't mind me staying here."

"Of course not. People stay here all the time."

"Like the French journalist you mentioned."

"Yes. We have lots of visitors."

"Why did you say he could write a story about you now?"

"I didn't. I said he could write about missionaries."

"Why?"

"Because he stayed here with us. That's why. And if he stayed with pygmies, he could write about them."

"I see."

"I enjoy visitors. More than my parents do." She looked to the house and Jack followed her gaze.

"Your parents don't?"

"It depends on who they are. Some they don't like at all. It's just that they don't want me unduly influenced." She looked down at her hands cradled in her lap.

"*Unduly?*"

"My father's expression. Inappropriately influenced."

"And what would be the appropriate form of influence?"

"The bible, of course."

"Not the other books you read then?"

She blushed. "What books?"

"Last night you said you weren't bored. That you read a lot of books. Are they appropriate influences is what I'm asking."

She took a sip of soda and smiled. "Not all of them. No, certainly not."

"When I was in college, a prof had us read Henry Miller. Ever read him?"

"Of course not."

"But you know about him?"

"Yes. I told you I read. Just because I've grown up here in the middle of Africa doesn't mean I don't have an education." She paused. "I read *Madame Bovary* in French when I was fifteen."

"How old are you?"

32

"Seventeen." She sat up straighter than she had been sitting before. "Almost eighteen."

"You're old enough to do what you want."

"I do."

"So you choose to stay here?"

"For the time being."

"Then what?"

"Travel, I think. I want to travel everywhere. I want to go to France and Italy and Spain, and I'd like to go to Australia." Her eyes took on a dreamy quality and Jack smiled.

"Why Australia?"

"You'll laugh."

"No I won't."

"Promise?"

"Sure. I promise." Jack held out his right hand and she shook it.

"I want to see the kangaroos," she said.

Jack laughed and she gave him a hard look. "I'm sorry, it's just that it seems a long way to go to see kangaroos."

Faith turned from him and crossed her arms in feigned anger. "You said you wouldn't laugh."

"I'm sorry."

"Faith," a woman's voice called from the porch of the house and both Jack and Faith looked up to see her mother standing there, a tall, pretty woman whose long, gray hair was tied back in a ponytail. She had a towel in her hand. Her face was soft and her eyes were kind, and she looked down at Faith with a maternal patience that even Jack could sense; it was as though she were looking down at herself and remembering something of her youth that made her smile, something she no longer had and would never have again, yet this longing, this nostalgia, was so tangible that Jack felt the two, mother and daughter, were, for that brief moment when time had stopped, united as one.

"Yes?" Faith stood.

"Come and help with dinner, please."

"Yes, Mother." Faith looked at Jack who was lighting another cigarette. "I'll call you when dinner's ready." She walked up to the house and Jack watched her, thinking about what type of woman would travel all the way to Australia to see a kangaroo.

They sat at the kitchen table and the father introduced himself as George and his wife as Lillian, and he said grace before the meal. It was roasted chicken that they ate and boiled potatoes and okra which Jack had never tasted and there were four tall glasses of water sweating on the red checkered tablecloth, and George said, "Goats are not as regular as milkmen," but more to be clever than to apologize for the water.

George was a tall, gaunt man who had the Bible in his head so that he spoke in the syntax of the book even when he spoke of the food. Lillian was quiet and deferred to her husband and Faith did as well, and Jack was uncomfortable sitting with this family and he ate as quickly as he could.

"The chicken is excellent, Lillian," Jack said.

"Thank you," she said, blushing at the compliment.

"God provides," said George.

"Jack is from Oregon," Faith said, pouring ice water from the white, ceramic pitcher.

"Really," was all George said. There was nothing Biblical about Oregon, Jack supposed.

"I understand you're from Alabama?"

"Indeed," said George.

"Never been there," Jack said as he held his glass out for Faith to fill.

"What religion are you, son?" George asked.

Jack looked at Faith and she smiled when he said, "Catholic."

"I understand that you're here to help a woman in jail? An African?" George said.

"Yes."

"What did she do?"

"Nothing."

"Then why is she in jail?"

"She's supposed to have killed a Frenchman who," and Jack thought about the word, but could think of no suitable synonym, "who raped her, but she didn't do it."

34

George looked first at Lillian and then at Faith. "A Frenchman, huh?" George said.

"Yes," Jack said. "A Frenchman."

"And an African," George finished. And that was all he said about the matter, but it was enough for Jack to take a great dislike for the man, and he felt sorry now for Lillian too because she had to live with this man who seemed to see everything quite literally in black and white, just like the pages of his Bible.

They talked about the town of Boda and the people there, George saying that the mission was doing its job of converting the Africans "from their heathen animistic ways." Lillian asked Jack about his family and about his work in Bangui, and Faith asked about Oregon and Jack told them about fishing for salmon in the coastal rivers when the rain was so heavy and hard there seemed to be no sky.

Jack excused himself and thanked Lillian for the meal, but he only nodded at George, and then he went outside into the night.

Faith stayed behind and washed the dishes, listening to her parents in the other room discuss her father's plans for a larger church, and as she dried the plates and put them in the cupboard, she thought of Jack and the world outside the Baptist mission, the world where it was possible for an American in Africa to travel to a far off town like Boda to help an African woman who was in jail for murdering a Frenchman.

She thought of Christophe, the journalist who only six months before had spent three weeks at the mission shortly after her two-month sojourn in Alabama. Christophe, she thought, his own name a lie. Each night after dinner they had sat on the front porch discussing books, and talking to him had been like traveling to other countries for he had been around the world and he described places she had only read about and his words made them real and concrete.

It hadn't mattered that he was Catholic. He was kind and handsome despite the brown goatee, and he had kind things to say to her parents, and at dinner he had made them laugh.

The second week of his stay he had asked her if she would like to take a walk after dinner. They took the path behind the mission, the path that wound up the hill past the *usine* where the coffee beans were shelled, and at the top of the hill he took her in his arms and kissed her long and hard, and that was the first time her lips had touched a man's lips, and she flushed with excitement.

The next day they had a picnic at the river, and he made love to her and it was the first time she had made love and her excitement was commensurate with her fear; later that night, however, she was afraid because she had no birth control and she did not know what she would do if she were pregnant. Have a baby, she supposed.

The next night they walked up the hill behind the house, and it did not rain and it appeared that the dry season had replaced the season of rains. He took her in his arms and kissed her before unbuttoning her blouse, and with his tongue he first tasted her breasts and then he took her nipples in his mouth and she told him no, not now, later when they were married, but he ignored her pleas and he reached down and unbuttoned her jeans and slid them down her thighs and then he unbuttoned his own, kissing her neck and telling her he loved her—*Je t'aime*, he said, *Je t'aime*—and he kissed her, his tongue in her mouth, and her father with his walking staff beating him on the back, beating him and how he scrambled in the grass, pulling up his pants with one hand as he warded off the blows with his other arm, and she buttoning her blouse and jeans, and now, in the kitchen over a sink full of dishes with tears running down her cheeks, she remembered how her father called her a whore, and she was not sure what had happened that evening, not sure at all, and she only knew that Christophe had left without saying goodbye and had never even written her a letter.

Now rinsing the plates, she thought of the only other man who had been forward toward her: Darrel Blankenship who was in the Baptist seminary in Georgia, the son of a friend of her father's, and the comparison of the two men was ludicrous, and now she felt guilty that she had been so attracted to Christophe, and though she was younger than Darrel, she had felt nothing for him but a kind of maternal condescension.

Darrel was nineteen and her parents spoke of him often, spoke of what a good family he was from and of what a good missionary he would make. Faith had known him since they were children; every summer the families would meet in Florida, and she had grown up with Darrel once a year meeting in Panama City for two weeks where they would compare their heights back-to-back in front of the families. This past summer, when she was visiting her aunt in Alabama, Darrel had made the drive from Florida and had proposed, proposed even though they had never even as much as kissed.

"Why, Darrel Blankenship, I cannot believe you asking me this now," she had said as they sat out on her aunt's porch-swing in the old country house outside of Birmingham. The magnolias were dropping their blooms, but still a hint of perfume lingered on the air. "We have never even so much as dated."

"But Faith, we grew up together. That's more than having dated. Besides, I love you." He had taken her hand, and she had pulled it away.

She had blushed, too, she remembered now, and she had been flattered, but she also had been flustered: she had never before considered marrying him, had not even so much as thought of marrying anyone. Then Darrel had frowned and said, "'And the Lord God caused a deep sleep to fall upon Adam, and he slept: and he took one of his ribs, and closed up the flesh instead thereof; And the rib, which the Lord God had taken from man, made he a woman, and brought her unto the man. And Adam said...'"

She stood. "I know, I know. 'This is now bone of my bones, and flesh of my flesh: she shall be called woman because she was taken out of Man.' But that has nothing to do with proposing marriage, Darrel. We're both young. We have plenty of time to think about marriage. Besides, I've never thought of myself as a rib."

Darrel had raised his eyebrows. "Then you're refusing me?" he had asked. In the shadows of the porch, she could see the hurt on his face, and she felt bad for it.

"It's just too early to talk about, is all."

Before she had flown back to Africa, he had asked her again, and she had only promised to think about it because she did not want to hurt him. It had been seven months since she had seen Darrel last and she had received one letter a week from him, and as she read each letter she could see Darrel on his knees, and she liked him less and less with each letter especially after Christophe had left, when she would go to the post office hoping for word from him only to find Darrel's missives, and she thought him young and foolish.

Her parents, George and Lillian, dropped hints as heavy as houses with each letter that arrived: "Oh, another letter from Darrel? He's such a nice young man. Whoever catches him will be very lucky indeed," her mother said. Her father, on returning from the post office and handing her a letter, said, "Darrel's writing you quite frequently, isn't he, Faith? He is going to be a fine missionary somewhere. I just wish there were more young men like him these days. He is a fine young man, just like his father." When her father said Darrel was going to be a fine missionary, she almost shuddered.

Faith wrote letters back, letters that mostly described her work at the mission school, but she did not address his repeated pleas for marriage. That is not to say that she did not think about marrying him: she thought about it all the time and it was like fingering a sore tooth; she imagined what it would be like and it was not a pleasant vision—she knew she did not love him. Then again, she thought, it was possible to be married and happy with someone you liked even if you did not love him. She had only to think of her mother. But marriage seemed to Faith not unlike an early death, the very wedding a funeral. She was only seventeen; she hadn't done *anything* yet.

Faith came out and sat next to Jack on the porch of the outbuilding where they looked at the stars as the cicadas and the crickets melded a metallic chorus that was a backdrop to the steady beat of the funeral drums. The heat of the day still rose from the earth in slow, simmered wafts, but the concrete porch was cool. The air was acrid with the stench of drying manioc, and the smell of tobacco that Jack exhaled through his nose.

"You smoke a lot," Faith said.

"Yeah, I guess. It kind of balances everything out because you don't smoke at all."

She didn't respond to that.

"That was funny what you told my father when he asked what religion you were."

"I wasn't trying to be funny. I just didn't want him to think there was some heathen sitting at his table."

"That's exactly what he thought when you told him you were Catholic."
They both laughed.

"Have you ever been to Australia?"

"Nope, never have."

"But you've traveled a lot?"

"Not really. Europe some. Right now, though, I like Africa. I like Bangui."

"Why?"

Jack looked down from the stars and turned to her. "What do you mean, why?"

"What do you like about Bangui?"

He flicked his cigarette out before him and it landed in the dirt and he watched the cherry burn in the dark. "I don't know. I guess I pretty much like anywhere I am. At least for a while, until it wears out."

"Wears out?"

"You travel to a new place you've never been, it has possibilities. But if you stay long enough, the possibilities wear out and you have to move again."

"But what do you like about living in Bangui? And its possibilities, of course."

"You've been there."

"Of course."

"What did you do there?"

"Not much. Bought supplies. We never stay there more than two or three days. Once we had dinner at the Rock Hotel."

"So you've never been to the *boites de nuite*? Never been dancing at the Rock or the San Sylvestre or the Byblos?"

"No. My father doesn't approve of dancing."

"How about you?"

"Oh, I think dancing is okay."

"Can I tell you a joke?"

"Sure." She looked at him and in the faint light of the moon she could see him smile. She liked his face, the lean cheeks with dimples when he smiled and the cleft chin that jutted out just a bit, and though he hadn't shaved for a few days, she liked his face despite the black stubble that now fielded it, the color of his short hair.

39

"Maybe I shouldn't tell you."

"Why? Go ahead."

"Well, it's got a Baptist in it."

"I can laugh at Baptists. I laugh at my father sometimes."

"In front of him?"

"No. You know what I mean. Go on, tell me the joke."

"Well, it also mentions sex."

She could feel the flush on her cheeks, but it was dark and Jack couldn't see the change of color. "Come on, Jack, what do you think I am, some kind of prude?"

Jack turned and looked at her and she looked angry and that made him smile.

"No, I don't think that. Okay, I'll tell you the joke, but there's been so much building up to it that it's probably anti-climactic now."

She sighed. "Just tell the joke, Jack."

"Okay. You know why Baptists don't fuck standing up?"

"Ha-ha, Jack. Everyone knows that. Because it might lead to dancing."

"You've heard that before?"

"More than once. It's old."

"Sorry. I told you it wasn't a very good joke."

They sat in silence and she asked him if he knew any other jokes, but he said he didn't. A dog howled and then another howled right back at the first and they took up a steady correspondence that made the night seem lonely in between, their howls maybe some esoteric foretelling of the day yet to come. The night was alive with the noise of the crickets and cicadas and dogs against the beat of the drums that marked each night, and yet it still seemed quiet.

"I hate those drums," Faith said.

"Every night."

"They remind me of all those who never had a chance to be baptized."

"And you think they'll all go to hell?"

"Of course. It saddens me." She sighed.

"Yes."

"Many of them will have never had a chance," she said and sighed again.

"A chance?"

"To be saved. That is what we do."

"I understand."

"Do you? Didn't you ever believe in God?"

He rubbed both his thighs. He crossed his ankles. "I don't know that I ever had a chance. My foster father was a minister."

"You said."

"Yes."

"Did he talk to you about God? Did he teach you?"

Jack spit off the porch. "What?" she asked.

"He was a minister. And he was a child molester." He paused and searched for words to follow. "How do you align that evil with the supposed goodness?"

"I'm sorry, Jack."

"He was an evil man."

They were silent. The generator hummed. The cicadas continued their chorus. And the funeral drums never missed a beat.

"Jack, I'm sorry. But just because this evil man posed as a pastor of some kind, a charlatan, that doesn't mean that there is no God." She paused. "You could still believe?"

He laughed, but it wasn't a laugh—sonically it only resembled one. "I can't believe in a God who created such people as him, who abandons the children here to dysentery and gout and malaria and filariasis and foul water and starvation and snakes."

"I'm sorry, Jack."

"Don't be. You do your work. You have a lot of work to do. Are you going to stay on here forever?" Jack asked.

"No, of course not."

"Then what are you going to do? Have you finished high school?"

"Yes. I've been home-schooled here. I finished all the curriculum almost a year ago."

"You're ahead of the game."

"Are you being sarcastic?"

"No. Just saying you're done with high school early. Are you going to go to college?"

"I want to."

41

"Are you going to?"

"Well, we haven't talked about it yet. My father, he's a bit protective, I guess. And a bit of a chauvinist."

"He doesn't want you unduly influenced?"

"Right. Nor inappropriately so."

"What would you like to study?"

"Biology."

"Pre-med?"

"Yes, if I can do it."

"Doctors make a hell of a lot of money." Jack lit another cigarette with his Zippo and the flame of the lighter lit his face and Faith could see that he wasn't being sarcastic, but that he was just making conversation and the light reflected in his brown eyes.

"It's not the money."

"What is it?"

"You live in Africa enough you would know."

"Yeah, I know. When I was in M'baiki teaching..."

"You used to teach?"

"With the Peace Corps."

"You were in the Peace Corps?"

"I was."

"When?"

"Before they left because of Bokassa."

"Why didn't you go?"

"Because I wasn't ready to leave then. I told you: I hadn't exhausted all the possibilities. Anyway, I was saying that I used to have to steal quinine from the Peace Corps to give it to my students."

"Steal it?"

"They said they didn't have enough for everyone and that was probably true, but at least I could give it to the kids I taught."

"When are you leaving, Jack?"

He turned and looked at her and saw her looking at him with eyes that were too earnest. "Day after tomorrow."

She leaned back against the wall and looked across the yard at her house.

"Why?" he asked.

"I was just wondering. I like talking to you. There's no one here to talk to."

"But you have visitors."

"Mostly other missionaries."

"And the occasional journalist?"

"Yes, the occasional journalist."

"Maybe you'll come to Bangui sometime soon and I can take you out dancing."

She laughed. "Baptists don't dance, you said."

"Well, we'll make you one who does."

"I'd like that."

"But your father sure as hell wouldn't."

"No, he wouldn't like it all. But he and I are different."

"How so?"

"We just are."

"I can see that. You're a hell of a lot prettier."

She blushed once again, and they were quiet and they listened to the night noise of the drums and the cicadas and crickets, and Jack felt uncomfortable with the silence between them because it was heavy and there were things that might be said next that would be awkward. It was getting late and time to go to bed.

"Not long until the rains," Jack said.

"What are you going to do? With your friend, I mean."

"Do? Hell, I don't know."

"Well, how are you going to help her?"

"That's a long story."

"I've got time to hear it."

Jack thought about telling her everything that had happened with Mari, and he decided he would tell her, but Faith's mother came out on the porch and called her in for the night. Jack continued sitting there after she left, and he watched as her father came out of the house and walked to the shed that stored the generator. Jack saw the lights fade as the hum of the generator died down to nothing, and then it was dark. The father walked through the moonlight to the house, and Jack heard the door shut. He sat

43

there for a while thinking about Mari in jail and how he had to get her out, and he worried about Dieudonne, the Chief of Police, worried that he might not do the right thing because Jack could not be in jail even for one day—he knew he couldn't. He thought of when he was a boy, and it hurt just to think about how the man in the second foster home had done those things to him, how that fat son of a bitch who was some kind of Baptist minister in Estacada, Oregon, locked him in the closet, days at a time, and, he just couldn't think of it because he'd get sick with anger and shame, and he hadn't thought about it for a long time. He only knew that he couldn't spend a minute in a place that locked him in. And if he were arrested, there was no guarantee that he would ever be free because African justice was, he thought, a crap-shoot at best and everything would depend on a judge believing that Jack had killed the man in self-defense, and sometimes, Jack thought, aggression was the best self-defense of all.

He went inside and got the bottle of Scotch and he brought it back out to the porch and he sat there sipping from it until he'd drunk about a quarter of the bottle, sipping the Scotch and smoking cigarettes, and then he went inside and went to bed, and he told himself, as he did every night before falling asleep, that he would never think of the past—of that son of a bitch who had raped him, or of Karen and her professor again.

Yet there was a past he could think of, the kind woman who adopted him, and her two daughters both of whom were in college and were like second and third mothers, three kind women who were nothing but loving and kind. Yes, he could think of them.

The next morning he woke to the rooster's call, and he tried to go back to sleep, but he couldn't as the room was too warm. He went outside and the rising sun shined through the green foliage of the orange and mango trees that surrounded the compound, the shadows long yet thwarted by the buildings themselves. He walked to the spigot and washed his face and wet down his hair, and as he was combing his hair he saw Faith walking up the path from the market. He watched her as she walked, and when she came up to him with a smile for a greeting, he said, "You're up early this morning."

She walked up to where he stood on the concrete slab by the spigot behind the small, wooden structure of the church, and she carried two pineapples and she looked fresh in the jeans and cotton shirt; she looked like she'd already had a whole morning's coffee.

"Good morning, Jack. Ready for some breakfast?"

"I thought I'd go down to the market and have my coffee there."

"Why don't you come eat with us? Don't want to eat with Baptists?"

He set the comb down on the shelf above the spigot, picked up his shirt from the hook it hung on and put his arms through the sleeves. "I'd just prefer to sit outside, I guess, but thanks." He buttoned the shirt top to bottom. "You want to come?"

She thought about that before saying just a minute, and she went inside with the fruit. She came back out and they walked down the hill through the fields of coffee on either side of the road until they came to the main road that led down to the center of town and the market. They walked past the adobe houses where women were starting fires in the dirt before their front doors, and children were playing and chasing chickens, and everyone on the road was walking toward the market, and many of these people greeted Faith. "*Bonjour, Mademoiselle*," they said, and she smiled and returned their greetings, and she knew many of their names.

In the market, they sat down on a rickety bench before a fire and each had a cup of coffee and some *beignets* made from manioc flour that were deep-fried in a vat of palm oil that hung over the fire. As Jack smoked, Faith spoke Sango to the lady who fanned the fire with her apron to charge it. She dropped the round doughnuts into the red palm oil where they sizzled.

"You speak Sango well," Jack said.

"You remember I grew up here."

"True."

"I was speaking Sango when I was three or four."

"French?"

"Later."

"Who taught you?"

"My parents taught me French."

"Sango?"

She turned and looked at Jack a moment, and then returned her gaze to the mug of coffee in her hands. "No one, not really. Our cook, Girard,

45

he had a son the same age as me. We used to play together." She smiled, recalling the memory, and when it fully arrived she was warmed by it. "His name was George. Anyway, I spoke Sango better than English."

"You still see George?"

Faith closed her eyes as if she were praying. "Yes, in a way. When I close my eyes, I can still see him. At age six. Barefoot. Smiling with a handful of peanuts." She opened her eyes. "But then I open my eyes, and he's gone."

"What happened?"

"We were playing behind the church. It could have been me. We were kicking a ball back and forth and I kicked the ball into the ditch next to the church. George, he crawled down to get it. I heard him scream. I ran to him. I saw the snake slithering away. A black mamba, my father said."

"I'm sorry, Faith."

She turned to look at him again and smiled. "Yes, so am I. George, I remember, he could make me laugh."

A little boy in tattered shorts was chasing a mangy dog with a stick and the dog ran past Jack and Faith and then the boy came running by and he knocked over the pan of dough the woman had prepared for doughnuts and now it was full of dirt. The boy ran off and the Africans around the fire laughed and the woman just leaned over and picked up the pan and scraped off the dirt with her hand.

Jack watched the boy run off after the dog. "He could use a little discipline."

"They don't discipline the children. Not much, anyway."

"I know. That's what I mean."

"But do you know why?"

Jack sipped his coffee. "No. Too lazy?"

Faith smiled, but it was not a happy smile. "The infant mortality rate here is about the highest in the world. The Africans figure if they're not going to live very long, they might as well let them do what they want. Let them be happy while they can."

"But he's five or six years old."

"The ones who live are considered lucky to have made it, special in a way. Just like George. And then George died."

Jack thought about that as he finished his coffee.

After breakfast, they walked back up the hill to the mission. Faith asked him if he would like to come with her to the mission school below the coffee plantation where she taught each morning. Jack told her no, that he had to visit his friend in jail.

Faith stopped on the path and Jack walked three more steps before he stopped and turned, and Faith looked up at him. "Is she your lover?" she asked.

Jack laughed because of the word she chose to describe Mari, a woman he indeed had loved, but the phrase sounded antiquated to him, stilted and not quite right, a phrase out of a romance novel, he thought. *Lover.* He resumed walking and Faith caught up with him.

"What's so funny?"

"Nothing, Faith." Jack smiled.

They stopped in the yard between the house and the outbuilding.

"Well, is she?"

"No, Faith, she isn't. She once was, though. Now we're just friends."

"Oh."

Faith turned to go up the steps to the house.

"Faith?"

She turned back to him. She looked like she was going to cry and there was no reason for it.

Jack walked up the stairs and took her hand. "Faith, I told you, we're just friends and I have to help her. We were lovers a long time ago."

Faith smiled, and took her hand from his.

"I've got to go to work."

"What time are you done?"

"Noon."

"After lunch, do you think you could get your father's truck? My motorcycle broke down about fifty kilometers back toward M'Baiki."

"I don't know. I'll ask him."

"Thanks."

"Where did you leave it?"

"In a ditch."

"You think it'll still be there?"

47

"It should be. It's in the middle of nowhere and you can't see it from the road."

Faith went into the house, and Jack wondered just what he was getting into here in Boda when he'd come this far only to help Mari. He hadn't come for anything else.

"Thank you, Jack," Mari said as the sergeant closed the door of the cell and Jack set the sack of provisions down on the floor.

Jack sat down on the stool next to where Mari now sat up on the cot. "How are you?"

"I'm okay."

"Are they treating you okay?"

"Yes, but the sergeant offered me one-thousand francs."

"What did you tell him."

"To go to hell."

Jack smiled and lit a cigarette. "When are you going to stop smoking?" Mari said.

"Sometime."

"You always say that. It is not good for the health."

"I know."

"You should quit."

"I will."

"Is it so difficult?"

"What?"

"To stop smoking."

"I don't know. I never tried."

Mari unwrapped the *mongbelli* from its covering of palm fronds and she took a bite and Jack opened the bottle of orange soda, prying the cap off with the tip of his Buck knife, and he set it by her bare feet. He watched her eat, and then he stood up and went to the barred window and looked out at the yard where the mango tree shaded the dirt. Chickens pecked at the earth, up and down like sewing machines in their robotic operation, and a goat tethered to an orange tree circled the tree so that the rope was wrapped around the trunk and the goat could not move in the direction it pulled. It bleated, but no one came to unravel the rope.

"It's hot in here," Jack said. He wiped his forehead with a bandanna. He looked out the barred window and then reached up and tried shaking the bars with both hands, but they would not budge.

"Soon the rains will be coming," Mari said as she watched him at the window.

Jack sat back down on the stool, and Mari finished eating and picked up the soda and took a sip.

"You want some?"

"No. No, thanks."

"Jack, thanks for coming here to help me." She looked at him and her brown eyes were serious and she didn't smile. She looked like a child, Jack thought. She set the bottle down and put her hand on Jack's thigh.

"It's nothing. I owe it to you."

"I wish everything were different."

"So do I."

"But it's not."

"No, it's not."

"Things can never go back and be changed, can they, Jack?"

"I know that."

"You don't love me now?"

"I love you."

"But things cannot go back to where they were before?"

"No. Because things have happened and everything is different now."

Mari lay back down on the cot, her hands cradling the back of her head, and her eyes took on a patina of glass. "I would still like to go to America with you."

Jack smiled. "I would have liked that."

"But we can't."

"Yes, things happened. I made mistakes."

She rolled to her side and propped herself up on her elbow. "Mistakes can be fixed."

"No, not really. When something is done, it changes everything that follows."

"What does that mean? You didn't understand about the baby and now you do, so why can't we go back to the way things were before?"

49

"Because I did what I did."

"I forgave you. It was a misunderstanding."

"But I did that and I learned something about myself."

"But it's done with. We can start over."

"You can't start over. You said that a minute ago. It would have to be, I don't know. It would have to be that we met for the first time and that can't happen."

"Jack." Mari sat back up and took his hand in hers.

"It can't."

"We can. When we are in Bangui, you could come to my house with flowers and pretend it was the first time we met and then we could go to the Rock Hotel for dinner and then go to the Byblos to dance, and it would be like the first time." She reached out with her other hand and touched Jack's cheek. "We could fall in love again."

Jack's eyes welled up, and he stood and went back to the window and looked outside at the goat still bleating and trying to extricate itself, and with his back to Mari he said, "I will always love you, Mari. But we cannot go back to the way things were."

Mari stood and came to him and wrapped her arms around his waist from behind him and she put the side of her face to his back and she could feel him crying silently. "Jack, let's try again. I love you."

He turned around and hugged her and then he kissed her forehead. "No, Mari." He pulled her tight, his cheek against her head, and her hair smelled rich and fertile, fecund like sex. "There is only once." He led her back to the cot and gently pushed her down onto it and then he yelled for the sergeant and he came and let Jack out and again, in the office, the sergeant asked if she were good, and Jack looked at him and tensed his body and in English he said, "Fuck you," and he walked out into the heat of the day.

As he walked up the hill to the mission, he felt that now he had done everything that had been done to him, that his betrayal of Mari was an echo, a ripple of Karen's betrayal of himself four years before, and he remembered the July day in Eugene when he had proposed to Karen after they had eaten lunch on the banks of the McKenzie River, and how she had cried and said yes. And then they swam naked in the river, coming out to the beach where the sun dried the water from their hair, and they made love in the sand, her hair smelling like a ripe future, and as winter folded into spring Karen told him that she was sorry, but she had fallen in love with someone else, a professor, and she wished Jack all the best because, she said, he was a good man.

All the best, she had wished him. *A good man.*

There had been no place for Jack to run forward to for his future had been ripped away like a page from the calendar, as if you could rip out the pages of the upcoming months and never go through them. He went through the motions of finishing school and the months slipped by slowly, and he only knew that he was to graduate in June. In March, the Peace Corps was on campus and he listened to their pitch about going to the Third World to work, and he was not interested in helping anyone, but he thought maybe he could help himself by escaping to Africa where there would be no evidence of his past to remind him of who he was, and in Africa, he felt, he might find a new identity to walk in, one that had not been rejected by a woman whom he loved. In Africa, he thought, there was always the possibility of escape.

They were driving back toward Boda with the motorcycle tied off in the bed of the Toyota Landcruiser, and Faith downshifted and turned left onto a narrow path five or six kilometers before Boda, and Jack asked where they were going, and the jungle was a thick, green wall around them.

"You'll see," was all she said, and she drove down the narrow road strewn with sharp rocks, dust billowing behind them, and as they descended the hill it became darker until they were submerged in a shaded world under the canopy of ebony and rosewood trees, and the air was cool and moist.

Faith turned off the road and onto a narrower path. She drove slowly as the branches scraped the side of the truck, and Jack had to roll up his window.

"Where are we going, Faith?" Jack asked again.

"To a little pool on the river my mother used to take me to when I was little."

They drove for another kilometer before Faith stopped the truck in the grass beside the road. They climbed out of the truck and Faith led Jack down a steep trail and he could smell the water, sweet and rich.

They emerged onto a beach from the thick green fronds of stunted palms, and Jack said, "Nice spot, Faith." They were standing next to a punch bowl, a waterfall spilling into the pool the only sound, mellifluous and sweet and pure.

"Want to go swimming?" Faith said.

"Sure, but..."

"You're not a prude, are you?" Faith smiled and Jack laughed.

"Not hardly. Is the water clean?"

Faith turned her back to him and began unbuttoning her shirt. "Clean enough. And too fast for schistosomiasis."

"I had to take the poison for schisto once and it made me sick as hell."

"It's clean, Jack."

"Okay then."

Jack unlaced his boots and took off his shirt and jeans and shorts and he dove in and when Faith heard the splash, she pulled her arms out of her sleeves and let the shirt drop to the ground. She turned and watched him swim with strong strokes across the pool and behind the waterfall, and through the water she could see him and he looked filmy through the falling water and she thought he looked like he was going both up and down at the same time.

"Okay," he yelled. "Your turn."

"Don't look."

"Of course not. You have my word."

Faith bent down to unlace her shoes, and then she pulled off her jeans as Jack waited for her behind the waterfall.

"You're not looking, are you?"

"No. And besides, I can't see through the water."

"How would you know unless you looked?"

She dove in and swam behind the waterfall where Jack stood on the sandy river bottom with the water up to his chest. She came up out of the water next to him and the water came to her neck and the water droplets beaded on her face and dripped from her hair.

"This is a beautiful spot, Faith."

"We used to come here for picnics."

"With your dad?"

"Sometimes. Mostly my mom. He was always so busy."

She dove under the waterfall and swam across the pool and Jack followed her and she turned and splashed him and he splashed her and they played in the water like children. He dove under the surface and swam near the bottom until he came up behind her and she did not know where he was and she spun around in the water looking for him when he came up behind her and yelled, "Boo," and she swam away from him across the pool and under the waterfall and Jack followed her. She was leaning against a rock with her hands brushing back her hair when Jack came beside her, and he stood and it was Faith who put her arms around his neck and Jack let himself be kissed, and then he kissed her back and they held onto each other kissing with their lips wet and pressed together, when they heard children laughing. Faith pushed Jack away and went down into the water and Jack stood beside her and they both looked out at the two little boys on the beach, not more than six or seven years old, and they knew that the boys were laughing at them.

The boys took off their shorts and dove into the water and swam up behind the waterfall and held on to rocks and both Faith and Jack could be seen only from the neck up.

"Hello, Phillipe. Jean-Jacques," Faith said with a frown that was not angry, but that was one of half-hearted reprimand.

"*Bonjour, Mademoiselle,*" the two boys said in unison. "You came to swim with your new boyfriend?" one boy asked and the other giggled.

"He is not my boyfriend," Faith said in French.

"But we saw you kissing," the other boy said, and now they both laughed.

Faith blushed and Jack could think of nothing to say.

"You are all red-faced," one boy said, and again they laughed thinking there was great humor under the waterfall.

"What are you doing here?" Faith said.

"We came to swim."

"Go swim, then," Faith said.

"Yes. We will leave you to your kissing."

They swam back out from behind the waterfall and they climbed to the bank and dressed and then picked up the clothes left on the bank, and laughing, they shouted that they were going to take Faith's clothes back to the mission, a favor for her, they said.

"No, wait," Faith yelled in Sango and swam after them, and in French Jack yelled for them to wait and he watched as the boys backed away from the pool laughing like this were the biggest comedy in the world. Faith swam to the bank and they were still backing up the hill to the road with handfuls of clothing when she climbed out of the water. She ran to them and they stood there and looked her up and down until she came to them. She pulled the clothes from their hands and now Jack was laughing as she covered herself with the bundle of clothes, yelling at them in Sango, and they laughed even harder at what she said. She turned away from them and Jack watched her as she bent down and pulled on her jeans. When she stood, he looked at her breasts which were full and they bent up toward the sky as if there were a sudden reversal of gravity. She put her arms through her sleeves and buttoned the shirt and Jack swam to the beach and got out and dressed and the boys were still laughing.

Faith told the boys to go home and one said, "Yes, *Mademoiselle*. We will see you in church on Sunday," and they laughed and turned to walk up the road, and Jack laughed and Faith turned and gave him a look that saw no humor in anything that had transpired.

Coming up to her, Jack said, "Sorry, Faith, but you have to admit, it was funny."

Faith almost smiled, but she restrained herself, and walked up to the truck and climbed in and Jack followed her and sat down beside her. They turned up the road and as they approached the two boys who stood on the side of the road laughing and waving, Faith stepped hard on the gas and shot up a mess of dust that covered the boys as they passed.

"Boys will be boys," Jack said, and he leaned to Faith and kissed her on the cheek.

They parked in front of the outbuilding. Jack wheeled the motorcycle onto the tailgate as Faith held the bike by the handlebars. Jack jumped down to the ground.

"Faith," they heard her mother call from the porch. "Your father's been waiting for the truck. Is everything okay?" She walked down the porch stairs and crossed the yard.

"Everything's fine, Lillian," Jack said. "Thanks for letting us use the truck."

"I'm glad we could help." She looked up at her daughter in the bed of the truck. "Faith?"

"We'll be done in a minute, Mom." Faith was still standing on the tailgate holding the motorcycle. Jack pulled the motorcycle down to the ground by the rear wheel as Faith guided it from the front.

"You two must be hungry. I baked a pie. Come on up and have a piece."

"Sounds good to me," Jack said.

"Is Dad angry?" Faith jumped down to the ground.

"No, not really. He was just worried, I suppose."

"We weren't gone that long, were we?"

Faith's mother looked at her daughter for a moment before responding. "No. It must have been farther than you thought, Jack."

"Yes, it was."

"Come on up and have some pie. I'll tell your father you're back."

Faith turned to Jack and said, "Boys will be boys and you're still one, too," and then she went up the stairs to the porch and into the house and Jack smiled to himself as he wheeled the motorcycle to the porch of the outbuilding, thinking about Faith; but then he thought about the mess of everything with Mari in jail, and he wished that everything were different, and he wondered if Fate were against him.

In the afternoon when the people were getting up from siesta, Jack squatted next to the Yamaha 175 parked in the shade of the porch. He could feel the rain coming as he changed the float in the carburetor, cleaned the plugs and adjusted the timing. To Jack, repairing the motorcycle was good, clean work—the kind that had a beginning, a middle and an end, and he worked slowly and enjoyed the accomplishment of each movement of his hands. The afternoon was still and the humidity was heavy, and when the wind came up, it blew hard and out of the east. The palm trees bent down under the weight of the wind and Jack hurried his job now. The orange light went gray as mountainous clouds with great peaks and valleys were pushed across the sky from the east by this wind that picked up dust and leaves and clothes left out to dry, carrying it all across the sky.

The motorcycle started on the third kick. Jack drove down the road through the coffee plantation, shifting through the gears one by one, and the bike ran well. The wind almost knocked him over when he turned around and rode back up the hill to the mission. He pushed the bike up the stairs and into the room where he slept.

He took the bottle of Scotch and went outside to watch the first storm of the year that would change the season from dry to rain. He wanted to see the first rain drop hit the ground because he knew he would be witnessing something that somehow defined this existence in Africa: two seasons, one with and one without, a rise and fall of the rivers, life and death in the middle of the continent where one year was really two, where life disappeared twice as fast as anywhere else in the world. You could be born in the dry season, Jack thought, and die in the season of rains.

The lightning streaked across the sky in a long, yellow bolt that cracked a seam through the clouds, followed almost immediately by an explosion, and Jack took a sip of the Scotch and watched another and another and as there were so many bolts of lightning reaching down and touching the ground at the same time, they looked as though they were legs connected to the clouds, running and pulling the clouds to the west and the thunder the sound of the whip driving them forward.

The lightning moved on across the forest toward Cameroon and the sea, and in its wake were other dark, billowy clouds the color of dark granite and they were full of rain. Sipping the Scotch from the bottle, Jack waited for the rain because when it came it would divide a year into two, and everything following for the next six months would be afternoon rain and then a swollen river that boats and barges could ply, and it would mean that Bangui, at the end of the river in the middle of the continent, would have cement, gasoline, kerosene, cloth, hardware, autoparts, everything that defined a civilization, or at least everything that helped people make it work.

There was a pause in the weather and the wind stopped as if it were deciding if this were truly the time, possibly considering itself a week too early, and then the clouds gave birth to a million drops of rain each the size of one's thumb. Jack could smell it before it fell, and then feel it as it fell, and he saw the first drop hit the orange laterite of the yard, and then the ground was a river and the wind came back on and blew the rain into the houses.

Now was a different season. There was no calendar to tell anyone that it was, but everyone knew. It rained hard for an hour before the clouds simply disappeared, and the sun was hot again in the late afternoon as it always was, only now the air was wetter and more stifling as it would be for another six months of the *saison des pluies*.

That night, after dinner, Faith went out to see Jack and he was already in his bed when he heard the knock on the door. He got up, opened the door and standing in his shorts was ready to come out to the porch to talk when she took him by the hand, closed the door and led him to the bed, and standing there she kissed him, and their hands explored each other, and Jack said no, what about her parents, and she kissed him again and they lay down and the lightning and thunder outside returned, and the rain beat down hard on the corrugated iron roof, the room alive with the sound of rain, so loud that neither Jack nor Faith could hear each other; they could only feel what the noise might have been as they sweat together, their lathered skin rubbing together, their panted breath together, the beating of their hearts together, each of them rising and falling with the rain that had been so long absent.

"Good morning, Jack," the Chief of Police said as he stood up from behind his desk when the sergeant showed Jack into his office. "This certainly is a surprise." He was a fat man who looked pained by the humidity as he wiped his forehead with a white handkerchief. Jack walked forward and shook his hand in the traditional handshake of friends, their middle fingers snapping before release. Dieudonne motioned for Jack to sit in the chair before his desk, and they both sat down.

"The rains have come again and the road to Carnot is a quagmire so that I was delayed by six hours in returning," Dieudonne said in French as he leaned back in his chair and loosened the collar of his olive-green uniform that was as neatly pressed as it always was for despite his own girth, his uniforms were crisp with starch.

"The rain makes it difficult to travel," Jack said.

"Yes, it does that, but at least it clears the dust." Dieudonne took a Dunhill from the ivory case on his desk and slid it across the mahogany surface to Jack who shook his head and took a Siat from his own breast pocket. Dieudonne leaned across the desk and with a gold lighter first lit Jack's and then his own, and then he leaned back in his chair again.

"The sergeant says you are a friend of the girl's."

"I am. I know her from Bangui."

"It's a terrible crime she has committed. I am sorry for her." He shook his head.

"It's a serious crime, but she didn't do it, Dieudonne."

Dieudonne raised his eyebrows as he exhaled the smoke and he leaned forward and stamped out the cigarette in the ashtray before he had smoked much of it at all. "What is this? But she has confessed."

"She is protecting someone."

"Really?"

"Yes."

"And how do you know this?"

"She told me."

"Really. And who is this someone?"

Jack turned from Dieudonne and looked out the door to where the sergeant sat behind his desk. He turned back to Dieudonne and said, "Me."

"You, Jack? But how could that be?"

"I killed the Frenchman and I would do it again."

Dieudonne frowned at this business of his first morning back after he had been to Carnot to buy a diamond for his wife. He looked across the desk at Jack, took a piece of paper from the drawer and picked up a pen and sighed.

"What is this you are telling me, Jack? That she did not kill the Frenchman?"

"Yes. I did it."

"But why would you kill him? He was just a *patron* of a coffee plantation. Why would you kill him?"

"He was in the act of raping Mari."

"That is what she said."

"And I had come to visit and I heard her cries and her sister was unconscious on the floor and the children were in shock and I pulled him off of Mari, and he pulled a knife from his pants and we fought."

Dieudonne sighed again. "I see, I see. But this complicates everything now."

Jack reached across the desk for the ashtray and Dieudonne pushed it to him.

"What do you want me to do?" Dieudonne asked.

"Let Mari go. I will go to Bangui for the trial. It was self-defense."

"I see that, but it complicates everything. The papers have been drawn up. They are waiting for her in Bangui. She is to be sent to Bangui today."

"I told you that I did it, but that it was self-defense. I will be, what is the word in French?"

"*Disculpe?*"

"Yes. Exonerated."

"Yes, I hope that you will. But still, this complicates everything."

"I know."

"I will have to arrest you." Dieudonne drummed his fingers on the desk, and then he stood and went to the window and looked out at the gray clouds that were swept across the sky. "The wind is beginning to blow again. Soon it will rain."

Jack stood and joined the fat African at the window. "I wanted to talk to you, Dieudonne, about arresting me. You see, I have a problem. But I am afraid of small places."

"*Claustrophobie.*" Dieudonne turned back from the window, returned to his desk and sat, opened a drawer and took out a pair of handcuffs. Jack went back to his chair. "That is something everyone is afraid of, Jack." He looked at the handcuffs in his hand. "The fear of small places. Of being locked up."

"Listen to me, Dieudonne. It is why I needed to speak to you. You know I won't run."

"No, that is probably true. But we have procedures that must be followed when one is suspected of a crime and incarceration is a large part of the procedure."

"But I told you it was in self-defense."

"And I believe you."

"Then why do you have to lock me up?"

"Jack, imagine you being in my position. You are an African and I am an American. I have told you I killed someone, but that I cannot be locked up. You believe me. You know I will not run. So, you do not arrest me, but tell me to go to Bangui to stand trial. Now, what would the people think?" He raised his hand. "Wait. I will tell you what they would think. They would think that I was crazy or that I was afraid of whites or that I was in the pocket of the white man. You see? I have to do my job."

Jack leaned forward in his chair. "Wait. Let me tell you something before you arrest me. It will explain why I cannot be locked up."

Dieudonne sighed again. "*D'accord*, Jack, but still I must lock you up. I promise we will give you the best of care. You have my word on that. And when this is over, you and I will go out and drink together and we will drink all night and laugh about this misunderstanding." He toyed with the handcuffs, passing them from one hand to the other as he leaned back in his chair.

"Okay. But please listen."

"You have my attention."

"It was when I was a child," Jack said, and he stood and went to the window again and with his back to Dieudonne, he told him about the foster home and the man there who would come home and strip down to his shorts when Jack was six years old, and he told him how the man would crawl on his hands and knees as if he were a lion, which he pretended he was, and how Jack would run from room to room to escape, and when the man caught him he would rip off Jack's clothes with his teeth as if he were indeed a feral beast, and he would pin Jack down to the floor and make Jack suck on his penis and when Jack once bit him, the man became enraged and beat him and locked him in the closet and after that episode, he would lock Jack in the closet for days at a time and would allow him out only if Jack promised not to bite, and Jack was stubborn and once he spent five days in the closet shitting and pissing on the floor because the man would not even give him a bucket. It was only after the first grade teacher came one afternoon to inquire about Jack that she heard his cries and the police came and freed Jack and he had been in the closet for five straight days and he was

60

covered in excrement and he would not talk and he was dehydrated, and the man was arrested and Jack was taken to Child Protective Services and later his teacher adopted him, and when growing up Jack would never sleep with his door shut and sometimes he would wake crying and screaming, and his new mother would hold him tight all night long.

Dieudonne fumbled for a cigarette.

"You see why I cannot be locked up." Jack turned and looked at Dieudonne. "Not even for a minute. It is impossible. I would go crazy."

"It is terrible what that man did to you. I hope justice was served and that he was killed."

"He was in prison for seven years."

"That is all?"

"I think."

"Here he would be killed. But here, I have never heard of a crime like that. Never."

"Do you understand why I cannot be locked up?"

"Yes, I do." Dieudonne stood and came to the window and put his hand on Jack's shoulder. "I understand." He pointed out the window. "Look at that house across the road where the old man sits under the eaves. You see him?"

"Yes."

"Well, he is blind, and he sits there all day. His daughter feeds him and gives him water and I have seen her give him *mbako* and when he drinks much of it, he becomes very drunk. Last week he was very drunk and he screamed obscenities at the children in the neighborhood, and he said terrible things."

"So?"

"Well, I like the man, but he was drunk and did something that was not good for the children, for the community, so despite his handicap I had to lock him up for three days."

"Wait, you are not telling me..."

"Wait. Listen. Then I released him and there he is now and he will sit there until it rains and then he will go into the house. He is free to do what he chooses. Now you, you have a terrible handicap as well, but in the eyes of the law you are the same as anyone else."

61

"You are going to lock me up, aren't you?"

"I have no choice. You will be given the best of care, I promise you. And then when the trial is over you will be free."

"Don't you believe what I have told you?"

"I do. I believe. But the man had sixeen knife punctures in his abdomen and it is necessary to have a trial. Then you will be free."

"I cannot be locked up. I just cannot be locked in."

"I understand that, but it will only be for a short while, Jack. Please understand that."

"Besides, what if the judge does not believe it was self-defense? What if I am convicted? They will lock me up for the rest of my life for killing a bastard who deserved to die."

Dieudonne held out the handcuffs before him. "Please, Jack. This is for the best. Cooperate with me. Please, take these. Put them on. Do not make me do it."

"I can't." Jack pushed Dieudonne against the wall and Dieudonne did not so much as struggle. Jack pulled the pistol from the holster and stepped back and checked to see if it was loaded before pointing it at Dieudonne who stood against the wall. "Sit down at the desk."

Dieudonne walked to the desk and sighing, he sat down. "Jack, you are making a mistake. If you will give me the gun, I promise you I will not report any of this. We can pretend this has never happened."

"I wish we could do that, but I told you why I cannot go to jail. You do not understand. Now, call in the sergeant."

"Jack, this is a grave mistake."

"Call him in."

"Jack, once I do that, there is no turning back."

"Now."

Dieudonne sighed, the exhalation seemingly depleting his body of all reserve. "Pierre, come here, please," Dieudonne shouted in a voice restrained of emotion.

The door opened and Pierre walked up to the desk. He looked at Jack who was standing by the window, but he did not see the gun because Jack had it behind his back.

"Yes, what do you need of me, sir?"

"Jack?" Dieudonne said.

"Sit down," Jack said and he pointed the gun at the sergeant who immediately raised his hands and sat. "Put your gun on the floor." With his right hand, the sergeant gingerly took the revolver by the handle and placed it on the floor. "Now, Dieudonne, please handcuff the sergeant's hands behind his back."

Dieudonne stood and did as he was told. "Lie on your stomach," Jack told the sergeant and he did. "Now, Dieudonne, I must handcuff you as well. Do you have another pair?"

"In my desk."

"Please, take them out."

Dieudonne walked back around the desk and removed the handcuffs. Jack walked up behind him and set the gun on the desk and Dieudonne put his hands behind his back and allowed himself to be handcuffed.

"Jack, you are my friend and I tell you, you are making a terrible mistake."

"There is nothing I can do about it. I am sorry."

"I too am sorry. When you are apprehended, I will still do my best to explain that you are a good and honorable man."

"Thank you. But if I am caught, you can say those words at my funeral. Now, please lie on your stomach next to the sergeant."

He did as he was told, and Jack gagged each man with a handkerchief, and he tied their legs with the rope Dieudonne told him was in the truck outside, and he took the sergeant's keys and his gun and went to Mari's cell.

"Mari, it's time to go."

"Jack, thank you. Did he allow you to remain free?"

"Yes and no. Come, Mari. We must hurry."

He took her by the arm and directed her out of the cell and as they walked through the foyer she looked into the police chief's office and she saw the two men lying on the floor. "Jack, what have you done?"

"Not now, Mari. We must hurry."

She climbed on the back of the motorcycle and they rode through town and up the hill to the mission.

From the kitchen, Faith could hear the motorcycle, and she wiped her hands and hurried down the back porch and into the yard where she was standing when Jack rode up with an African on the back, and her smile faded.

Mari dismounted and Jack leaned the motorcycle on the kick stand.

"Jack, what's wrong?" Faith said.

"Mari, wait here," Jack said and walked quickly to the outbuilding and Faith followed him and on the porch she grabbed his arm.

"Jack, what are you doing?"

"He was going to lock me up."

Jack went inside and picked up the clothes on his bed and stuffed them in the leather bag, and he turned and Faith took hold of both his arms. "What did you do?"

"Nothing. I tied them up. No one is hurt." He started to move toward the door, but she held him.

"So you're just going to leave?"

"I have to help Mari."

"You still love her."

"This has nothing to do with love. It's just that I had to make it right. She didn't kill the man. I did. Now the police know, so she'll be okay."

"You killed the man?"

"Yes."

"But why?"

"Because he raped her. I went to her house and he was raping her. The fat son of a bitch was raping her."

"You killed him?"

"Yes. I killed him. I killed the son of a bitch."

"What are you going to do?"

"Take her as far as M'Baiki, maybe, I don't know."

"And just leave? Leave me?"

"Faith."

"After last night? Just leave me? Without an explanation?"

"Faith, I'm sorry. This is not about love. This was simply about making right what was wrong, and I could not spend one night in a jail because if I did I don't know what would happen."

Faith took him in her arms. "I know. I know that. You told me. But

64

Jack, you can't just leave like this. Not without me. No one is going to leave me ever again." She leaned back and looked in Jack's eyes and tears welled up in her own. "I'm going with you."

Jack leaned forward and kissed the top of her head. "I'm sorry, Faith. I really am. But I have to hurry. The police will be looking for me as soon as they find them."

Faith looked up at Jack and she had tears running down both sides of her face. "Faith, I can't go to jail."

"I know."

"I just can't."

"I know. Jack?"

"What?"

"I love you."

"You don't know that. You don't even know me. Remember? I'm the guy who won't eat with Baptists. I'm trouble. I came here and interrupted your life. Remember?"

"I told you I love you. And I know you. And trouble? Trouble would be never seeing you again. Trouble would be you leaving me the way... you can't just leave me like this."

"I killed the Frenchman. I stabbed him sixteen times."

"Because you were protecting the, the..."

"*African*. Mari is her name."

"Mari."

"But sixteen times?"

"You did what you had to do."

Jack squeezed her with both his arms wrapped around her and he kissed her on the mouth and she kissed him back, and when they heard the door open, they looked up and saw Mari. She stood there without saying anything and then she turned and went back out.

"Jack, I have to know something. Do you love me?"

Jack didn't say anything, but Faith's arms were still around his shoulders and her tears were still on his lips. "I can't go to jail, Faith. I can't."

"I know, Jack. I know. But do you love me?"

"I don't know what love is, Faith. What happened to the tough missionary?"

"I was never tough, Jack, and love is what we had last night."

Faith put her face against his and they hugged, and she thought about Christophe and how he had left and never written and she thought of Darrel Blankenship and his letters and about Florida and about her mother and father and about how they loved the notion of Darrel Blankenship because to them he was really only a notion or an ideal, but he was certainly not real, *I just wish there were more young men like him these days...whoever catches him will be very lucky indeed,* and then they went outside and found Mari sitting in the shade.

PART TWO

It was raining hard and heavy, a wash of water angling down from the east, and there were puddles in the dips in the road. Jack downshifted the Landcruiser at each one, and finally he had to stop, climb out into the rain and lock the wheel hubs for four-wheel drive. The wipers couldn't swing fast enough to wipe away the rain that beat down on the metal roof of the truck sounding hollow and metallic, and Mari sat in the middle and Faith sat by the door, their bags on the floor. The only things in the bed of the truck were the motorcycle tied off to the rack behind the rear window and a fifty-gallon drum of diesel fuel roped off next to the motorcycle.

Jack silently reproached himself for allowing Faith to come, but she had made it clear that there would be no truck without her and without the truck the travel would have been dangerous. He now wondered if he allowed her to come because of the truck, or because he liked the idea of loving her, or whether it wasn't something of his to allow—that she came of her own accord, and he was confused and tried not to think about it. As he drove, Jack worried about many things, but he was more concerned about himself than the others because they were not at the risk that he was after having confessed to killing the Frenchman, and now there was a probability that Faith's parents would think that he had stolen their truck or that he had kidnaped Faith and no matter what they thought, they were sure to contact the police. Still, though, he at least felt relieved on the account of Mari; no longer would she be accused of a murder she had not committed.

Five kilometers east of Boda was the barrier, and Jack slowed to a stop and wondered if he should crash through the wooden beam that blocked the road.

"Mari, lie down," he said and he motioned for Faith to get out of the truck with him and as he stepped down, Jack stuck the revolver under his belt in the back of his pants and he pulled his shirt tail down over it.

"*Bonjour, Monsieur,*" Jack said to the gendarme dressed in camouflaged fatigues who sat behind a desk in the wooden hut next to the barrier. Jack handed him his papers and so did Faith.

The gendarme looked first at Jack's and then at Faith's, and he slid the papers back across the desk. "Is there anyone else in the truck?" he asked. "I thought I saw someone between you as you pulled up."

Jack started to answer, but Faith interrupted him and spoke in Sango and after she had finished speaking, the gendarme looked nervous and he stood and backed away from them and told them to get out of the hut. Only when Faith and Jack climbed in the truck did he come out of the hut to open the barrier, and Jack started the truck and drove through before he asked Faith what she had said.

"I told him Mari was a leper and that we were taking her to the leprosarium in Bokanga."

"How did you think of that?"

"Haven't you ever read *Huckleberry Finn*?"

Jack smiled, and Mari asked what had transpired and Faith explained to her in Sango, and Mari laughed, then caught herself and said to Jack with half a smile, "Missionaries have the ability to lie well."

Faith ignored her comment.

The rain stopped and the clouds moved west and the sun was hot and it was steamy in the cab. Jack opened the window and black flies bit at their faces and hands, and they drove and swatted at the flies that left welts the size of small coins.

There was little traffic on the road between Boda and M'Baiki, only an occasional *voiture en occasion*, and when one approached, Jack drove as close to the shoulder as he could. The butterflies were thick in the forest and Jack had to stop the truck every ten or fifteen kilometers to scrape them off the radiator to keep the truck from overheating.

This far south from Bangui it was deep jungle that the narrow road carved through. Ebony and rosewood trees with branches intertwined like the fingers of clasped hands towered over the palms and citrus and banana and papaya trees. It was dark even with the sun somewhere over head, dark and green and dank and rich, a miasmic fecundity that was pregnant with the small life of black flies and mosquitoes that buzzed in the air, and beneath them the snakes, the spitting cobras, the green mambas and black mambas that spiraled through the vines. Above the narrow slice of road, the branches reached across and mingled and the light that filtered through was a reluctant diffusion. Occasionally there were termite mounds, Matterhorns of laterite soil three meters tall, and when it rained the termites crawled out for water. During the dry season, the village children would beat pots and pans next to these mounds in an effort to replicate the sound of rain, and the termites would come out only to be snatched up by bony fingers, dropped in burlap bags to be taken home for dinner. Now it was the rainy season and there would be termites and the rivers would rise and the roads would be a deep, rutted mud for the half year before the next season would erase everything sodden.

Mostly they were quiet as they drove, but Mari would talk from time to time, commenting on a village they passed or asking Jack to stop when she saw pineapples for sale, or manioc, or fish from the river, and once they did stop so she could buy antelope meat, and with this she planned to make a profit in Bangui where the price would be higher than in the jungle. Bangui was the concrete hub of the Republic and the roads that led to the city from east and west and north and south were lined with pedestrians, bicycles and trucks, all laden with everything the city did not produce on its own: chicken and goat and cow and snake and monkey and fish and manioc and papaya and oranges and limes and lemons and avocado and mango and bananas and palm wine, and charcoal made in smoldering fifty-gallon drums. In Bangui, these commodities were sold and the people would trudge back to their villages with coins in their pockets, small coins called francs because this African republic had been minted in the image of France.

As they passed other villages, Mari asked Jack to stop, but he told her no, they had to hurry now, there was no time but to go forward, to keep moving away from the law.

The sun dried the mud-slicked road and except for the puddles in the low spots, the road was dry again and bumpy as ever from the rocks that protruded from the laterite. Jack drove fast but was careful to avoid the sharp rocks, and it had been four hours since they had left the police station in Boda. He was worried about being pursued. He seemed to be the only one of the three who was worried about anything because Mari's comments concerned the villages they passed, and Faith was generally quiet; she thought about what it would be like once they had disposed of Mari, what it would be like with only the two of them alone in a truck driving to some frontier, two of them driving like any couple in love.

71

Jack looked at Faith and her face was relaxed and she smiled at much of what Mari said, yet it was not a condescending smile, and Jack thought that if he were to make it out of the country he would have to be rid of both these women—the two women he loved in separate ways. He wondered about the two women sitting next to each other, wondered what they thought, but mostly they ignored each other and the silence grew more uncomfortable with each kilometer of jungle.

Cresting a hill south of M'Baiki, the engine sputtered and died. Jack shifted into neutral and rolled down the hill and pulled to the side of the road. "We're out of gas," he said in English, and Faith said, "Diesel, Jack. It's not gas," and Jack frowned and said, "Whatever." He got out of the truck and climbed into the bed and unscrewed the cap on the fifty-gallon drum, inserted a hose, jumped down and sucked on the hose and spit out a mouthful of diesel before inserting the hose in the truck's tank.

As it filled, Mari went into the bushes to relieve herself and then Faith did the same, and when Mari got in the truck, Faith asked Jack what they were going to do.

"I don't know, Faith. Right now we're just running."

"Where to?" She stood next to Jack as the diesel overflowed from the truck's tank and Jack pulled out the hose and kinked it and screwed in the gas cap, climbed into the bed of the truck and replaced the cap on the big, metal drum.

He stood above her and looking down at her he said, "I've got to get out of the country. I'll leave you and Mari in M'Baiki and then I'll go south and cut up north by Berberati and cross into Cameroon. To Douala. It's the best way out."

"And then what?"

"A ship. I don't know. Maybe I'll go to the American Embassy."

"That would be best. If we go to the American embassy, we could explain everything, and then everything would be all right."

Jack climbed down from the truck and stood next to Faith. He put his hands on her shoulders. "Listen, Faith. It would be stupid for you to go with me."

"You think I took my father's truck just for a drive in the country? You can't just keep leaving people. Like you left Mari."

"What?"

"She loved you, too."

Jack removed his hands from her shoulders. "That's over," he said.

"Yes. But we're not." Faith walked around to the passenger side of the truck and from over the hood she said, "I'm going with you. And that's that."

Jack looked at her across the hood. "Faith, you don't know what love is."

"And you're the expert?" Faith looked through the windshield at Mari who was watching them. "Don't patronize me, Jack. Never, never patronize me. I've had enough of that from my father and you are not my father."

"Faith, damn it. This is stupid. You're too young to get involved in this."

"You don't listen, do you? I didn't know there was an age limit on stupidity." Faith climbed into the cab next to Mari. "You're only twenty-five," she said as Jack climbed into the driver's seat.

Jack began to say something, but he stopped himself just short of regret; he started the truck and put it into gear, resuming the slippery road, and after an hour they came to the barrier before M'Baiki, and when he stopped Jack said in French, "Mari, we'll take you to the market. You can get a *voiture en occasion* to Bangui from there." And he took out his wallet and gave her five thousand francs.

"Thank you," she said, and she looked at the money in her hand and folded it and put it inside her bra under the sari she wore, and she looked like she was going to cry.

"Mari, you stay in the truck. Faith will tell them you're sick. It worked before."

Faith smiled at Mari and patted her thigh and climbed down out of the truck and followed Jack to the hut where three gendarmes were playing cards at a metal table behind the desk.

The gendarmes were dressed in camouflaged fatigues and they looked up at Jack and Faith and they frowned at being interrupted, but there was something else in their looks as well and Jack thought he could feel it. Jack handed both his and Faith's papers to the gendarme who was closest to the other side of the desk, and he picked them up as though they were dirty and looked at them with disdain, and then he passed them to the man who was sitting on his right, and he, in turn, passed them to the man sitting next to him who gave them back to the sergeant after having given them a cursory examination of his own.

The sergeant said, "Where are you coming from?"

"Boda," Jack answered before he could think better of it, and then he added, "From Carnot. We only stopped in Boda for the night."

The sergeant looked at Faith. "You are a missionary in Boda?"

"Yes."

"And this is your truck?"

"Yes."

"What are you doing with him?"

"I was going to Bangui for supplies and offered him a ride as he only had a motorcycle," she said in Sango.

"You speak Sango very well," said the sergeant. "Does he?" He motioned to Jack.

"No, very little."

Jack watched the conversation he could not understand. The two other gendarmes sat straight up in their chairs like wooden soldiers.

"Who is in the truck?" the sergeant asked Faith.

"A woman. She is a leper. We are taking her to the leprosarium at Bokanga."

"And you are not afraid of getting sick?"

"No. We have both been inoculated."

"I see. Very well, then. Have a good journey."

As he passed the papers to Faith, a voice came on the short wave radio. Jack and Faith walked back to the truck. As Jack turned around on the other side of the truck, he could see the sergeant talking into the microphone, and before Faith had her door open the sergeant yelled for them to stop. The three soldiers came out with their guns drawn and from the other side of the truck Jack reached in the open window and picked up the nine millimeter pistol and from behind the hood he aimed at the sergeant and in French told him to drop the weapon, but instead the sergeant aimed at Jack and fired and Jack shot back.

74

From a distance of ten meters the two men missed each other, and then one of the other gendarmes fired and the bullet hit the hood of the truck. Jack aimed and shot at him, but he missed again, and then he once more aimed with two hands, and he pulled back the trigger, and the gun exploded and kicked back in his hand as the gendarme fell down with a wound in the chest, and the other gendarme turned and ran inside the hut, maybe to call for someone on the radio or perhaps in fear, and the sergeant shot again as Faith was closing the door behind her and she slumped and fell out onto the ground, and Mari screamed. Jack took aim and shot at the sergeant, the first shot missing, the second two hitting him in the chest, and he slumped to the ground, knees buckling first, then the body as if he were being sucked down into the earth by some alien worm.

Jack ran around the truck and helped Faith up and eased her onto the seat next to Mari. Faith moaned and said as if in great surprise, "He shot me. I was shot. The man shot me." Jack slammed the door and ran around to the driver's side and climbed in and started the truck. He stepped on the gas and rammed through the barrier and drove toward M'Baiki. He looked over at Faith as Mari held her with her arm around her shoulder. Faith was groaning now and Mari held her and Jack asked Mari where Faith had been shot.

"In the arm, I think."

Jack held the wheel with one hand and pulled his arm out of his shirt sleeve, and then the other, and he handed the shirt to Mari and told her to use it to apply pressure to the wound because he couldn't stop now, he said.

They entered the town of M'Baiki and Jack was in fourth gear going up the hill with his hand on the horn and children ran off the dirt street in front of him as he passed the market on his right and the ramshackle bars that lined the street on his left, and he came to the intersection where he had to turn right by the police station, and he skidded through the turn, the rear end of the truck fishtailing so that it hit a goat tethered to a sign post, and people were running out of houses to see the commotion of a wild truck with a blaring horn. Then he drove up the hill above M'Baiki to the intersection where the paved road to Bangui went left and the dirt road to Scad, the village near the French lumber mill, went right, and at the crossroad Jack hesitated for a moment before making the right turn on the dirt road that took them south again into the deep jungle where the only roads were labyrinthine and were for the logs trucks that brought the timber to the mill.

"How's she doing?" Jack asked as he drove hard and fast down the rutted road toward Scad with Mari leaning over Faith, holding the shirt to her bicep, the shirt soaked with blood.

"It hurts," Faith said. "It hurts. It's bleeding. It won't stop bleeding. I'm running out of blood."

"Hold on. I'll stop as soon as I can. Is there a first aid kit?"

"Under the seat. Am I going to die? I'm bleeding. It won't stop. Oh, please, God, no."

"It'll stop, and no, you're not going to die. Try and be calm." He asked Mari to look at both sides of the arm to see if there were two holes, and Mari said there were, and Jack felt that at least there was some luck in the shooting, that Faith would be all right if the bullet were clean, but hoping for sterility in a place where germs met and festered in the very air was perhaps too much to desire.

They drove through Scad and past the lumber mill where huge logs were piled high and barefoot Africans ran between the machinery that moved the giant logs.

It was late afternoon and the clouds were gathering in force. Once they passed through Scad, they entered the deep jungle that went south for thousands of kilometers through Zaire, The Congo, Angola, Zambia, and he wasn't sure where to go, but he knew that they had to keep going. The road narrowed and was full of tributaries, but he stayed on the main road until he came to a narrow fork far enough from Scad that Jack felt it safe, and he slowed and turned off and drove another kilometer down the narrow path with the branches of trees scratching both sides of the truck. Lightning and thunder cut loose, and the rains followed hard and heavy. Finally he pulled off into a small clearing on the side of the road where someone had cut the trees and planted a hectare of coffee.

He reached under the seat for the first aid kit, and with the rain pounding on the roof of the truck he had to shout to Mari for her to switch places with him. He looked at the arm, and it was only a flesh wound. "Faith, how are you doing?"

"It hurts. Jack, I'm scared. I lost a lot of blood."

"It's not serious. This is going to sting a little."

"My parents must be worried. I'm sorry. If I die, tell them I love them. God, don't let me die. Please, God."

"Easy, Faith."

He poured hydrogen peroxide on the wound and it bubbled and Faith stifled a scream, and he applied antiseptic and bandaged the wound, and Faith leaned on Jack's shoulder and cried.

"Jack, he shot me. I'm bleeding to death."

"You're not bleeding anymore. You're fine."

"I could die."

"Faith, god damn it, you're not going to fucking die."

Mari said something to Faith in Sango and Faith replied, and her crying slowed and Jack still held her.

"What did she say?" Jack asked Faith.

"Nothing."

Jack turned to Mari and in French he said, "We should all speak French so there will be no misunderstandings."

The rain continued to come down in torrents and the noise of the rain kept them from hearing the truck until it was next to them, a log truck pushing through the mud toward Scad, and the driver may not have seen them in the clearing beside the road for he did not stop. As they waited for the rain to let up, Jack looked through the glove box and found matches and a compass, and he switched places with Mari and sat back behind the steering wheel. He cracked the window and lit a cigarette, and Mari told him to put it out because it would bother Faith. He took two quick drags before going outside to smoke.

When the rain stopped, it was dusk. Jack started the truck and pulled farther off the road into the jungle. He got out and cut palm fronds and did his best to cover the truck so that it would not be visible from the road. Mari gathered firewood and she tried to start a fire, but the wood was damp and would not burn. She filled a cup with diesel and with the fuel was finally able to get the small twigs to catch fire, and she slowly added bigger sticks until the fire would continue on its own. Jack helped Faith out of the truck and she sat down on a log by the fire as dusk fell to night.

Mari boiled water and made a broth with the smoked antelope and then she made a *boule* from the ground manioc she had boiled, and they sat by the fire and ate and they knew they were far from anywhere because there were no funeral drums to be heard; only the cicadas and crickets sounded the night and the occasional screech of a monkey or of some foreign bird.

Jack got up and returned with the Scotch and he took a sip and handed it to Mari who also took a sip before she offered it to Faith.

"No thank you, Mari. I don't really drink."

"Why not?"

"I just never have."

"It might help you sleep."

"How can I sleep? I've been shot."

"How's your arm now?" Jack asked.

"It still hurts. A little. Not like before. I'm not going to die." She started to cry again. "I wonder what my parents are thinking."

"If it doesn't get infected, it'll be alright," Jack said.

"They must be scared to death. I need to write them soon. My mother, she'll be going crazy. My father, God, he'll be in shock."

"We should change the bandage again, Jack," Mari said.

"What are we going to do?" Faith asked Jack.

"Jesus fucking Christ, I don't know." Jack stood and paced before the fire. "I think I killed the man. Maybe both of them."

"It's too bad," Mari said. "It was all an accident."

"All an accident? I killed the bastard. I shot him. My God, can you believe this shit? I killed the man. I'm not supposed to kill people. I build schools. I build schools for the fucking United Nations."

"Jack," Faith said.

"And now I'm running through Africa with guns, shooting gendarmes at barriers, killing people. Do you understand that? I killed that bastard who raped you, Mari. I had to do that. But this? Killing gendarmes like some damn cowboy shooting his way out of town? No, God, this isn't the way it is supposed to be. It was supposed to be simple. Mari goes free. I'm exonerated for self-defense. I go back to work at the UN. Simple. But no, now I'm driving wild through Africa shooting my way out, and with a god damn missionary no less, and... Sorry, Faith. I didn't mean that."

"Jack," Faith said again. She stood and Jack looked at her standing in the light of the fire, her right arm in a sling made from his shirt. "Jack, calm down."

"Calm down? Look at you. A seventeen-year old girl who should be home with her parents. I take you for a drive in your father's truck and what happens? You get shot. A gendarme shoots you through the arm. Can you believe this?"

Mari stood. "We're in trouble, Jack, but we can repair this; we can, we can do something."

Jack backed away from Faith and looked at both women standing by the fire. He looked first at Faith and then at Mari and it was as if the significance of all the day's events, as if the significance of everything that had happened since he had walked into Mari's home and found her being raped—it was as if he now realized the gravity of what he had done.

He sat back down on the log by the fire. He looked at the flames. Then he looked back up at Faith and Mari. "I just don't know what we can do now. I mean, if those men are dead. Even if they're not. At least the two of you are still innocent of anything."

"But I was with you," Mari said. "I was with you when you killed the Frenchman and when you killed the sergeant."

"We don't know that the sergeant is dead," Faith said.

"Shot twice in the chest? He's dead," Jack said. "But Mari, the police know you are innocent. I told Dieudonne that. You can go back to Bangui."

"How?"

"Once we get you near a town, you'll be able to take a *voiture en occasion*."

"And where will you go?" Mari asked. "They will be looking for you everywhere after what happened in M'Baiki. At every check point in every road."

Jack sighed. "I know. I don't have any choice now. If I can make it to Cameroon or The Congo, I can make it to a port. I don't know. I just have to get out of this country before I can decide what to do next. I have to cross the border. That's the only thing I know. I have to cross the border." And as he said this, he thought he may already have. The African continent was like a vast ocean.

Mari was quiet and she looked at Faith who studied Jack in the flicker of fire light. "We," was all Faith said, and Jack got up to make the arrangements for sleeping as Mari put a clean bandage on Faith's arm.

It rained that night and under the canvas tarp Jack had tied off over the truck bed, Mari and Jack pushed against each other to avoid the dripping of rain. Faith slept in the cab after protesting that Mari should sleep there, but she gave in when Mari said that because of her wound, she should sleep where it was dry. A bat flew under the tarp and fluttered in confusion on Mari's chest, and she screamed and Jack swatted the bat away, and then Mari fell asleep again. Jack lay awake thinking about all of the nights he had slept with Mari under her mosquito net in the stucco house in Bangui and how they had made love and how they would never make love again, and he was sad because he felt he would always love her in some way; it was as if all his love had been grounded in her before, but that he had pulled away much of the love, but not all of it for there would always be a single strand of love that tied them together, even when he was very far away.

After breakfast, they turned back to the main road and turned right and continued south toward The Congo or Zaire, Jack wasn't sure which, and after a hundred kilometers during which they passed three log trucks, Jack turned west on a narrow track and he drove slowly in four-wheel drive because the laterite surface of the road was as slick as ice from the previous night's rains, and there were potholes a meter deep and they were full of water which had to be carefully traversed. The wind had blown down branches that crossed the road, and the road itself was anything but straight; it was so serpentine that without the compass Jack would have thought they were making circles, and still, it was possible they were. The jungle was so thick they could only see cracks of sky.

At noon they came across a coffee plantation buried deep in the jungle. Jack was not sure which country they were in or, indeed, if they were in any country at all. He had marked the odometer from Boda and they had gone three hundred kilometers; it was possible, he feared, that they were just south of Boda now because they had first driven north from Boda and then east to M'Baiki and then south and then west, and though they were lost, it was possible, he thought, that they had not gone far enough south to avoid Boda and Carnot. But there was no town here in the jungle, just a border of coffee on the left side of the road, coffee plants two meters high for as far as the eye could see, and the jungle that stood towering above them.

Jack turned into the plantation to see if it were possible to purchase some fuel. He drove down the narrow track through the coffee fields until he came to knoll in the center of the plantation on which stood a stucco house and in the yard two dogs barked and chickens ran from the truck and a goat looked up from her grazing. He stopped the truck below the porch and an African came out of the house and greeted them.

"Is the *patron* in?" Jack asked through the open window of the cab, and the man said no.

"Do you have some diesel we could buy? And some gasoline?"

"*Un peu peut-etre, mais pas beaucoup.*"

Jack got out and Mari and Faith followed him up to the porch, and the African told them to please sit down in the *chaise longues* on the porch. He came out with beer and he poured four glasses. They all drank, Faith too, but she took but a small sip of the warm beer.

"Where is the *patron*?" Jack said in French as he leaned forward and offered the man a cigarette. The man took it and put it in his mouth and Jack lit it, and the man, who looked old and who was dressed only in shorts, his midriff an undulation of ribs, exhaled.

"He went to Bangui a month ago and has not returned."

"Is that unusual for him to be away for so long?" Faith asked.

"Yes, considering he had planned to return ten days after he left. But Dubois always changes his plans."

"What is his name?" Mari asked.

"Dubois. Maurice Dubois."

Mari did not hide her gasp, and both Faith and Jack understood the significance.

The African turned to Mari. "Do you know him?"

"No, no, I thought for a moment he might be my sister's friend's friend, but it could not be."

The African laughed. "If you knew him, you would remember him for he has a face like a horse and weighs one-hundred-fifty kilos at least." He laughed again.

81

"So he should be back soon," Jack said.

"I think. He was to have met his wife in Bangui. She was coming from Paris to stay for three months as she did the year before, but it is possible she changed her mind."

"What do you mean?" Jack said.

"Well, he is not the kind of man a woman would want to live with for long, I think."

"Why?" Jack said.

The African looked at the two women and shook his head. "He is a very rough man. Sometimes he takes the women who pick the coffee."

"What will you do if he does not return?" Faith said.

"What do you mean? He always returns. But if he did not return, it would not make the gods weep."

They finished their beer and the man sold them fifty liters of diesel and twenty liters of gasoline, and he gave them fresh water and told them that Boda was sixty kilometers due north.

When they were back in the truck, the man came to Jack's window and asked Jack what was wrong with Faith's arm.

"Nothing. Just a snake bite," Faith told him.

"What kind?"

"Black Mamba."

The man's eyes went wide as he leaned on Jack's door. "When?"

"This morning," Faith said.

"You had the serum?"

"No. I sucked out the poison and spit it back in the snake's eye, killing him instantly."

"My God," the man said backing away from Jack's door. "You are magical."

"No," Faith said. "No magic. Just a strong belief in God."

Jack started the truck and thanked the man. They pulled out of the drive and drove through the fields of coffee and back to the road. "What was that all about?" he asked Faith.

She smiled and Mari looked at her with a new curiosity. "Well," she said, "he seemed too curious for his own good was all. And besides, why did he ask you about my arm and not me? Chauvinist. So I thought I would give him something to think about."

"You did that," Mari said. "He might even move to a village with a church in it."

Faith laughed and said her arm was feeling much better now.

They drove west and the first road they came to, they turned south and drove toward the equator and away from Boda and the nation of the Central African Republic. Jack said that he hoped the African at the plantation could inherit the land, and Mari laughed at that.

"What is so funny?"

"The French would never give an African his land," Mari said.

Jack stopped in the afternoon to refuel and again he was too late with the hose and he got a mouthful of diesel. Mari gave him a cola nut to chew, but its bitter taste was as foul as the diesel and he spat it out the window.

They drove south through the afternoon. The road was barely the breadth of Jack's outstretched arms and they had to drive with the windows rolled up because branches scraped the sides of the truck as they drove. The heat in the cab was suffocating and Jack and Faith perspired profusely but Mari much less so, and Faith asked Mari about growing up in Kisangani, and Mari told her about the revolution when her grandfather was killed, when the troops from Belgium came in to stamp out the rebellion and the stories she told were ones that were passed down to her from her mother for she had been too young to remember anything but the hunger of growing up.

Jack listened as she spoke because he had never heard these stories before, he had never heard how Mari and her sister Francoise had taken a boat from Kisangani down The Congo River and then how they waited for weeks to catch a ride on a barge up the Ubangui River to Bangui where their cousin said there was work, and how they arrived to find that there was no work at all except for the work of a prostitute. Francoise had been eighteen and Mari had been fifteen when they first arrived three years before, and she spoke of how life was better in Bangui than it had been in Kisangani; in Bangui, they had a house with a concrete floor and a corrugated iron roof, she said. But still, she missed her mother and father and brothers and sisters and wondered if they were alive.

Jack thought about Mari's house in Bangui, a house that seemed so much to her, a house where he had slept, and thinking of it now he could smell the open sewer that ran down both sides of the dirt street in the Lakounga Quarter, a relatively affluent neighborhood of Bangui, and he could smell the woodsmoke from the charcoal that burned before houses three times each day for although there was electricity in Bangui, few people had anything to plug in; driving now, he could hear the buzz of mosquitoes that hovered at night and he could hear the mangy dogs bark outside and the echoed crying of children—children who were sick with amoebic dysentery or malaria or filariasis—and he thought that if this life of Mari's in Bangui were so much better—a life where she would dress up each evening, take a taxi to a bar or disco where white men would pay her three thousand francs, *she had been just fifteen*—then her life in Kisangani must have been very bad indeed.

"Will you go back to visit your family?" Faith asked.

Mari thought about that for a moment before saying, "Yes, if we save enough money, we will go back. There is not much left in Bangui for me now." She smiled, and Jack listened to what she said and he felt bad for having heard it.

"They must be worried about you," Faith said.

"Maybe, but we write."

"When we get to Cameroon or wherever we're going, I need to write my parents as well," Faith said.

"They'll be very worried about you," Mari said.

Faith said yes, and then fell silent.

Mari asked if she had brothers and sisters, and Faith said no, she was an only child.

"It must have been lonely growing up," Mari said.

Faith thought about that for a moment. "No, not lonely exactly, I don't think. I was too busy. My mother home-schooled me which meant I was essentially in school all the time. And when I wasn't, I was playing outside in the compound, playing mostly with George."

"George?" Mari asked.

"A childhood friend. I shouldn't have made that joke about the snake at the plantation. George died of a snake bite. I kicked the ball into a ditch,

Mari, and he went to retrieve it. That was a real black mamba that bit him. He was only six."

"There are so many snakes everywhere. You have to be careful," Mari said.

"Yes."

Faith went on to tell Mari how she had grown up in Boda, first learning Sango, then English and French, and how she would go back to the states each summer, but that the states was a foreign country to her where she did not feel she belonged, and though she did not tell Mari about the racism in the south among the Baptists her father and mother knew, she thought about it and she knew she could never be that way and that she could never live with those people on the their front porches where they drank iced drinks and sitting high in their porch swings they thought they were so much closer to God than the blacks they joked about, although they never called them blacks--they used another word, a word, maybe the only word of English that every single African knew.

They talked for sometime about their respective childhoods, and each woman knew not to ask Jack about his own.

Jack ignored them and wondered just what it was he was going to do. Whatever it was, it would be soon; as soon as they got to a border, he would make a decision. But he had no idea what that decision would be. As he drove, he replayed the scene in M'Baiki over and over again, and there was no way out of it. The sergeant must be dead. Maybe both of them. He had to admit he had killed, yet he went round and round with what had played out and he changed each version with the hope that he had not killed, or that if he had, he had had no choice.

But he knew that in every action there was choice, and he had made his own.

Driving around a sharp bend in the road, Jack hit the brakes hard and the truck went into a skid. It was too late. The truck crashed into a tree that had fallen across the road. Mari hit the windshield with her head and Jack was braced by the steering wheel and Faith was the only one wearing a seat belt, but she hit her arm against the door, the arm that had been wounded, and she moaned.

Jack opened the door and helped Mari out, and Faith walked around to where Jack was holding Mari and the two of them helped her to the side of the road where they had her sit down. She was bleeding from her forehead.

"Are you okay, Mari?" Faith asked.

"My head hurts." Mari leaned against the base of an ebony tree, and Jack brought the first aid kit and Faith started to bandage Mari's head, but Jack could see how her right arm hurt, and he took the tape and the gauze from Faith. She watched and told him not to bandage it too tight.

When he was done, Jack tried to open the hood of the truck, but it was badly crumpled, and he looked at the tree and it was as big around as the girth of five men. "Fuck," he said in English, and Faith turned to look at him but said nothing, and Mari smiled and said to Faith, "That is one of his favorite words."

"I heard that, Mari," Jack said.

"Jack taught me all of the bad words in English," Mari said. "Son of a beech, motherfucker, fuck you, dick head, shit and cocksucker."

Faith restrained a laugh and stood. She frowned and said in English, "You're a fine teacher, Jack. Very utilitarian prose, indeed."

Jack said nothing and went to the base of the tree a few meters off the road. The roots were gnarled and full of orange soil. "We'll have to cut a path around the tree to get back to the road," he said to no one.

"What did he say?" Mari asked.

"That we have to cut a path through the jungle to the road," Faith told her.

They could hear the crack of thunder in the distance and Faith said it was going to rain soon and that they should make camp at this spot. Jack agreed and went into the jungle with the machete that Faith had told him was behind the seat in the truck. Mari unfurled and then tied off the canopy over the bed of the truck, and as she worked she watched Faith struggle to make a fire.

"That wood is too big," Mari said. She tied down the last rope and went to help Faith gather dry pieces of wood from under tree trunks and together they kneeled and using some of the gasoline this time, started a small fire. Mari sat next to it and stoked it with larger pieces of wood until it was burning well, and Faith gathered more wood and

Mari poured water into a pot and set it to boil. Mari showed Faith how to make a *boule* from the manioc, and as they worked together they could hear the machete cutting vines and hacking at wood and Jack's intermittent cussing.

The lightning came closer and it was dusk and dark in the jungle, and Mari called Jack to come to dinner, but he yelled that he would eat later. As Faith and Mari sat eating with the thunder exploding in the distance, they could hear Jack working the machete and they could hear him swear, and when it began to rain, they called Jack again, but his answer was the swish of the machete through vines. Mari and Faith took the leftover food and set it under the canopy and went inside the cab of the truck and waited for Jack to return.

Both women were wet from the rain and Mari took off her sari and hung it over the steering wheel and it was almost dark in the cab and Faith took off her shirt, pulling it carefully over her right arm, wincing as she did, and she took off her jeans and spread them out over the dashboard as best she could so that they hung down to her bare feet. The cab smelled of the rich fertility of the damp forest floor, and the two women could smell each other's sweat and the wet clothes and their matted hair.

"How is your head?" Faith asked in French.

"Fine. It hurts only a little. Is your arm still hurting?"

"Not so much as before. Jack should be coming back soon. It is almost dark."

"Yes, but he is a stubborn man."

Faith laughed at that and the rain came down harder, rattling the roof of the truck, so loud they almost had to shout.

Mari turned to look at Faith in what little light there was. "You love Jack?" Mari asked.

Faith didn't say anything for a moment, and then she said that she thought she did, but that she had never been in love before, "and I'm afraid of this feeling I have for him because I have never had it before. It's like some nervousness in my chest. I can't put it in words. I once thought I was in love before, but I was only in love with the idea of love, of going off with a man I hardly knew." And when she said this, she thought that this was just what she was doing now.

"He is a good man, but he refuses to admit that," Mari said. "I loved him, too. But for us it is over."

"What happened?" Faith took the bandage off her arm and felt the wound and it didn't hurt as it had before.

"Nothing much except we lost a baby and Jack did not understand. He moved out and left me. Are you going to put on a new bandage?"

"In the morning. This one's wet." Faith wrapped the bandage in a ball and set it on the floorboards. "He shouldn't have moved out, Mari."

"No, it was only a misunderstanding. It was not his fault."

"What didn't he understand?"

"He thought I aborted the baby."

"And you didn't?"

"No."

"So, he wanted a child, Mari?"

Mari pressed her lips together and was silent a moment before saying no, she didn't think he did.

"Then why was he angry?"

"I don't know. Maybe just so he could be angry with me? I don't know."

Faith thought about that for a while and said nothing, and then she said, "He was wrong to do that."

"Yes, he was wrong, but he apologized and he said there is no going back to what once was."

"He said that, did he?"

"Yes. Maybe he is right."

"No, Mari, he is not right. We make a mistake, we ask for forgiveness. That is the nature of humans. We make many mistakes. And we must forgive ourselves. Then we can go back and try again." Faith put her hand on Mari's shoulder, and Mari turned to look at her in the dusky gray light of the cab. There were tears on Mari's cheeks. "Don't for a minute think that just because he is a man he is right, Mari. That is a mistake too many women make."

"Yes."

"And sometimes a woman becomes in awe of the man she loves, and then she must be very careful."

"What do you mean?"

"Sometimes a woman becomes blinded and thinks the man is always right. And that makes the man even more full of what he thinks of manhood, this self-righteousness of being male. I know. My father is that way."

"That is the way all men are," Mari said.

"I know, but it is stupid to be like that. And because men are that way, they are really much weaker than women."

"That is the way with men. I don't know about men in your country, but men in Africa let the women do all of the hard work, and they take credit for the ideas."

Faith laughed.

"It is not so much funny as it is sad, Faith. If the men worked as hard as the women, this would be a rich country, but it is the women who do all of the work. It is often the same with sex."

Faith felt the rise of blood in her cheeks. "My mother says that we need to let men think they are in charge to keep them happy," she said.

"What do you mean?"

"Well, if we can put an idea in their heads and let them think it was their idea, then they will do what we first thought of. But if it is not their idea, they feel that they are not men."

Now it was Mari's turn to laugh. "Yes, I know what you mean. Once I told Jack that we should go to Mongoumba to buy fish, and he thought the idea silly. It was too far to go to buy fish, he said. So I forgot the idea. And then one month later he said that he heard that Mongoumba was a place to buy fresh fish cheaper than Bangui and that it would be a nice drive and that we could have a picnic, and I told him it was a wonderful idea and we went." The windows were steamed now from the wet clothes and the heat of their bodies and their talk.

"It's ridiculous, isn't it, Mari? The way we have to herd the men into doing what is right without letting them see our ropes?"

"It is the way with men. The same in your country, too, then?"

"The same everywhere." Faith laughed. "One time my mother decided that we needed a new propane stove. She had been cooking on a wood stove for years. With my father, it is always the same: to get something new it must be his idea. My mother knew this, of course. I was seven or eight

89

and I remember we had one whole week of burned dinners and when my father complained, she said it was hard to cook on the wood stove and he suggested that we buy a propane stove and my mother told him that was a wonderful idea."

"I guess men are all the same, then. Even Jack, but he is not quite so bad as most. He never was cheap with money and whatever he had, he gave me."

"Sometimes I wonder why we love men at all," Faith said.

"It is the biology of the body. The chemistry of a man and woman in bed together. It is the children that we create, I think. It is nature's need to continue being nature. It is like gravity that pulls us together."

Faith didn't say anything.

"But it is still funny how most men love women and want a son for a child."

"It is, isn't it?" Faith said.

"But I think what it is is that when they were young they remembered how they lusted over girls and they do not trust other boys with their own daughters."

Faith laughed and then so did Mari, and Faith said, "It would be a simpler world if there were no men."

"But what would we do in bed?" Mari asked, and Faith blushed again, but it was dark in the cab and Mari could not see the color of her cheeks. They both laughed again when they saw Jack walking out of the jungle in the gray light of dusk, a machete in his hand, the shirt soaked to his back so that it outlined his body, his black hair slicked down over his forehead. They were still laughing when he opened the door.

He looked at the two naked women. "*Qu'est que ce?*"

They laughed harder.

"What's so funny?

"Men," said Mari, and the two women laughed some more, and Jack sighed and closed the door and went to the back of the truck and took a drink of water from the canteen.

The rain stopped and the fire was out, and Jack stripped down and crawled in the bed of the truck under the tarp, and he heard the door open and shut, and Faith was still naked when she slid in next to him under the blanket and lay down on her back, sliding her arm under his neck.

"Jack?"

"Yes."

"What are we doing?"

"What do you mean what are we doing?" He lay on his back and Faith propped herself up on her left elbow.

"I mean out here in the jungle. Do you think we'll really make it out of here?"

"If I didn't think so I wouldn't have spent the last three hours cutting a path."

"And when we make it, what happens?"

"What do you mean?"

"With us."

"I don't know. Right now we just have to worry about getting out of here. That's enough to think about for now."

"So much has happened since yesterday. Since you came to Boda." Faith lay back down and sighed.

Jack turned his head to look at her, but it was too dark to see. "I'm sorry, Faith. Sorry that you got into this. You should be home with your parents teaching at the school."

Faith was silent a moment, and then Jack could hear her cry.

"Faith?" Jack said.

"I was just thinking. Things happen for a reason."

"That's your religion talking."

"Yes, but how can you live without a religion? It helps you understand."

"Sure. Can your religion help me understand how I killed the men in M'Baiki? How the three of us are here in the middle of nowhere? Tell me the answers to that, Faith. Help me understand that. If you can make me understand that, then I'll say you've got some religion."

"Oh, Jack, I don't know that. But later, we'll understand."

"Later's no good, Faith. I need to understand now. I need to understand just what the fuck it is I need to do. How we can get out of here."

"We'll get out."

"And then?"

"And then life will take care of itself."

91

"I wish you were right, Faith. I wish I could believe that. But right now I'm wanted for murder and I'm starting to think that maybe it was murder. There are dead men now who should be alive. I killed them. In all my life, I could never imagine that I would kill someone. And now I've done that. Two, maybe three times."

"No, Jack. You killed the man in self-defense. And the gendarmes, if they're even dead—and we don't know that they are—that was self-defense too."

"Sure, Faith. It is all self-defense. Is that what you will tell your parents? That you ran off with me in self-defense?"

"I don't know what I will tell them. I try not to think about them now. I pray to God that He will let them know I'm alright. Later, I'll tell them myself."

"Tell them what?"

"That you're not the man everyone thinks you are."

"I'm not even sure of that, Faith. Maybe everyone else is right."

"Who, Jack? Everyone else? Everyone that matters now is me."

He took her head with his hand and kissed her on the lips, and she winced, and Jack apologized and asked her if her arm hurt, but she said no, not much, and a soft rain fell on the tarp above them as they held each other, and the rain fell steadily and later the pitter-patter of the rain on the canvas tarp sent them far away in sleep.

The sun rose without clouds. It was hot, humid, and after breakfast Jack went back to chopping a path through the thick vines and dense underbrush that grew from the forest floor. Above him, the parrots called out to each other and the monkeys screeched at the disturbance of the man hacking away at the bushes and vines. Although Faith said her arm no longer hurt, Mari made her change the bandage once again before she led Faith along a game trail into the jungle, the trees towering above them allowing only thin beams of sunlight to filter down as if the sun were searching them out, but even on the shaded floor of the forest the heat was stifling, the air humid and rich with the scent of pregnant earth. Mari carried a pan and Faith asked what they were doing, and Mari only said, "Termites."

They came across a termite mound constructed of the orange laterite soil. It was a tower two meters high and Mari knelt next to the base and turned the pan over and beat gently on it with a stick. Faith asked her again what she was doing and Mari didn't answer until the steady stream of termites came out of a hole from the depths of the mound, and Mari snatched them up and put them in the burlap bag, and Faith knelt down to help her.

"Why do they come up when you beat on the pan?" Faith asked, and Mari told her that it was the sound of the rain that made the termites come out of their home and the beating of the pan was so similar to the sound of rain if you beat it gently that the termites were fooled.

"Have you ever eaten termites?" Mari asked.

"No."

Mari snatched one up and put it in her mouth and chewed. "They are not bad raw, but cooked in palm oil they are good."

Faith continued to pick up the termites as they crawled out of the mound, moving lethargically to the false call of rain. "Do you want to try one?" Mari asked.

"No, no thank you. After they're cooked, I'll try them."

They worked in silence, both women on their knees, plucking the unsuspecting insects between forefinger and thumb as they lethargically plodded out of the earth and into what they must have thought was rain. It was humid as it always was during the rainy season and Faith perspired, the sweat running down her neck and down her chest. "You know something, Mari?" Mari looked up from her work, and then looked back down at the termites she was engaged with, picking them up and dropping them into the sack, one after another. "What?"

"I was just thinking. It is strange for both of us to be here with Jack."

"Yes."

"It is awkward."

Mari laughed, but it was a laugh without mirth. "Yes."

"I was only thinking that if it wasn't for Jack, we could be great friends."

"And why can't we?"

"I don't know. I just, I, well, I don't know. I guess we can."

Mari said that it was possible, and then she asked Faith if her arm hurt.

93

"No, it's fine."

"I'm glad."

"Mari, I just wish things were different between us."

"I suppose that is true. I don't imagine this is much easier for Jack either."

Faith got off her knees and sat down and sighed. "This is hard work."

Mari looked at her and then continued with the task at hand. "Yes. But don't worry. I'll be leaving the both of you when we come to a town."

"I didn't mean that."

"I know."

"Do you think it is possible for a man to love two women?" Faith asked.

Now Mari turned and sat down. "I would not know, but I imagine that more possible than a woman loving two men, more possible than two women in love with the same man getting along for more than a short time."

"It's funny, isn't it?" Faith said.

"What?"

"The two of us here like this with Jack."

"No, not funny, I don't think."

"I wonder, though, what would have happened if Jack would have stayed at the Catholic mission in Boda instead of with us, with my parents and me."

Mari looked at her, turned back onto her knees and resumed the harvest. "Yes, Faith, don't think that I have not wondered the same thing."

Faith and Mari worked for an hour more until they had almost half a kilo of termites and Mari tied off the top of the bag. Back at the truck they could hear Jack cutting through the jungle with the machete and they made a fire with small branches of rosewood and prepared lunch and soon Jack came back hungry.

"We're having fried termites, Jack," Faith said in English in a tone of warning, and Jack sat down lathered in sweat. Faith fetched him the canteen. He took a long drink before saying anything.

"I'm done. I think we can get through."

Mari fried the termites in palm oil and they ate them and Faith grimaced at the first bite before she decided that they weren't so bad, that they didn't really have much taste—that it was all texture, crisp and crunchy like potato chips—and Jack ate his without saying anything. When they were done, Jack started the truck and Faith guided him through the narrow path from in front of the truck and Mari rode in the cab. The branches scraped at the side of the truck like finger nails on a chalkboard, and Jack drove slowly over gnarled roots and small logs.

Back on the road on the other side of the fallen tree, Faith got in beside Mari and Jack said, "We made it." They drove on and the morning was hot and the road was slick from the previous night's rain. The road was as narrow and serpentine as it had been before, and Jack looked at the compass every ten or fifteen minutes and saw that they were headed both south and west, but mostly south, and with each passing kilometer he felt a clearer sense of security because they were so deep in the jungle no one would follow them; they were in the middle of the continent, probably still in the Republic, but no longer did borders have meaning. There was nothing this far in the jungle but trees and more trees that had a thickness to them that could not be penetrated and in between the trees was just a tangle of vines, verdant webs of growth. It was just deep jungle in the middle of the continent and one did not require a passport to be lost.

Jack stopped to refuel and this time it was Mari who sucked on the hose. She did not take a drop of the fuel into her mouth. Jack watched her as she kinked the hose and again did not spill any fuel.

In mid-afternoon, the clouds gathered again and crushed the heat of the day with their rains. It rained so hard that Jack had to stop because he could not see where he was going and they sat in the cab for an hour waiting for the rain to stop and as quickly as it had started, the rain ceased, and the quiet was almost as loud as had been the rain on the roof of the cab.

They drove until dusk when they came to a river and it was too dark to cross, so they made camp and ate the remnants of the smoked antelope and a *boule* of manoic, and they sat around the fire until it burned out and there were no clouds this evening. Sitting on the clearing beside the river bank, they could look up and see the stars and it was still and quiet except for the gentle lap of the river current as it stroked the shore. They did not speak as they sat there, none of them willing to be the first to break the silence that was like a blanket, and each of them was alone with separate fears that could not be connected and shared: Jack's were mature as if they had been planted as seeds many years before and with all of his years they had grown and now the fears were as big as they could be and they were fears for his own life; Faith, she had not experienced fear like this before because she had never been separated from her parents, she had never been off in the jungle with a man who had killed, and she was as confused as she was afraid; and Mari, she was only afraid for her sister and her niece and her nephew who were like her own children, and now she felt disconnected and alone, more alone than ever because she was with Jack and she could not be with him.

In the morning, Jack and Faith woke to Mari's pounding on the back window of the cab, and when they looked out to the river where she was pointing, they saw three elephants watering themselves on the river's edge. Jack dressed and pulled on his boots and he stood by the truck and watched as the elephants drank, and Faith joined him and when Mari closed the truck door behind her, the elephants turned and looked and then they waded through the water and loped into the jungle on the other side, breaking branches and small trees with great noise. Then, after they had disappeared, there was the sound of an elephant's trumpet.

The river was shallow, no more than a stream, and they were able to cross it without mishap. It was six hours south of where they had camped that the truck broke down. The gears slipped and when Jack couldn't keep it in gear anymore, he coasted the truck to a stop near a stream and he had to pry open the hood with a tire iron because it was bent and crumpled from the accident the day before, and looking over the engine told Jack nothing. He looked under the chassis and saw a red liquid dripping into the mud. The cover of the transmission was cracked. He checked the level of transmission fluid and it was empty and it was no use to do anything else because they couldn't drive without transmission fluid.

"We're shit out of luck," Jack said in English as he pushed himself up from the ground. He explained the situation and said they had little choice but to ride three on the motorcycle. He said that it would be rough and uncomfortable but that was all they could do.

As Jack and Mari unloaded the motorcycle from the back of the truck, Faith made a bundle of the food she had hurriedly taken from her mother's pantry, canned sardines and canned mackerel, a bag of ground manioc, three oranges and a papaya, and the remnants of the termites. Jack tied the twenty-liter gas can to the front forks. "Your father is not going to be too happy about where we left his truck, Faith," Jack said.

"No, he won't be, but I'll tell him it was God's will," she said and laughed, but it was hollow and empty of anything resembling humor. More a plaintive lament.

When Jack was done with his job, he stripped down and dove into a pool downstream from where Faith was bathing and where Mari splashed herself in the shallows. It was cool in the water in the afternoon heat and when they climbed out of the water and dressed, the clouds came as they did every afternoon. They sat in the cab of the truck waiting out the storm, but it was a long storm and the wind picked up and took the rain horizontal to the ground and the lightning and thunder were incessant. The storm didn't dissipate until dusk so that they stayed one more night before continuing toward Cameroon on the motorcycle. Jack figured they had enough gasoline to go four hundred kilometers and he didn't know where the end to four hundred kilometers was. He hoped it was in Cameroon or The Congo, anywhere but in this republic where the laws might have him hanged for murder.

Jack was tired and went to sleep in the truck bed, and Mari and Faith sat next to each other on a log by the fire. Above the river where there were no trees, they could see the stars, but as there was no moon, it was dark, the only light a small circle of yellow afforded by the fire.

Mari said she was afraid.

"Of what?" Faith asked.

"Pygmies live in the forest."

"So?"

"They have all of the evil spirits on their side."

"That's nonsense."

"How do you know? Have you ever met a pygmy?"

"No."

"So you don't know."

"I don't believe in sorcery either."

"How can you not believe in sorcery? It exists everywhere. Bangui is full of sorcerers. Everyone believes in sorcery."

"And what do they do?" Faith asked.

"Terrible things. They turn into crows and can fly anywhere."

"Mari, I don't believe in that sort of thing."

Mari was silent for a moment and then she said, "But maybe you do," and Faith said nothing in reply.

"How's the arm?" Mari asked.

"Oh, it's better. It doesn't hurt."

"*Et comment va tu?*"

"Me? I'm okay. Worried. About my parents."

"Yes, I can imagine that. They must be worried about you."

"That's what makes me sad, that they are worrying, that they do not even know if I am alive."

"That is only for now. You'll be able to write them soon."

"That doesn't do any good tonight. They are there in bed in Boda now, wondering where their daughter is, maybe thinking I am dead. I feel like I don't have any power now."

"Exactly. You do not. Not now, not here in the middle of the forest. But soon, maybe a few days or a week, you will be able to contact them and tell them you are fine. That you are in love."

Faith was silent and Mari could see the tears on her cheeks, yellowed by the flickering flames. Mari put her arm around her.

"It will be better soon, Faith. We're almost there."

"Where?" She wiped her tears with her hand. "Where are we? Where are we going?"

"Somewhere safe."

"Where is safe? Jack, he shot those men. The police will always look for him."

"Once we cross the border, you'll be safe."

"And then what? Where do we go? He'll be wanted by the police."

"You can't worry about that now. First, we need to cross the border."

Faith looked at Mari.

"What happened at your house? I mean that night the man was killed."

Mari removed her arm from Faith's shoulders. She clasped her hands and with her elbows on her knees, she bent toward the fire. She stared at the flames as Faith watched her, waiting for her to say something. The flames burned in her eyes. "I was home with my sister and the children. It was a Sunday evening. We'd finished dinner, had done the dishes. Roger and Mari were playing in the street in front of the house when Francoise, my sister, called them in from the porch to go to bed.

"I was taking the laundry off the line when a truck pulled up before the house. A white man got out of the truck. I recognized him. A Monsieur Dubois. I had met him at the New Palace Bar a month before.

"He was drunk. He told me he would give me ten thousand francs to sleep with my sister and me. At the same time, he said. I told him to leave. That I would scream and that the neighbors would call the police.

"He laughed. He grabbed me. He is a big man. Fat. He smelled of whiskey. He dragged me into the house and locked the door. Francoise was putting the children to bed. Our house is two rooms. The children sleep in the front room on the floor near my bed. Francoise, her room is in the back.

"The children were on the floor. They looked at this man. They were afraid. Francoise told him to leave. He pushed me on the bed. He swore. He yelled at Francoise, told her to take off her clothes. He grabbed her, ripped off her sari, pushed her down on the floor. He was on her and I was beating his back with my fists." She paused, caught her breath, trembled and began to cry. Faith put her arm around her shoulders.

"He was angry. Violent. He was crazy from whiskey. He grabbed Francoise by the hair and beat her head against the concrete floor until she passed out. Blood came from her nose.

"I backed away from him. I wanted to run. But the children. Francoise. I couldn't leave. I told him to leave us alone. He grabbed me, ripped my sari, forced me onto my back on the bed, and I screamed. I screamed and screamed and screamed. I tried to scratch his eyes from his sockets, but he pinned me down by the arms and he was laughing.

"Someone called my name. It was Jack outside. I heard the pounding on the door. He must have kicked it in.

"There was Jack. He pulled the man from me. I sat up. I watched Jack kick the man in the face. His face was covered with blood. When I saw Jack take the knife from his belt, I screamed. I didn't want Jack to kill him, not then, not in front of the children, not kill him because then Jack would be in trouble.

"But Jack took his knife and I saw the terror in the man's eyes. In his eyes I saw the terror of Francoise's eyes. And Jack stabbed him again and again and again until I stood and took Jack in my arms, pulling him away from the man who was covered in his own blood, lying there on the floor. Dead.

"Jack was crying. He was crying and he was apologizing as if it were his fault. We stood and I held him as he cried, and he cried for a long time.

"Later we took the truck and the body to the dump."

Mari stared at the fire. Her jaw was clenched. "He deserved to die."

"I'm sorry, Mari. I'm sorry. It is horrible." Faith hugged her close.

"Yes. He deserved to die. Jack did what he had to do."

They were silent, both of them staring at the fire that was now dying, a bed of red coals, and Faith was thinking that she loved a man who had killed a man in what they called *cold blood* despite that Jack called it self defense. But then, she thought, we rationalize the worst of our lives and it could well be for Jack that it had been a kind of defense of the self for his guilt concerning Mari was justifiably profound.

And she loved a man like this? she thought. This bothered her because everything in her life preceding Jack could be explained by her religion, but falling in love with a man who killed could not be readily explained that way or any way of which she could conceive.

"And before this, I'm sorry, Mari, but before this happened, you were pregnant?"

"Yes."

"With Jack's baby?"

Mari turned to look at Faith, but it was too dark to see, just the red glow of coals against her face.

"Yes."

"What would have happened if the baby had lived?"

"If it had lived? If it was a boy I would have named it Jack and if it was a girl, Jacqueline."

"No, I mean between you and Jack." Faith looked toward the truck five meters away. Its silhouette was barely discernible.

"I don't know. Maybe he would have married me. If not, he would have gone back to *Les Etats Unis* sometime. The baby would have been a part of him I would always have had." She paused and looked into Faith's eyes. "I don't know if he could be a father."

"Why?"

"I don't know. His own childhood."

"You still love him, don't you?"

Mari yawned. "I told you I did. But not like before. We can be friends. Now it is time to go to sleep."

Mari climbed in the cab and shut the door behind her and Faith sat by the dying fire for a few more minutes wondering who was *we* that could still be friends, and she thought that Mari was a much stronger woman than herself for she would never have been able to travel with Jack and another woman who loved him, but then she thought that maybe she was doing just that and she was surprised at herself; she thought that in three days she had aged more than in her previous seventeen years combined and that now she would never again be the same Faith who taught in the school at the foot of the hill, who spent her evenings knitting uniforms for the children.

She crawled into the bed of the truck and lay down next to Jack and as she listened to him snore, she thought about her parents and how far away she was from them, and how far away she was from whom she had always been, and she wondered if the events of the last three days had created a deep and permanent chasm separating who she had been before Jack had walked up on her porch at the mission in Boda, and who she would be from now on and forever more.

It was rough going on the motorcycle. Jack had to drive slowly and with great care as he was sitting so far forward that his legs were behind him on the pegs and the gas tank was between his legs and any bump would jar his groin. By noon they had already crashed twice, each time gently with Jack's leg breaking the fall, but still it had frightened them and the road was so slick, it was not possible to go over thirty kilometers an hour. Cameroon seemed very far away, beyond even the realm of their imagination. Faith sat behind Jack with her left arm around his waist, and Mari sat behind her in a similar fashion. When it rained that afternoon, there was no shelter save the dripping trees and they stood there under the canopy of ebony trees, soaking wet when the sun broke through and no one was very happy when they got back on the bike in sodden clothing on a slippery road with Jack unable to shift higher than third gear.

At dusk, Jack checked the odometer and saw that they had gone one-hundred kilometers and he thought they were two or three hundred kilometers from running out of gas; then they would have to walk. There was no traffic on these narrow roads because it was only the log trucks that used them and none of the roads had destinations except the one being the mill behind them and the other being the trees that were in every direction. It was only the compass that kept them moving west now.

They had no more water in the canteen and they could only fill it when it rained with the water that filled the pan during the storms, and then they would drink it and fill it again as long as the rain fell, and it always fell in the late afternoon and sometimes at night when the clouds would gather en masse and at some esoteric but cosmic signal they would let loose a torrential downpour that created new rivers and streams.

They finished the termites and antelope and manioc that night and there was nothing left for the next morning except one tin of sardines and one tin of mackerel. It rained again that night and the lightning and thunder preceded and then followed the rain and they had made a shelter of palm fronds, but it dripped all night and no one slept much and in the morning they were tired.

They rode for three hours, stopping every thirty minutes because they were saddle-sore and their backs hurt, and in mid-morning they came to the river that blocked their way. The road led to the bank of the river and on the other side they could see that the road left the river, but now it was swollen with water and the current was swift. The water was the color of mud and there were small trees and branches being carried downstream and when they stopped on the bank, they each knew that they were going to have to cross the river because to not do so meant to turn around and go back and after all the work of having gone so far, going back would have been tougher than swimming their way across.

They sat on the bank and rested from the ride before anyone said anything and then Jack asked Mari if she could swim.

"*Un petite peu.*"

"We'll have to leave the bike here," Jack said.

"There's no way we can get it across?" Faith asked.

"I don't think so. We could try to make a raft, but in this current we'd probably tip over and lose the bike. Anyway, we've only enough gas for another hundred kilometers or so."

"I'd rather walk, anyway," Mari said. "*C'est mon derriere que me merdre..* I'll never ride a motorcycle again."

Faith looked at Mari and laughed, but then she looked at the water rushing by and she didn't smile and the three of them were silent as they watched the river that was fifty meters wide and a torrent of wild water now when only a week before it had probably been a dry, hollowed bed of rock.

The sun was out and there were no clouds. The sky looked innocent through the canopy of trees. Birds were singing and monkeys cackled high in the trees and it was a very peaceful place in the middle of the jungle if they didn't have a river to be crossed, but there was also the sound of the rushing water and there was no peace here for the three of them.

Jack smoked a cigarette slowly like a man who knew it would be his last, as if he knew that he would have none left to smoke after swimming the river. Mari stood and took off her clothes and so did Faith and Jack stood and stripped down to his shorts as well and they made small bundles of their clothing. Faith had her back to Jack and she was naked except for her underwear and the white bandage on her arm. He watched her as she took the bandage off and dropped it to the ground. He asked her if her arm still hurt.

"No," she said with her back to him. "It's okay. There's no infection."

"Good. You'll be able to hold on to a log?" he asked, and she said she would. He stood and entered the water and waded up the river next to the bank and he had to hold onto the branches that reached out from the bank to keep from being swept away with the current. He dislodged a small log from the roots of the trees it was entangled in. It was three meters long and had the girth of a single man. Jack dragged it down the muddy bank before Mari and Faith, and he broke off the longer branches, but left the shorter ones so that they could tie on their bundles of clothes and what few provisions they had left.

"Is it cold?" Mari asked, her arms crossed before her chest.

"Not at all," Jack said and smiled. He stood in the water that was up to his chest and he felt the chill in his groin. He held the log and Faith came into the water and tied the three bundles of clothes to a branch.

"Listen to me, Faith," Jack said. "I want you and Mari to be on either side of the front of the log and I will stay in the back. Both of you hold on with both hands and kick and I will kick, too. Don't worry if we get washed down the river because that is what will happen. There is no way we will come out by the road there. If we're lucky, we will end up only a kilometer downstream from here. So don't worry. Don't panic, Mari. It will be fine. And whatever you do, do not let go of the log. As long as you hang on, you'll be okay, even if we are swept all the way south to Angola." Jack paused and looked up the river and then he looked up at Mari who still stood naked on the bank. "Mari, Faith, do you understand?"

"Yes," Mari said, and Jack told her to come into the water and she stepped in and the water was above her chest and Faith held out her hand for Mari and helped her to the log and Mari held her hand so tight it hurt. Mari took hold of a branch on the front of the log and Faith waded to the other side and took hold of a branch across from Mari. Jack pushed off from the bank and the log was pointed downstream and Faith and Mari were in what was the bow and Jack was at the stern. The current was strong and they rode down the river near the bank from which they had cast off.

Jack tried kicking from the side of the log to move it toward the middle of the river, but each time the bow of the log started to move to his right, the current would push it back again. It was as if they were hanging on to a torpedo the course of which had been preordained, and the branches from the trees on the river bank hung low and scratched their faces and backs as they were swept beneath and then through them. The water was gray and muddy and they bobbed in it, only their heads and arms above the surface.

"Mari," Jack yelled. "Try kicking sideways."

Mari didn't respond, but maybe she had heard and maybe she tried to kick sideways, but Jack could only see the terror on her face as she held the branch with both hands, her head just above the surface of the water. "Faith. Faith. Kick beneath the log." Neither did Faith respond, and Jack wasn't sure if he could be heard above the roar of the water.

They rounded a bend, and the bend in the river kicked them out away from the bank and now they were in the middle of the river and Jack saw three antelope swimming with their heads bobbing up and down, fear stretched across their eyes as they struggled against the implacable force of the water. The antelope were so close that Jack could have reached out and touched their antlers. Seeing the antelope being swept away frightened Jack because the antelope did not need to be in the river as did Jack, Faith and Mari, and that the antelope were there at all was because of the violence of the weather, and now that they were being carried downstream on a log through wild water, Jack felt that now, for the first time since leaving Boda, he was no longer in control; all their fates were designed by the rushing water and the only way to take back control was to fight their way to the other side in a battle of wills, theirs against nature's.

The water took on a quality of waves like rapids that were not quite rapids because the water was so high above the rocks. The log bobbed from end to end and when the rear of the log rose, Jack looked down at the front where Mari and Faith were submerged and he could not even see their hands holding the branches. Then the front of the log came up out of the water and Jack held his breath as he went down under for what seemed like a long time. When he was under the water, he hoped only that Faith and Mari were still hanging on.

He came back out of the water and they were still in the middle of the river and other logs passed them and he looked to the front of the log and Faith and Mari were still there. Faith was silently praying to God to let them live through this and Mari was too frightened to pray, but her grip was ferocious and the bark cut into the skin of her hands; she didn't even know she was bleeding.

The sky became as dark as the water in a conspiracy of the brothers Zeus and Poseidon. Lightning lit the black of the clouds and they couldn't hear the thunder that followed as the roar of the water was deafening. Jack began to wonder if they were going to make it across or if they would even make it to either shore or if they would all drown or if any one of them would drown.

Then it began to rain.

First the rain came down from above, but then the wind picked up and took the rain horizontal so that it blew with the raging current of the river and almost seemed a part of the river itself. No longer was there a sky. Just water above and below them. A world of wet.

They came around another bend of the river and there were no more waves, but the force of the turn pushed them back to the side of the river where they had started. Jack pulled himself to the side of the log and kicked with everything he had to push the tail end of the log toward the opposite shore, and as he neared the shore where they had started, the front of the log, where Mari and Faith gripped the branches with both hands, turned toward the middle of the river, and Jack pulled himself back behind the log and kicked now with everything he had left and with everything he did not know he ever had, and the log moved toward the middle of the river. Jack could see both women kicking as well. This was the first progress they made as they passed the middle of the river and approached the other shore when a log as big as any tree Jack had ever seen rushed toward them. Faith couldn't see it coming because she was on the up-river side of their own log, but both Jack and Mari saw it barreling straight at them with branches sticking up as big as the masts of a cutter. Jack yelled to hold on. He kicked as hard as he could and as the log approached them as if propelled by some force greater than nature, Mari screamed and Faith turned and watched it crash into the middle of their own log and because of the branches she could no longer see Jack. For the briefest of moments the two logs formed a perfect T in the middle of the swollen river, the impact sending each of their thoughts in separate directions.

The collision spun the log around so that Jack was closest to shore, maybe five meters away that he could have swum, but when he looked out at the other end there was only Faith and he started to yell at her when she let go of the log and began to swim downstream amid the flotsam and jetsam, a roiling stew of debris. The rain beat down on the river so hard that Jack couldn't tell where the surface of the river met the edge of the sky; it was as if the two had melded and now they were in a netherworld of water and they were breathing the water and he couldn't see Faith or Mari, so he hung on to the log and rode it downstream in the rain.

He looked for any sign of Faith and Mari as the current rushed him through the overhanging branches near the shore, but he could only see gray water, and he could only feel the branches raking his head and neck and arms and shoulders.

He couldn't hold on any longer. He grabbed two of the bundles tied before him and then he pushed off and he reached at a tree root and pulled himself to shore where he rolled over and lay on his back with his feet still in the river. The rain beat down on his naked body and he couldn't feel it or anything besides the ache in his muscles and the exhaustion of his lungs.

He shivered in the rain. He lay there for a long time, and when he was somewhat less exhausted than he had been before, he sat up and dressed with great difficulty, pulling the wet jeans up over his legs as if he were a very old man. He rested for a few minutes and then stood and carried the two bundles as he walked through the vines and the thick foliage that lined the bank. He kept his eyes on the river and the branches scratched his face, and his face and neck and shoulders and arms were lacerated and bleeding. He worried about the snakes, always the snakes. As he walked, he again reproached himself for having brought both Faith and Mari on this brutal escape to Cameroon when he knew he should have gone alone, and then he thought back to everything that had happened since he had killed the Frenchman and then, before that, the seed of it all: not trusting Mari when she told him of the miscarriage. If he had only believed her, he now thought, then maybe he would have been there when the Frenchman had come. But then, as he thought about that, he knew it was probably not true, and he wondered what was true and what was not. He only knew that he was alone in the jungle in the very center of the continent of Africa and any truth beyond that simply did not matter. If there were previous truths in his life, they were now as inconsequential as all past mistakes. To wish things were different was of no use, that such wishing was an otiose exercise. He had tried that for years and longing for Karen after she had left him had been nothing more than a sedentary exercise of melancholy; it was as foolish as Hamlet's soliloquy about existing, or acting, and Jack realized after lying awash in his own self pity that in order to truly exist one must act and even running off to Africa with the Peace Corps was an action better than none; better, surely, than wishing for Karen to come back to him because there was no hope of that, and longing without action was as weak and empty as asking for absolution for some sin.

Yet even action could be futile: his beating of the professor was a temporary elixir only palliative in its exertion that when ceased, he felt a two-fold resurgence of pain. Beating the man had felt real, though, the fist into flesh and bone and cartilage satisfying in an atavistic way, and the moment of seeing the man crumpled in his chair beneath a wall of framed diplomas, the face bloodied, eye glasses smashed and on the floor, had filled him with an ephemeral elation, but as he walked out the office door and down the hall where students milled about, the elation seeped away and he was saddened because Karen must now and always be gone from his life. That chapter was closed.

His legs were heavy and he wasn't sure where he was going now except there had to be some hope that Mari and Faith were alive and on the shore somewhere downstream. The rain stopped and the sun broke through the clouds and in the shade the air was as wet as the river. He was thirsty and the canteen was empty but he didn't dare drink the river water until it was boiled. He tried to remember when he had last taken his quinine because he felt feverish, but then he was probably just tired and it was hot and this might not be the onset of malaria, but still he perspired and his body ached, but that could have been from the swimming and the struggle with the log. He sat down in the shade to rest.

He opened a bundle and took out the bottle of pills. He took two. If this were malaria, he thought two would at least help and if he woke with fevers and chills he would take six and then six more and then six more three hours apart and then he would probably get better; with the medicine, at least the odds were with him.

When he woke, it was dark and it was raining again. He crawled to the base of a tree and sat with his back against it and his head was so hot that the rain felt cool and refreshing and he sat there and fell back asleep. On and off through the night it was sleep, wake, dream, sleep, fever, chill, fever, chill, and the dreams were colorful and wild and drunken, Dionysian affairs. When he woke again, he knew it was the beginning of malaria and he took six more pills.

It was quiet in the dark except for the cicadas that now buzzed. It was one thing to be in the dark of the jungle night with Faith and Mari, but to be alone was something quite different. Sitting against a tree as the river rushed by and not knowing where he was, thinking of snakes, Jack could feel the tinges of doubt that were the precursor of fear and there was nothing to be afraid of. Jack had never been afraid of death, but that was because he was always sure he would die somewhere with people nearby, someone to watch him leave, but here in the middle of the African continent in which country he was not even sure, he thought he might die because of the fever and chills and no one would ever find him by this river in the jungle. To die alone was not to die and if one did not die, one was to have never been alive. He took six more pills and slept until morning.

At dawn, a half dozen gibbons looked down at him from the branches of trees, their white beards like forest gnomes'. He pushed himself up. His head felt like an anvil that had been through a night of hard service. He walked down the river. The branches and vines were thick and in two hours he had gone half a kilometer at most. He sat down and drank from the runoff that spilled into the river hoping that it was clean, rain water that had yet to be tainted by the earth. His throat was like tree bark, and the water soothed it as it rinsed down.

He took off his shirt and tied it to a tree branch overhanging the river where someone might see it. He lay down to rest and when he awoke he was dreaming that Faith and Mari were bathing him with water, and Faith cradled his head in her lap as Mari squeezed water onto his forehead from a bandanna and he heard them speaking in French as Faith said, "*Il est la paludisme*. Give him six tablets of the quinine."

"Where is it?"

"In one of those bundles."

Mari reached over to the bundles and went through them. "I can't find it," she said.

Jack felt a hand in the pocket of his jeans and Faith said, "Here it is."

Faith put the tablets in his mouth and Jack tasted the bitterness and she told him to swallow and he did, and the dream ended when he went back to sleep and it was dark when he awoke and the fever was gone and he looked up to see Mari boiling water over a fire.

"Mari? Faith?" Faith was sitting next to the fire and she came over to Jack and kissed his forehead and sat down next to him and Jack saw Mari smile.

"What happened?" Jack asked.

"You had malaria," Mari said. "We gave you quinine. You probably ought to take some more. Shouldn't he, Faith?"

"Yes, six more, I think."

Faith gave him six tablets and Mari brought him a cup of water and he took the tablets and drank the water. Then he asked for more.

"What happened?" Jack asked again.

"Faith saved me from drowning," Mari said. And then she explained how she had been knocked off the log during the collision, how she went under and then bobbed up and how Faith had gripped her arm and how she had held her as they went down under the water, then came up again and how Faith then grabbed hold of a branch of the huge tree that had rammed them, how they drifted down the river hanging onto the huge log for what had seemed to be several hours before they came close enough to shore to swim, how tired they were and how they sat and watched the river for Jack, how he never came, and how they slept that night—afraid, Mari said, afraid of everything around them—and then how they hiked up the river the next morning looking for any sign of Jack until, after walking for what must have been nine or ten kilometers through the thick jungle, they came across a clearing and saw the shirt hanging above the river from a branch. They found him sleeping against the tree, Mari said. "And I thought you were dead."

They rested another day on the bank of the river. Mari gathered berries and nuts and they ate what little they had. The following morning they cut upstream through the jungle and it took them several hours to make it to the road where they had originally tried to cross. Looking across the river they could see the red motorcycle leaning on its kick-stand under a tree, an anachronism shining in the sun.

The road, a thin slice through the forest, was muddy and they had to circle the puddles. The sun was hot and the puddles evaporated and it was muggy as they walked. Jack took the lead and he carried the pistol in his hand because he had the notion that if he saw an antelope or a boar or some kind of game, he could shoot it. Mari and Faith followed, each carrying a bundle of provisions and they had everything they needed almost except for food, and they only had a little water but it would rain again; that was all they could be sure of, that it would rain.

They came around a bend and ahead of them and with her back to them was a pygmy woman who had a basket full of red palm nuts riding on her back supported by the thick bark strap that wrapped around her forehead. She heard them and turned and she held a baby sucking her breast. She quickly turned back and walked on and then she cut into the jungle and when Jack, Faith and Mari arrived at the spot, they saw the narrow game trail that she had taken. Jack suggested they follow it because the pygmies would have something to eat and he was hungry.

"But, Jack, she is a pygmy," Mari said.

"I see that, Mari," Jack said.

"Jack," Faith said. "Mari is afraid of pygmies."

"Why?"

"Because they have evil spirits or something."

"That is true," Mari said.

"Nonsense, Mari. We're going to follow her."

They walked along the game trail and she never turned back to look at them and they had to walk quickly to keep her pace. Jack was the slowest, and once he slipped and fell and Mari and Faith each helped him up. After thirty minutes, a man came out of the jungle with a crossbow and he stopped next to the woman and Jack said hello, and the man replied in a language Jack didn't recognize. He looked at Mari, but she said she did not understand either and nor did Faith.

Jack walked up to the man and smiled and they shook hands and the man looked up at Jack and he could not have been more than five feet tall. He wore only a loin cloth and his thighs were wide and muscular and his back was a ripple of strength and when he smiled his teeth were filed to sharp points and they were stained with berries and his nose was flat and wide like the nose of a boxer who has been hit too many times.

The pygmy motioned for them to follow him. He led the way, followed by the woman and her baby and then Jack and Faith and Mari. They walked along the narrow trail and after a short time they came to a clearing in the forest where a dozen huts were scattered around the clearing, small huts shaped like igloos and built of palm fronds, each only a meter high. When they entered the clearing, a dozen or so pygmies gathered in a circle around the three of them and they smiled. The man who had led them to their camp spoke to the others in a language neither Jack, Faith nor Mari could understand.

An old woman with breasts that sagged limply to her waist motioned for them to sit down on a bench of sticks underneath a shelter with a roof of leaves. When the three of them sat, the entire band of pygmies gathered around them and stared, and Jack felt closed in. His fever had abated, but he was still weak, and his head still ached as did the joints of his arms and legs. One of the men climbed a palm tree ten meters high, his legs and arms wrapped around the narrow trunk as he shinnied toward the sky. The tree swayed with the weight of the man, and everyone looked up at him as he climbed. He came down with two gourds and the old woman made cups from broad leaves and gave one each to Jack, Faith and Mari and the man poured them full of palm wine and it was sour and tasted refreshing and Jack drank three servings and the woman laughed at this and then everyone was laughing and Jack asked for another which quadrupled the mirth. As they laughed, a woman stoked a fire in the center of the clearing and next to her two women worked at quartering an antelope.

An old man Jack took for the chief said something to Jack and in French Jack said, "I don't know what you're talking about, but the palm wine is excellent. I would like some more."

Jack held out his cup and it was filled.

"Don't drink too much," Mari said. "It is stronger than you think." Faith and Mari each had another cup.

The children were shy but curious and peaked at them from behind their parents and when Jack looked at them they ran off giggling and then they came running back. An old man sat down next to Jack and he had a gray beard and his eyes were glazed white from glaucoma. He had a pipe and he took out a leather bag and he filled the pipe with what Jack thought was marijuana and when the man lit it, Jack recognized the sweet

112

smell and when the pipe was passed to him he hesitated because it had been many years since he had smoked marijuana, but then he took it and inhaled and held the smoke in his lungs and then he coughed and the children laughed. He passed it to Faith who declined and who said in English just what she thought about Jack smoking dope and she passed it to Mari who also declined and the man and Jack smoked and then Jack passed it to another man who inhaled deeply, and he handed it to another and then a young boy no more than seven reached out and took it from the lips of a man who may have been his father and the boy ran off and several children gathered around him and they smoked in a huddle of giggles. All of the adults except for Faith laughed hard watching the children imitate the adults.

Jack was high, and his aching was alleviated so that he felt renewed yet somewhat ethereal, but being the latter prevented the possibility of discomfort for there was nothing solid an ache could attach to. He smiled at the sight of the children crouched around the pipe. He caught eyes with the old man who had glaucoma and he couldn't be sure his own vision was returned, but they both laughed and drank more of the wine. It was late in the afternoon when the clouds gathered and everyone stripped down and washed in the rain except for Faith, and when the storm had passed it fell dark and the fires spat sparks into the blackness of night, the orange flames lapping at the darkness, illuminating the green jungle around them. They sat under the shelter eating antelope and berries and some kind of root that was sweeter than manioc. When they were done eating, the pygmies danced around the fire in a circle that swayed in and out of time, but one that moved around the fire all the while, a languid loop moving around the flames. The old man with glaucoma came out of the circle to where Faith, Mari and Jack sat watching, and he bent down and took Faith's hand and tugged it. She shook her head, but he laughed and pulled again. Faith looked first at Jack and then at Mari, and she stood and laughed. It was a nervous laugh, forced yet controlled.

"Well, Jack," she said in English. "Who said Baptists don't dance?" She was led to the fire where the man released his grip, and she began to sway slowly in the flickering firelight, following the lead of the others.

"How about you, Mari?" Jack asked.

"D'accord."

They danced for some time, and Jack sweat and was tired. When it seemed very late, a man showed Jack a hut with a small opening and Jack had to get down on his knees to look inside where two beds made of long sticks were on either side of the hut. The man looked at Jack and held out two fingers and pointed to both Faith and Mari who were sitting in the light of the fire under the shelter, and then the man pointed at Jack's crotch and laughed.

Mari and Faith fell asleep before Jack. As he lay there, he could see the flames of the fire outside and as he watched, a child came and peeked in the opening of their hut and Jack sat up and the child giggled and ran off. Soon the child returned with several other children and they peeked in at Jack, said something, and then started giggling so that Jack said in English, "Good night. Don't let the bed bugs bite," and the boys and girls ran off laughing loudly.

Jack slept on the ground between Mari and Faith and he slept well because of all he had eaten and drunk and smoked. His head still hurt some, but not as before, and the fever was gone. It rained again that night, but the hut stayed dry, and in the morning they ate smoked meat of some kind that after they had eaten it they discovered was monkey and it was sweet and red with the smoke from the fire. Jack made a motion with two fingers that resembled walking and he pointed to Mari and Faith and everyone understood that they were moving on that morning, and the women prepared a bundle of nuts and berries and smoked meat. The old man with glaucoma came to Jack with a pipe and a leather pouch of marijuana and smiling, he handed it to Jack. Jack was warmed by the gesture and was putting it in his shirt pocket when Faith took it from him and gave it back to the man and everyone laughed except Faith and then she smiled, too.

The entire band of pygmies followed them down the game trail to the logging road. The man they had first encountered the day before came up to Jack and handed him his crossbow and a quill of a dozen arrows each with a dark, sticky poison on its tip, and Jack shook his head, pulling the gun from the bundle he carried, and then they shook hands, said goodbye and Mari and Faith and Jack waved to them and turned down the road.

114

After they had gone one hundred meters, Jack turned around and still the band of pygmies was standing there. Jack waved and yelled goodbye in French and they all waved and yelled something that could have been goodbye and good luck on the road ahead. The morning was still young when they found themselves with another river to cross, but one much smaller than the first and this time they were able to make the crossing without mishap.

The road went due west and it narrowed and the vines from each side touched in the middle. It had been a long time since a truck had passed this way. They walked with the sun on their backs in the morning and in the afternoon it was in their eyes until the clouds covered the sky and the rain fell again.

They walked like this for three days seeing no one, and with each step their pace slowed, the blisters on their feet growing with the kilometers, and no one complained because no one wanted to be the first to give voice to the pains in each muscle, the aches in each joint. The trek was without event except for the first night when a spitting cobra came into their camp at night. Mari screamed and was foolish enough to beat it with a stick until it was no longer recognizable as a snake and Mari was fortunate enough that it had not spit the deadly venom in her eyes but instead had missed and hit her cheek.

On the fourth day, the road began to widen and there were fresh tire tracks in the mud. They came across a clear-cut and they could smell the sweetness of the freshly sawed trees and there was a field of sunlight where the trees had recently stood.

Jack didn't need to look at the compass to know they were now heading north; this was good because they had to go to Bouar to the frontier where they could cross into Cameroon, Jack said. The farther they walked, the better the road became, and each of them wondered where this road was taking them and the fears they had had of encountering the police returned as they closed in on civilization.

They walked slowly and their feet rose less with each step. Sometimes Jack would hold his stomach, and Faith would ask him what was wrong and he said that nothing was wrong, he just had a slight ache in his stomach was all. They were dirty and tired and hungry and thirsty. Jack scratched at the whiskers that had grown into a beard covering his thin face, and both Faith and Mari were quiet as they walked, sweat running down their necks, all three of their lives a great discomfort.

It was in the afternoon after the rain and they were walking through the mud when the log truck came from behind them. They could hear it coming for a long time before they saw it. They heard the air brakes hiss as the truck stopped along side of them, and the driver leaned out the window of the big blue Mercedes diesel and asked if they needed a ride, and the very question seemed ludicrous like asking did you think it would snow.

They climbed up into the cab and Mari sat next to the driver and Faith was in the middle and Jack was by the open window because, he said to Faith, he couldn't sit in the middle, and the driver was a large African with a gold tooth and a wide smile and Jack wondered if he developed the smile after he had paid for the tooth. He introduced himself as Pierre and he said he had once been a police officer in Berberati, but that there was more money in driving the trucks for the French, and he asked what the three of them were doing walking in the middle of this forsaken jungle.

"Our truck broke down several hundred kilometers east of here," Jack said, and Pierre was impressed.

"You have been walking for several days like this?"

"Yes," Jack said. He leaned forward so that he could see Pierre who sat three bodies away with one hand on the wheel and one on the gear shift, his eyes steady on the curvy road ahead.

"What are you doing out here?" Pierre asked.

"We are missionaries," Jack said and he looked at Faith and then Mari. "We were out visiting the pygmies."

"Pygmies," Pierre said. "They have no god except the forest."

"The forest is their God?" Faith said.

"*Mais oui*, they are heathens," Pierre said. "They believe the forest is God. If someone is sick or if the hunting is poor, they believe that the forest has fallen asleep and is no longer providing. So they dance."

"Dance?" Jack said.

"They have a party all night and they are as loud as can be in their effort to wake the forest up and they do this for as many nights as it takes to wake up the forest."

116

"How do they know when the forest is awake?" Faith said.

"I don't know. When the hunting is good again, I suppose."

Jack thought of the old man with glaucoma and he said that he thought it was a good religion and Pierre turned and looked at him. "What religion are you?" he asked.

"Baptist," Jack said, and Pierre said nothing. Faith and Mari both fell asleep and Jack tried to keep his eyes open, but his lids were heavy and in the warm cab Jack fell asleep, too.

When he awoke, they were parked in front of a barrier and Pierre was in the hut talking to the gendarme. Jack woke Faith and Mari.

"What is it?" said Faith.

"A barrier."

"Where are we?" Mari asked.

Jack pointed to the sign fifty meters down the road on the other side of the barrier. "Berberati is ten kilometers."

Pierre waved at them from the hut and signaled them to come down.

"Listen," Jack said as he opened the door. "we lost our papers. We are missionaries from Mongoumba. Our truck broke down and we lost our papers swimming across the river. Okay?" Both women nodded and said they understood. "Let's go."

Jack climbed down and Mari and Faith followed. Their clothes were torn and dirty, and Faith's face was both colored by the sun and the dirt. Jack rubbed the stubble on his face that was now a black beard the color of his hair as he followed Mari and Faith to the hut where a gendarme sat behind a desk. He was young, not more than twenty.

The gendarme handed Pierre his papers and Pierre said he would be waiting in the truck, and then the gendarme held out his hand and asked for their papers.

"We lost them swimming across a river," Jack said. "I am sorry. We are missionaries from Mongoumba."

The young man looked at each of their faces before saying, "I must have some official identification from each of you. It is the law."

"Our truck broke down and we had to swim across the river. We almost drowned," Faith said.

"I am sorry. The law says that to pass a barrier each passenger of each vehicle, no matter if they are white or not, must show identification. Now, do you have any?" He looked up at them from behind his desk, his arms crossed.

"Look," Jack said and his accent went from French to American despite the words because his tone was harsh. "We told you, we lost our papers in the river. We almost drowned. We have not eaten for days. We are missionaries from Mongoumba. We were bringing the word of God to the pygmies."

The gendarme made a spitting noise and said, "Pygmies, what do they know of God or anything else?"

"That is exactly why we were with the pygmies. We were bringing them the word of God. Do you think we would go to Rome to preach?"

"What kind of missionary did you say you were?"

"Baptist."

"I am a Catholic."

Jack leaned on the desk with both his hands. Faith and Mari stood behind Jack. Pierre honked his horn. Jack turned to Pierre through the opened door of the hut and raised a finger and shouted it would be just a moment, and he turned to the gendarme and with a smile said, "Catholicism is a beautiful religion."

"I need your papers if you are to pass. If you have no papers, then you must stay here until we can verify your identification."

Jack frowned and then he said, "Mari, Faith, go back to the truck a minute."

In English, Faith said, "Jack, what are you going to do?"

"Don't worry. Just go to the truck."

Faith took Mari's arm and they walked back out to the truck and the gendarme stood and called them back and Jack told them to keep going and then he turned to the gendarme and said, "I am sorry about this misunderstanding. I am with the CIA. Do you know what that is?"

"*Mais bien sur.*" The gendarme sat down and looked up at Jack appraising him from head to foot. "However, you do not look like you are with the CIA." He smiled nervously. "You said you were a missionary."

"Of course. You, being in the military, know that I cannot look like I am in the CIA if I am to carry out a secret mission."

"That is true, but what are you doing here with these women and why are you on foot?"

"Can I trust you? Can I trust you not to say a thing to anyone including your commander?" Jack turned and looked out at the truck and then back at the gendarme before continuing: "There could be a reward in this for you."

"Agreed." But his look was dubious.

"We are investigating some activities in the jungle. We believe that Mobutu in Zaire is sending agents into the country in an effort to create rebellion so that he can invade."

"No, really?" The gendarme's eyes were wide with expectation.

Sighing, Jack sat down on the chair across from the gendarme. "Yes, this is true. The African woman there, she is my interpreter, and the American, she is an agent as well."

"A woman agent?"

"Indeed. Our very best. She is an assassin."

The gendarme looked out at the truck where Faith and Mari stood and he was impressed.

"An assassin?"

"She is skilled in every art of hand combat and she is ruthless."

"Really?"

"Of course. Now listen to me, please. This is very important. Do you have a piece of paper and a pen?"

"Yes, here." He handed the paper and pen to Jack who leaned over the desk and wrote something and handed the paper to the gendarme.

"That is our secret address in Bangui. Show it to no one. What I want you to do is this. When you are next in Bangui ask for The Rabbit."

"The Rabbit?"

"Yes, that is my code name. Never mention it to anyone for there are few men alive who know it. Mention The Rabbit and tell them that the sun was high in Berberati."

"The sun was high?"

"Yes, they will know what it means."

"What does it mean?"

"You do not need to know that. You want to work for the CIA, do you not?"

He nodded. "But of course."

"To help your country?"

"Of course, anything."

"Good. Just tell them the sun is high, and that will be enough. And mention The Rabbit. They will understand. There will be a reward in it for you and when I am in Bangui I will put in a favorable word with my commander and I think, if you do this right, we will be able to hire you from time to time for work of the greatest sensitivity."

"You hire Africans?"

"Often. We call them foreign nationals. And you look to be of the caliber of man we could use. The money, by the way, is very good. If you succeed with this, I can guarantee you a bright future. How old are you?"

"Eighteen."

"Good then. That is a good age to start a career with the CIA." Jack stood. "Stand up."

The gendarme stood up and Jack reached out and shook his hand. "Remember, The Rabbit said the sun is high in Berberati. Please repeat that."

"The sun is high in Berberati. The Rabbit said this."

Jack walked around the desk and slapped him heartily on the back. "Good work. Welcome to the CIA. I will be meeting you in the future, I am sure."

"Thank you, sir."

Jack walked out to the truck and Mari and Faith climbed up into the cab and Jack climbed in next to them and slammed the door. The gendarme lifted the wooden barrier that blocked the road and he saluted and Jack returned the salute and the gendarme held the salute until the truck passed through the barrier. Jack looked in the mirror and saw the young man still saluting the departing truck.

"He must know that I was once a police officer," Pierre said with a smile. "I was a sergeant. It is good to see such respect from the young."

Faith asked what that was all about, and Jack told her that he would tell her later; Mari, however, knew it was something devious because she

120

recognized Jack's smile, a smile she had not seen for a long time.

At dusk, Pierre dropped them off at the central market in Berberati. It was a much bigger market than Boda's, and Faith and Mari bought *mischwee* and *mongbelli* with the money Mari had carefully tied up in her pouch and they went across the street to a bar. Jack ordered orange soda for himself and Faith, and Mari ordered beer.

"Orange soda, Jack? Have you been so easily converted?" Mari asked.

Jack poured two glasses and he drank his and then he grimaced and held his stomach. He got up and went outside to the toilet which was a hole in the ground inside three corrugated iron walls behind the bar, and his stomach was tumultuous.

Once again in the bar, he sat down and Faith asked him what was wrong.

"Amoebic dysentery, probably. My gut is a mess."

"How?" Faith asked.

"I drank some water from a stream that day we crossed the river." Jack bent over the table with his arms crossed at his waist, and then he stood and hurried back out behind the bar.

"He will need some medicine," Mari said. "I'll go see if the pharmacy is still open."

It was dark and the street lights near the market were not on and the market square was lit by sundry fires. It was smokey and the night air smelled of barbecued beef and the smoke from the fires hung over the market like a heavy fog. Mari walked up the hill past the market and knocked on the door of the pharmacy, but it was closed, and a man came out of the adobe house next to the white stucco building that was the pharmacy, and he asked her what she wanted.

She explained and the man told her to come back the next morning, but she persisted and said it was for an American who was a missionary and he was very sick, and the pharmacist sighed and walked with reluctance to the door of the pharmacy.

It was dark inside. He lit a match and then a candle and behind the glass counter he looked through three drawers before he found the bottle of poison that would kill the amoebas that were swimming inside Jack's intestines. He explained the dosage and Mari reached beneath her sari and paid the man more than the medicine was truly worth; because she had said it was for an American, he had overcharged her.

As she walked down the hill toward the market, there was a crowd gathered in front of the police station and she saw Pierre, the driver of the truck, talking to an officer and from the shadows she watched as Pierre walked down the steps and mounted his motorcycle. She watched as he drove off into the night.

Several people stood on the porch of the station and one held a lantern up to the wall. They were reading a handbill that had been posted next to the door where the handbills of the wanted criminals were always posted. Mari waited until the crowd dissipated, and then she walked up the steps and lit a match and read of the reward of one hundred thousand francs for information leading to the apprehension of an American who had kidnaped a young American missionary by the name of Faith Sellers. If Faith were found alive, it said, the reward would be paid by her parents to anyone aiding in her recovery. The handbill described Faith as a seventeen-year-old girl with light brown hair and blue eyes who could speak Sango and French.

Mari tore the poster from the wall, folded it and tucked it beneath her sari and hurried to the bar where she gave Jack the bottle of yellow liquid. She told him of the dosage and he opened the bottle and took a swallow, and the taste of the poison was strong and like a flammable fuel. After he had drunk it, he could still breathe the fumes.

"We need to get going," Mari said as she handed the poster to Jack. "This was at the police station."

Jack read it and handed it to Faith, but he said nothing. The sound of thunder cracked once and then again, and the rain began to fall.

"Have you been in Berberati before?" Jack asked both of them.

Mari shook her head, but Faith said yes, she knew the Baptist missionaries here.

"Do you know where the Catholic mission is?"

"Yes, but why?"

"Because we need a place to stay tonight and the Catholics are better with secrets than most."

"I saw the truck driver at the police station," Mari said.

"Pierre?"

"Yes, he was talking to the policeman at the station."

"Then they know we're here in Berberati," Faith said.

"Then the Catholic mission is the best choice," Jack said.

"Why?" Mari asked.

"Because I told Pierre we were Baptist missionaries."

They paid for the drinks and walked out into the dark rain.

As they passed the market, people were hurrying with their wares, gathering under the eaves of the Arab stalls that formed a square around the open market itself. As they walked up the hill, the rain came down hard and the water washed past their ankles and it splashed up to their knees. It was cold in the rain and they hurried as best they could. Both Jack and Faith felt visible in their whiteness and walked with their heads bent under the rain. Faith led them off the main street onto a myriad of labyrinthine paths that wound around small adobe houses with roofs of thatch and no one was out and it was so dark they bumped into each other. Faith led them up a narrow road strewn with rocks, then up a drive that was steep and slippery. When the lightning cracked again, Jack could see the coffee plants and with the next bolt the stone cathedral that rose above them and then the brick house off to the side of the cathedral.

The porch was covered and they stood out of the rain. Faith asked Jack in a whisper what they would say to the priest, and Jack said that they would tell him they needed refuge from the storm, that their truck broke down and they were on their way to Bouar to visit friends. "And I will say I am a Catholic."

Jack knocked on the door, and for some time no one came to open the door and they wondered if whoever lived here was asleep or gone away. Then the door opened and an old man, balding but with white tufts of hair on the sides of his head, stood before them with a lantern in his hand, the surface of the tiled floor sparkling in the yellow light.

"Father, do you have a place we could stay tonight? Our truck broke down and we are on our way to Bouar," Jack said.

"Come in, come in," the priest said. He was wearing a robe over his pajamas and he led them into the house. "It is a miserable night," he said

123

and though he spoke in French, Jack could tell the accent slurred and that he had been drinking. Then they could all discern the sweet smell of whiskey on his breath. "Have you eaten?"

"Yes," Jack said. "We just need a place to sleep, if it is not too much trouble."

"But of course. Would you not care for something to drink at least, before you retire?"

"No, no thank you."

The priest sighed. "Then come, come with me to the back and I will show you where the guests sleep."

They followed him through the dining room and his steps were without measure. In the kitchen, he opened a cupboard and took out another lantern and he lit it and handed it to Jack. "This is not the night to be traveling," he said.

"No, it is not," Jack agreed.

He opened the back door and the wind blew in the rain and he handed Jack a key. "You see the dormitory there. There is one other guest, but there are plenty of beds."

Jack stopped. "Who?"

"The guest? I forget his name, but he is from Bangui. An American. And I am Pere Jean-Paul."

The priest said breakfast was at seven, and after saying good night they crossed the muddy yard in the rain. The door to the dormitory was unlocked and Jack walked in first with the lantern and it yellowed the concrete room. There were eight beds and the one on the farthest end of the room was draped in a mosquito net under which was the blanketed figure of a man, and Faith whispered that they should take the beds nearest the door. They began to get out of their wet clothes and Mari and Faith were in bed when Jack sat down on the third bed from the door. He set the lantern by his feet, and was unlacing his boots when the American said hello in French.

"Hello, sorry to disturb you," Jack said in English.

"Is that you, Jack Burke?" The man sat up and pulled the mosquito net up. He sat on the edge of the bed and in the yellow light of the lantern Jack recognized Terry O'Malley, a thirty-five year old architect with whom he had played poker at the American *charge d'affaire's* home in Bangui.

O'Malley was a large man with a belly that hung over his belt for his fondness of beer, and he was one of those large men to whom violence was anathema so that his physical presence and his words and gestures never quite matched.

"O'Malley? What are you doing here?" Jack asked.

"I was going to ask you the same thing."

Jack walked over to his bed and they shook hands and Jack set the lantern on the floor and sat on the edge of the bed across from O'Malley's. Mari and Faith lay on the dark side of the room and they may have been sleeping they were so quiet.

O'Malley said he was on his way up north to a small village north of Bozoum where he was on a new project designing and building a cotton factory for the Germans. "Good money, Jack. The fucking Krauts pay well. I could probably get you on, if you wanted."

"Great, Terry. That's great. But I'm happy at the U.N. for now," and after he said this, he thought how he would never show up at the office in Bangui again and he wondered what everyone would think when they heard the reports that he had kidnaped a missionary and a prostitute and when he thought it, it seemed ludicrous to him, too, because of the combination of kidnap victims that he was said to have chosen.

"And what about you? You're traveling with an entourage?"

"Friends, Terry. Two friends of mine."

"I could have sworn that was Mari."

"It is."

Terry reached down to his bag on the floor and took out a pack of Dunhills and lit one and offered Jack one and they both smoked. "I thought the two of you were no longer a pair."

"We're not."

"I heard you fucked her over."

"I guess I did."

"Then what are you doing together? Making amends? I was in Bangui day before yesterday and, wait a minute, Jack, no," he paused and Jack watched his chubby face in the lantern light as the cheeks sucked in with the pull on the cigarette. "Jack, what are you doing up here? You hardly ever go up-country."

"Only when I have to." Jack bent down and ground the cigarette on the concrete floor with the toe of his boot and left it there.

"Are you in trouble?"

"No, why do you ask?"

"Because I was at the New Palace Bar in Bangui day before yesterday and I was sitting out on the veranda with Yvette and a couple of her friends and they were talking about how Mari was supposed to have been sent back to Bangui, except she never arrived, and here I see Mari in Berberati with Jack Burke. Kind of coincidental."

"Listen, Terry. If you just be quiet and listen, I'll tell you what's happening and yes, I am in trouble."

Jack told him what happened in Boda with the police chief and then what happened at the barrier in M'Baiki and how they had been in the jungle for seven days and how they got the ride to Berberati and then he told them that Mari had seen the poster, and "no, I didn't kidnap Faith. She just happens to be with me, is all."

Faith lay there listening under the mosquito net, and she frowned.

"It doesn't look like either of them have been kidnaped."

"Thanks for the vote of confidence."

"But you're in a hell of a mess."

"No shit."

"But you don't know that the sergeant in M'Baiki died, do you?"

"Shit. Just one died, though?"

"As far as I know. There was a big hassle at the M'Baiki barriers both coming in and going out yesterday, and they gave me the third degree on my papers before letting me pass and I asked what was the deal. They said some American gunman had come through shooting the place up like Billy the Kid, and I thought, right, sure, that happens all the time, an American with a gun in Africa."

"It was all an accident."

"So you did shoot the guy?"

"Hell yes, he was shooting at me."

"Man, Jack, you are up the fucking creek. You know that, don't you?"

"Yeah, I know. That's why I've got to get out of here."

"What are you going to do?"

"Go to Cameroon."

"How?"

"Sneak across the border."

"You're crazy."

"I don't have much of a choice."

"No, I suppose not. Not now, anyway."

Jack turned and looked at both Mari and Faith in their beds behind him. "Can you give us a ride to Bouar tomorrow? It's on your way."

Terry was silent and didn't answer.

"Hey, I'll understand if you won't. You could get screwed. They think I'm a murderer."

"You killed the Frenchman at Mari's, didn't you?"

"The son of a bitch was raping Mari, Terry. I killed the motherfucker. You bet I did. You would have done the same thing."

"With your knife. They say the guy had something like fifteen stab wounds. Said he was all carved up like a pumpkin at Halloween."

"Forget it. We've come this far and I guess we can make it to the border by ourselves. I don't want you getting into any trouble." Jack stood and picked up the lantern. "Hey, I'm glad about the new job. We'll see you in the morning at breakfast." He walked back to his bed and turned down the wick until the flame died. He took off his boots, pulled the mosquito net down and tucked it in under the mattress.

"Hey, Jack," O'Malley whispered, as if the darkness itself muffled his voice.

"What?"

"Remember that hand I had in Bangui? Flush to the ten? And how you bluffed me out of that big pot with two lousy pair?"

"Yeah, I remember. Twenty thousand francs."

"More like twenty-five. Well, you might just get out of this yet. I'll see you all in the morning. After breakfast, I'll give you a ride to Bouar. It's on my way."

After breakfast, Pere Jean-Paul took Jack aside as the others returned to the dormitory to pack. They stood together in the kitchen. The priest reached out and put his hand on Jack's shoulder. Jack backed away. "Are you in some kind of trouble, son?"

127

"No, none at all." For a moment, Jack had the urge to tell the priest everything that had happened, tell him how he had killed the sergeant and before that the man who had raped Mari; he wondered what the priest would be able to say to make him feel less responsible for the man's death, less responsible for Mari and now Faith. Did the priest have that magic, Jack wondered. Could confession wipe away all the guilt he was feeling, the guilt he felt whenever he thought of the dead sergeant in M'Baiki? Could the priest say something that would make him less afraid? Could the priest give him some safe plan to live by? Could the priest tell Jack to forget about it, forget about the past, tell him to go on ahead and live a new life as he himself wanted to do, yet he knew it was impossible because some things you could never forget no matter how hard you tried.

"The reason I asked is that I heard of a young Baptist who has been kidnaped, or so her parents believe."

"Faith? Does she look like she's been kidnaped?"

"No. She looks like she's in love."

Jack didn't say anything and the priest continued. "I also heard that this American is accused of killing two people and that he is on the run with this missionary and an African woman, a prostitute from Bangui."

"We fit the description pretty well in all that, but we are different people than the ones who are being looked for by the police."

"Yes, I can imagine that you are different people. I heard that the Frenchman who was killed, I cannot remember his name. Was it a Monsieur Dubois?"

Jack did not take the bait.

"Anyway, I have heard that he was a terrible man with the women." He sighed. "Well, I am glad that it is not you the police are seeking. Go with God, my son, and remember that God is always with you; you only have to reach out and take his hand."

Jack shook the old man's hand and went to the door.

Before Jack stepped out on the porch, the priest asked, "Are you Catholic?"

Jack turned and looked at the man. For some reason, he wanted to make the man happy; he also wanted to tell the truth. "Yes, I am catholic, but in a different sense of the word and in all the wrong ways," he said.

He walked down the porch leaving the priest to ponder what this meant, a difficult game of diction this early in the morning.

Faith, Mari and Jack suffocated under the canvas canopy tied down over the iron frame above the bed of the Landcruiser pick-up where they sat crowded with O'Malley's provisions, and before the barrier on the north end of Berberati, they lay under bags and covered themselves with blankets. They perspired and it was difficult to breathe. Jack closed his eyes and pretended this was just a dream, but still everything around him was tight and oppressive, and it was all he could do to stay still and quiet. The truck stopped and a gendarme came to the back of the truck and pulled the canvas flaps back to look into the bed with O'Malley at his side. Jack listened as O'Malley explained in his American accent that there was nothing but three months of provisions. Jack smiled at O'Malley's French and the American accent that was still as heavy as the man himself.

"Then you would not mind giving me ten liters of gasoline, since you have so much," the gendarme said.

"I can't do that. I only have enough for a few months."

"But you have two barrels of fuel here."

"But even this is not enough for as long as I will be *en brusse.*"

"Really? You only have enough for yourself?"

"Yes."

Come on, Jack thought. *Give the man the god damn fuel.*

"It seems to me that you have plenty of everything including the fuel."

"Look, I am going to be up-country for three months. Do you know of any gas stations up there?"

"Maybe your truck is over-loaded. I think that it may be."

"There's no weight limit on these roads."

"No, but a truck as loaded as this could be a danger to the villagers as you pass. You could roll over, maybe kill someone."

"That's ridiculous."

"You think my concern for people ridiculous?"

"That's not what I said."

Give the man the fuel.

"No?"

"Look, possibly you're right. Maybe I could spare five liters."

"That is all? With two barrels? Only five liters?"

"Okay, ten."

"Good. Let me get my can."

O'Malley pulled back the canvas near the cab and opened a fifty-gallon drum and put a hose in it and the gendarme came back and O'Malley filled the can. The gendarme thanked him and opened the barrier and they were on the long, rough road to Bouar, the three of them sitting under the canvas and when it rained they were glad they were dry, but it was stifling hot, and O'Malley drove like he was in a terrible hurry to get somewhere and he was; he was in a hurry to have these three people out of his truck. He hit the rocks and bumps with great speed and the three passengers in the back were jarred and they bumped heads and it was hour after hour of this with infrequent stops well off the side of the road, and the farther north they went, the sparser the vegetation became until there was no more forest and the land was open savannah stubbled with occasional acacia trees, and when, after seven hours since leaving the mission, they slowed and O'Malley cut off the road and parked behind a clump of acacia trees, Jack and the two women climbed out into the open air as O'Malley refueled.

Faith passed out from the heat and Mari called for Jack. They helped her back to the truck where they gave her water and fanned her on the east side of the truck where there was shade.

Mari kneeled over her and Jack stood and O'Malley came down from the bed of the truck. "We've got to get going, Jack."

"I know. Give her a minute."

"Okay, but let's not make this too long."

"All right."

"Is it the arm, Faith?" Jack asked.

"No. My arm is fine. I just fainted. The heat, maybe."

Faith sat up and said she was okay and that they could go on, and Jack suggested she ride in the front until they got close to Bouar which, he reckoned, was still a hundred kilometers away. O'Malley was reluctant but he saw that Faith was in bad shape and he acquiesced.

O'Malley talked as he drove and Faith mostly listened. He talked about Jack and what a good guy he was and he told anecdotes of the poker games they had in Bangui. He said that Jack was a card and that everyone liked him and then he asked Faith if they were in love.

"Yes," was all she said and O'Malley let it go because he could see she was tired, but he said that he was happy for them and that he hoped they would get out of the country all right and that she should remind Jack to write once they were settled somewhere, but he didn't really think he would hear from Jack ever again. Faith thought about that, about settling somewhere, and she hoped it would be soon because she was so tired and she wanted a normal life with Jack; that was all she wanted. When she thought of a normal life, she thought of her parents behind her in Boda. The truck was headed north away from Berberati and Boda in the south, and behind her were her parents and she wondered about what she was doing and the doubt that she had first felt after she had been shot in M'Baiki, that doubt that had surfaced again when she was alone in the jungle with Mari after having crossed the river, that doubt that rose in her each night as she lay down to sleep, that same doubt that she had quelled each time it climbed to the surface of her conscience— that doubt was now stronger than it had been before and she wondered if she were doing the right thing. Her parents, her work, her students, everything that had defined her existence, was now in her wake. It was as though she had completely shed her identity. Was love worth all that? Was that part of love, this liminal stage of in-between, a point in time when she no longer knew who she was? And the doubt, was that part of love as well? The constant questioning of oneself and of what one was doing? Then she wondered if this feeling for a man, this feeling she had never had before, this feeling that made her blood run faster and thinner and caused her heart to beat and glow—she wondered if this was what was called *love*. Then she thought of the Roman poet Ovid and of his descriptions of love, of eros, and she thought he would commend her for having attained such a beautiful moment in life, and at this she smiled.

"Thanks for giving us the ride, Terry," Faith said. "I know it was a risk."

"Ah, don't worry about it. I guess I can look at it as getting Jack out of the country and I'll have a better chance in those poker games with him

131

gone. The man can bluff like no one else I've ever seen."

It was thirty kilometers south of Bouar that the police had the road blocked. O'Malley pulled up to a halt where the two Peugeot 404's were parked bumper-to-bumper across the road. An officer came up to O'Malley's window and Jack and Mari could hear him from where they were covered with a tarp in the bed of the truck under the canopy of canvas.

"Your papers, please," he said in French. He wore a white helmet and a crisp blue uniform, and he looked very serious about his job; he held the papers in his white gloved hand and he read them and handed them back to O'Malley. "*Et votre papiers, s'il vous plait, Mademoiselle*," he said to Faith. These were not the usual police who drank palm wine at the barriers, whose main business was to extract bribes with which to purchase whiskey and beer and cigarettes.

Faith looked in the glove box and she was wan with fever; the officer could see that she was sick. Another officer came up to the passenger side window from behind the truck. "There is no one in the back of the truck," he said through the window to the officer standing next to the driver-side door. He watched as Faith looked for her papers. Finally, Faith said, "I'm sorry. I can't seem to find them."

The officer at O'Malley's window opened the door and asked O'Malley to please step down. O'Malley looked at Faith and then he got out of the truck and the passenger side door was opened and Faith was asked to step down. One officer questioned her and asked if she were a missionary from Boda who had been kidnaped and she said no, she was Mary Lord, the first name that came to her mind. She said she was with the *Corps De La Paix*. She did not speak Sango, but French, and she said she was sick and could she please sit down, and the officer walked her to the folding metal table they had set up in the sparse shade of an acacia tree where she sat on one of the three metal chairs.

"Your name is Jack Burke, Monsieur?" The officer asked as O'Malley stood by the door of the truck.

"No, you can see from my papers who I am. I am Terry O'Malley and I am an architect on my way to the north of Bozoum to build a cotton factory for the Germans."

"Why do you have so many names?"

"Because I'm Irish."

"Your papers say you are American." The officer smiled, thinking he had caught him in a lie.

"Irish American. Nobody is really American. Except the Indians."

"No one is American?"

"Look, I'm American. My ancestors were Irish."

"I see. And you work for the Germans?"

"Yes."

"And where is the whore? The African named Mari Mbarza?"

"I don't know who that is."

"Are you sure?" The officer still held O'Malley's papers and he looked at them from time to time as he spoke.

"Yes." O'Malley was much bigger than the officer and the officer had to look up at him even though O'Malley was leaning back on the door of the truck.

"And your friend, the Mademoiselle, she is not Faith Sellers?"

"No."

"She has no papers?"

"Apparently she cannot find them."

"And what was her name?"

"She already said. Mary. Mary Lord."

"Ah, yes. Mary Lord. And what is she doing with you?"

"She is on vacation and is traveling with me."

"And you are lovers?"

"That is not your affair."

"No? Everything here is my affair, Monsieur." He looked up the road toward Boaur, and then south towards Berberati. "Everything."

"We are friends."

The officer sighed. "Come with me." O'Malley followed him to the table and he took a seat next to Faith and he said, "Mary, these guys are assholes. Just stick to your guns."

Faith nodded her head, but she was weak from fever, and she could do little more than sit in the chair.

The officer who had questioned O'Malley said, "Please, no English.

133

We are just ignorant Africans and do not understand English."

O'Malley sat next to Faith and the younger of the two officers, the one who had questioned Faith, stood from his chair and offered it to his colleague who sat down and continued with the interrogation as the junior officer stood behind the two Americans. "Now, let me see if I have this right. You are Terry O'Malley and not Jack Burke and you are Mary Lord and not Faith Sellers and neither of you knows a whore from Bangui by the name of Mari Mbarza."

"That is true," O'Malley said and Faith said nothing. "Look, my friend is sick. Could you please let us pass on."

"Of course. But a few more questions. Where are you coming from?"

"Berberati."

"Where did you stay?"

"The Catholic mission."

"And before that?"

"M'Baiki. Bangui. Look, please, we told you who we are."

"But Mademoiselle Sellers has no papers."

"Lord. Her name is Lord. We can't find them. I'm sorry."

"Yes, you are sorry."

Thunder could be heard in the distance. "It is going to rain soon," the junior officer said to his senior.

"Yes."

"The roads will be a mess," he went on.

"I know. I know. We are through here, anyway, with Monsieur O'Malley and his *copine*. Please," he stood and motioned for Faith and O'Malley to stand. "You may go." He handed O'Malley his papers.

"Thank you," O'Malley said, and as they walked to the truck he thought nothing of the motorcycle that he could see approaching from the direction of Berberati.

As O'Malley started the truck, Faith climbed in the passenger side door. The motorcycle pulled up next to the truck and the motorcyclist looked through the window at O'Malley and then at Faith and there was mutual recognition.

"It is she, the missionary," Pierre yelled to the officers and they ran up to the truck.

"And who are you?"

Pierre told him his name and said he was a truck driver but had once been a policeman in Berberati and he went on to explain how he knew Faith, that he had seen the poster at the police station in Berberati and that he was after the reward.

"And this is Jack Burke?" The senior officer asked him, pointing at O'Malley who held the wheel tensely with both hands, the engine still idling.

"No. I have never seen him before," Pierre said.

"Mademoiselle Faith," the senior officer said. "Where are your friends?"

"I am Mary Lord and I have never seen this man before. It may be that we whites all look the same and that this is a case of mistaken identity."

"I doubt that very much," the junior officer said as he opened her door and took her by the arm and led her to the driver's side where O'Malley was now being escorted out of the vehicle.

"Let us look in the back of the truck again," the senior officer said and he led the others to the back where he pulled back the canvas flaps.

"See," O'Malley said. "There is nothing. It is as she said. This is a case of mistaken identity."

"We shall see," the senior officer said.

"She is the missionary," Pierre said.

"Shut up," the junior officer told him.

The senior officer climbed up to the bumper and behind him stood O'Malley and Faith and Pierre and behind them was the junior officer with his gun drawn but pointed at the ground.

The senior officer pulled back the flap and folded it back on the canvas roof and from inside the bed of the truck he again said, "We shall see," and he moved boxes and pulled back a tarp and the last thing he saw was the barrel of a gun almost touching his nose and Jack's face looking up at him with a clenched jaw and eyes that squinted.

The others heard the explosion and they first looked to the sky, and the senior officer's face was no longer a face and much of it fell on Jack, and hair and blood and brain stuck on the canvas ceiling. Mari screamed as Jack pushed himself up from under the body of the gendarme, and the

135

four people at the tailgate did not know that they too were splattered with the senior officer's blood because all they could do was stare at Jack whose own face was red with the man's blood and on Jack's chest were pieces of teeth. As Jack sat up, he pointed the gun out at Pierre because he could not see the junior officer behind O'Malley, and Pierre made the mistake of lunging toward Jack.

There was a blast from the gun and gripping his chest, Pierre fell forward, and Jack had no more bullets and he took up the other gun he had taken from the sergeant in Boda so many days before. He cocked the hammer and there was an explosion but not from his own gun, and he saw O'Malley fall forward and hit his jaw on the tailgate of the truck and behind him was the junior officer with a gun pointing at him and Jack fired twice and the man fell to the ground.

Jack climbed out of the truck and it was quiet. Mari pushed herself up and climbed down beside Jack and the junior officer was not dead and neither was Pierre, but when Jack bent down and felt for O'Malley's pulse, there was none.

Jack stood up with the gun pointing to the ground and he looked down at Pierre and the officer who was still alive and he did not say anything. He just looked from one to the other with the gun in his hand. He raised the gun and pointed it at the junior officer who lay on his back and covered his face with his hands. "You motherfucker," Jack screamed. "Motherfucker, motherfucker," and with his arm outstretched he still pointed the gun at the prostrate junior officer. "You son of a bitch. Why, motherfucker, why did you have to kill O'Malley?" Tears spilled from Jack's eyes, and he whimpered, "Why? O'Malley's dead, for God's sake. Why?" Mari took Jack by the arm and led him to the front of the truck where he sat down and cried, his head on his knees, still holding the gun, and he said, "Motherfucker" over and over again, tears streaming down into his beard where they were lost.

Faith stood numbly and then she began to cry, slowly at first, but then the sobs came in torrents. Mari left Jack at the front of the truck and took Faith by the arm and sat her down by the side of the truck, and then she went for the first aid kit.

The officer's wound was in his arm and Pierre was shot in the chest and had blood coming through both his mouth and his ears and he tried to speak, but then he just lay there and it was apparent to Mari that he was dead.

Jack was leaning back against the truck wiping his face when Mari came around to the front of the truck.

"Pierre's dead, too, but the policeman is alive."

"Motherfucker."

"Faith is in bad shape."

"He killed O'Malley."

"Faith needs help, Jack."

"O'Malley's dead."

"Help her, Jack."

"He shot O'Malley. The motherfucker shot O'Malley in the back."

"Jack."

"He's dead."

"What about Faith, Jack?"

"Help her, Mari."

"Are you okay?"

"Help Faith, will you?" And then, as Mari left him, she could hear him say that word again.

Jack could hear Faith's crying that had been like a kettle on the boil but that now was simmering. Mari knelt next to her and hugged her and talked quietly, and Faith looked up at her and said, "Mari, everyone's dead. Everyone's dead."

"Quiet now, Faith. It's over. We have to get going before the police come. We have to help Jack."

Mari helped her stand and they found Jack wiping the blood from his beard with a bandanna, his right hand still holding the gun. His shirt was covered with blood and there were still pieces of flesh and small chips of bone stuck in his hair and in his beard.

"Jack," Faith said. She touched his shirt, withdrew her hand and looked at the blood on the tips of her fingers. "What are we going to do?"

Jack didn't seem to hear her, although he looked at her and the expression he wore was one of surprise, as though someone from his past had arrived after a long absence, someone he did not expect.

137

"Jack, did you hear me? What are we going to do now? O'Malley's dead. We killed him, too."

The glaze of Jack's eyes faded. "We've got to go. They'll be traffic. They'll stop and find the policeman. Is he bad?"

"No," Mari said, and she took the gun from Jack's hand and set it on the hood of the truck.

"Jack, look at me, will you? What do we do now?"

Jack looked up from the road at Faith. "I don't know, Faith. When we get to Bouar, you and Mari can stay. You haven't done anything yet. O'Malley hadn't either. If you stay with me, you'll wind up dead. Same as O'Malley."

"What do you mean we haven't done anything?" Faith said. "They're dead. You don't seem to realize what we've done. How many people we've killed."

"Oh, I realize it; hell, I killed them. I killed them all."

"*We* killed them all."

"Easy, Faith. That's not true."

"No. No. This isn't the way things are supposed to be, Jack. No, not like this."

Jack put his hands on Faith's shoulders. "Listen, Faith. Mari. If you come with me, well, we might not make it. Get out while you can."

"No," Faith said.

"We should bury the dead," Mari said.

Jack looked at her, and then he turned and looked at the bodies of O'Malley and Pierre. "We don't have time. Someone will be by here before long. Cameroon is not more than a hundred kilometers west of here. I've got to go to the border."

"No, no, no," Faith said. "This is not right, Jack. This isn't right."

"Faith, get a hold of yourself. Of course it's not right. This is not about right and wrong. It's about getting the fuck out of here before the police come. That's all it is. Right and wrong have nothing to do with this or with how we get out of here."

"Get out of here, Jack?" Faith said. "Get out of here? To where?"

"I told you. The sea."

PART THREE

Jack took the officers' guns and Mari and Faith helped him lift the injured officer onto the back seat of one of the 404's. Mari had bandaged his arm and he was not badly injured and would live. Jack climbed in the driver's seat, turned and looked at the man lying on the back seat. The officer's eyes were large and white with fear. "*Vous etes l'American? Le bandit?*"

"Yes, but I am not who you think I am." He turned back around and parked the car on the side of the road. He got out and lifted the hood up.

They took the body of the dead officer from the back of the truck and placed it next to the others and Jack kneeled next to O'Malley, removed O'Malley's wallet from his hip pocket and took out the wad of crisp bills. He whispered something to O'Malley, but Faith and Mari could not hear what it was he said. When he came back to the truck he had tears in his eyes.

They drove north for fifteen kilometers toward Bouar before abandoning the road and driving west through the open savannah, and that night they camped near a river far from any village and none of them would sleep in the back of the truck even after Jack had cleaned it. They sat in the cab as it rained and in the morning they drove west until the terrain was no longer passable. They abandoned the truck and they hiked up and down ravines and in the far distance to the west they could see the hills of Cameroon and seeing them gave them their first tangible destination. They trudged on, Jack in the lead with two revolvers in his belt and O'Malley's backpack full of food on his back, and Mari carried a cloth bundle that held more food and a blanket and a canteen. Faith was over her fever, but she only carried a canteen because Mari would let her carry nothing else.

That day they came across a group of Muslim cow herders guiding cows through the savannah, the men carrying staffs and the women with their faces covered, and these nomads dressed in the flowing robes of the bedouin did not stop to talk or even look surprised at the three of them trekking toward Cameroon.

That night after Jack had gone into the river to clean his jeans and plaid shirt of the blood of the policeman, he and Mari sat by the fire as

Faith slept wrapped in O'Malley's sleeping bag. Jack sat with a fifth of Irish whiskey tucked between his legs.

"How's your stomach?" Mari asked.

"Better."

"You still have another day with the medicine."

"I know."

"You shouldn't drink."

"I know."

"The medicine won't work as well if you drink."

"I know that, Mari. But my stomach's better."

Mari didn't say anything to that, and Jack took another sip of the whiskey. "If I could get you to Kisangani, would you go?" Jack asked.

Mari took the pan of water off the fire and set it in the dirt. They were camped in a hollow by the river bed and it had not rained since the afternoon and now the stars were glittering above them.

"Yes, but only with my sister and the children."

Jack struck his Zippo and the flint sparked but there was no fuel. "*Merdre*," he said, and he leaned forward and took a twig and poked it in the fire. It glowed and he lit his cigarette and leaned back against the stump. "I know, Mari, but I don't think even you can go back to Bangui now. You go to Kisangani and we will send a letter to Francoise and make a wire transfer to her from Cameroon and you can meet her there."

"Do you think we can do that?" She looked up from where she squatted and then she continued pouring the water from the pan into the canteen.

"Yes. It will be no problem."

"Then yes, I would like to go."

"Good. It is settled, then."

Jack took a drink of the whiskey and he offered it to Mari, but she shook her head. "Jack?"

"Yes."

"I wish everything were different."

"*Moi aussi*, Mari. Me also."

"It could have been different."

"It could have been, but it is not. Everything is this way because of what I did after the miscarriage. Everything. I'm sorry, Mari. I am sorry for everything. It's my fault. But there's no changing it."

"No." Mari put another piece of wood on the fire and arranged it in the coals and the sparks shot up into the dark sky and the fire lit both their faces as Faith slept in the shadows away from the fire.

"What do you mean, no? I came to the house and I struck you and I moved out, and that was it. That is why we are here today. That is why O'Malley is dead. That is why the policemen and the truck driver are dead. Everything is because of what I did that afternoon at your house."

"No, Jack. You cannot take all of the responsibility for this."

"Why not? It's true. It's funny, though, that I don't feel much about all this. I mean, I *am* sorry. But I am more afraid than anything. Afraid for you. Afraid for Faith. And afraid for me, too. All's I can do now is run. And then I'll be sorry for the rest of my damn life." He took a sip of the whiskey. "You know, a man has to be responsible for his own actions. That's all there is. And he has to be able to live with the result of those actions. And that's what I'm trying to do: live."

Mari looked at Jack across the fire and the orange flames lit his black beard and his brown eyes. She watched him as he smoked and sipped from the bottle of whiskey.

"What about before what you did?"

He wiped his mouth with the back of his hand. "What are you talking about, Mari? Everything that has happened is because of that afternoon and me moving out because if I would not have moved out, I would have been home with you when that man came and maybe he would still be alive. Maybe everybody would still be alive."

"No, Jack. What about everything before that afternoon."

"Like what?"

"Like the miscarriage itself, for example. What caused that?"

"I don't know."

"But you see if the miscarriage had not occurred, then you would not have moved out."

"So?"

"So you cannot look at everything today and see one seed for its birth. There are many."

"I don't know about that. I only know that it was me who set these events into motion. I stabbed the bastard, I squeezed the trigger every time." He paused, looked up at the stars and sighed. "And I might as well have been the one who shot O'Malley."

Mari reached for the bottle, took a sip and handed it back to Jack. "No, not only you. There was me. There was that Frenchman who raped us."

"I know, Mari, but can't you see that none of that would have happened if I had not hit you and moved out on you?"

"And you would not have done that if there had not been a miscarriage."

Jack didn't say anything. He took another sip of the whiskey.

"Jack? You see? Everything is more complicated than you want to believe and it is complicated in such a way that we cannot always understand."

"I don't know. It's not all that complicated. I stabbed him. How many times did they say? Fifteen, sixteen times? And then I shot the gendarmes in M'Baiki, and then the gendarmes on the road, and I just keep killing people. Mari? I keep killing people. And I would never hurt anyone if I had a choice."

"You killed them, yes, you did. But what if you did not?"

"They would still be alive."

"When something happens, you always look back to everything that preceded it in time and you try to find a cause, but it is not always so simple."

"It is, usually."

"Well, what if we had not met?"

"I don't know what you mean."

"None of this would have happened. So you cannot take all of the responsibility. What made us meet?"

"What do you mean?" Jack flicked the cigarette into the fire.

"If you look at the time of our meeting, can you look before it and see something that caused it?"

"Sure. I went to the New Palace Bar and so did you. I thought you were pretty and I bought you a beer. Simple."

144

"Maybe it is. But then what made you go to the bar?"

"I was thirsty. What made you go to the bar?"

"I went to the bars every night. Why did you go to the New Palace Bar and not the Rock or the San Sylvestre? That is my point."

"Mari, I'm tired and I don't see your point." He threw his cigarette butt into the fire.

"My point is that you Americans always try to discover all the causes of each moment and my point is that there are not necessarily those causes. So you cannot think that it was Jack Burke who made everything happen here in Africa since you arrived." Mari touched Jack's face and he turned and looked at her. "And besides, you would not even have come to Africa if it wasn't for that girl who cheated on you in America. You said that. You said you would have married her."

"Yes. I said that. So why does everything happen?" Jack tossed his cigarette in the fire.

"There is no answer to that."

"Faith would say it was God's will," Jack said.

"Which God?"

"I don't know. What would you say?"

"I would say we are foolish to live our lives trying to discover the answers when the questions we ask are so foolish. Everything we want to know we will know."

"When?"

"When we die, of course." Mari stretched her arms wide.

"That's good. I might get those answers pretty soon."

"Jack, don't say that. Besides, it may be there are no such answers, and so the questions are foolish." She paused. "You know Faith loves you?"

"She thinks she does."

"And you love her?"

He hesitated and then said yes, he thought he did.

"Then you have to live. For her, anyway." She laughed.

"What's so funny?"

"I was just thinking that you need to live for me as well if you are going to give me enough money to get to Kisangani and then send my sister money for the trip."

Jack smiled and Mari lay down and wrapped herself in the blanket and Jack watched the two women sleep in the light of the fire. When the fire was out, Jack took a blanket and lay down and it was dark and it didn't rain that night, but it was cold and Jack did not sleep well.

The rain started before they broke camp. It was steady and thick and after five minutes they were soaked. They walked west but could not see the mountains because there was only the gray of the clouds and the rain that fell, and in the distance the lightning could be seen and the thunder seemed to be an echo of itself again and again. They walked slowly and the rain dripped from their foreheads into their eyes and the clouds seemed to move at the pace which they walked so that the rain was always with them, a constant companion, and Jack needed the compass just to tell which direction they were going. Without it, he only knew what was in his wake.

After three hours, he knew that they were getting closer to the border because they were walking up a gentle but steady incline; they could feel it in the calves of their legs, a tightness in the muscle. No one spoke as they walked and despite the chill of the rain, they perspired under their clothing and their feet were wet. Jack led the way and Mari followed and Faith was not far behind. They had walked six hours before the rain stopped and then the clouds moved on into Cameroon and they were on a small hill when the sun came out and once again they could see the mountains near the border and they looked as far away as they had the day before. To the north, they could see the road that traveled to the border and the road was not a kilometer north of where they walked and Jack could see some huts of a roadside village.

"Jack, let's stop and rest," Mari said.

"Okay, but not too long."

They sat down on some rocks in the sun and their clothes steamed. There were no trees here, not even any acacia trees that would have offered at least thin hints of shade, and they were hot as they sat in the sun. As far as they could see the land sloped up toward the mountains, a muddy terrain studded with rocks and occasional clumps of grass. Faith opened two tins of mackerel and they ate and drank water from O'Malley's canteen. Before taking a sip, Jack held the canteen at arm's length and stared at it as if in a trance, and then he bent his head back and took a long sip before handing it to Faith.

"O'Malley filled that canteen," was all Jack said.

"Jack?" Faith asked.

"What?"

"What did you whisper in O'Malley's ear before we left him?"

"Whisper?" Jack smiled thinking of times before. "I told him that I had told him before never to draw to the inside straight."

"What does that mean?"

Jack stood. "Nothing, really. Maybe one shouldn't count on beating the odds, is all." Jack began walking north toward the village they had seen. Mari watched him go, but said nothing.

"Jack? Where are you going?" Faith asked.

Jack turned around. "To check out the terrain, see where we are, where we're going." He turned again and began walking.

"Jack?" Faith said. "Sometimes you can beat the odds. You just have to believe. You have to have faith." But she could not be sure he had heard for with his back turned to her, all he did was wave his hand and keep walking.

Faith stared after Jack as his silhouette grew smaller; she stared silently until Mari interrupted her reverie, saying only, "Men."

Faith turned to see that she, too, was watching the retreating figure of Jack, oblivious of Faith's presence. "What is it with them?" Faith asked.

"Arrogance. Fear of showing weakness. Fear of showing emotion. That is their greatest problem." Mari was sitting on a boulder above Faith's, and Faith looked up at her.

"I suppose. He seems so distant now, Mari. I can't seem to connect with him."

"A lot has happened in the last few days."

"But I am afraid that I will never be able to connect with him again. I almost feel—I have to be honest, Mari—I almost feel that I should just give up, that I should leave, go home."

"But you love him?"

"Yes."

"Then you'd be turning your back on love. And if you do that, it may never come again."

147

Faith looked at Mari, stared at her until Mari turned away to look off to the north where Jack could no longer be seen.

"But I don't know if I want love like this, Mari."

"Like what? Love is not supposed to be easy. And it's never a choice. If it gets too rough, you are just going to quit?"

"No. But this is like it will die around the next corner, the next bend. I want to know the love that will last until I'm dead."

"There is no love like that."

"Yes, there is. God's love."

"Sure, if you believe in God."

"I don't want the man I love to go off and die in the dark."

"Better that than to run away from him. Besides, we all die in the dark."

"Mari, I'm just afraid of being alone. I'm afraid maybe that I have done the wrong thing running away with Jack."

Mari stood and climbed off the rock she sat on, and sat down next to Faith. Faith leaned forward with her hands in her lap. Mari reached out and touched her hands. "We are all afraid of being left alone, Faith. But better that than having been always alone."

"What do you mean?"

"Better to have known love and lost it than to have never known it at all. That way, at least there are memories to embrace."

"But I don't want to be left alone."

"We all are. That's the way we start our life and that is the way it ends. There is no one who does not die alone. You cannot change that, and you cannot change Jack. If you ran away now, Faith, you will have forsaken your very name and you will still be alone, more alone than ever because you will have chosen to be by abandoning Jack."

"I know. It's just that nothing is working the way it is supposed to."

"If you had not come with Jack, if you would have stayed at the mission in Boda with your parents, would your future be the way you would want it?"

"I don't know that."

"But tell me, what would your future be like?"

"I told you, Mari, I don't know. No one can know that."

"But would you fall in love?"

"Yes, I think so, sometime."

"Then you do not believe there is just one love meant for each person?"

"I don't know." Faith stood and climbed off the rock and looked at Mari. "I don't know that. I only know that if I hadn't come, I would be home with my parents teaching at the school..."

"And everything would be safe."

"Safe and oh, I don't know, Mari. It's just that I am so afraid now."

"Safe and you would long for Jack and you would know you had made the wrong decision by staying because you would never see him again."

"Yes. But now I am afraid I am going to watch him die."

"You don't know that."

"I'm tired, Mari. I'm very, very tired." Faith sat down with her back to the rock on which Mari sat, and she closed her eyes and said, "I think I will sleep until Jack comes back."

"You sleep. I'll keep watch for Jack."

There were no clouds that afternoon and it did not rain. The sun was hot and they weren't sure which was worse, the sun or the rain. As they walked, they could see the mountains looming above them and it was difficult to judge the distance to the mountains, but that night they camped in their shadow as the sun set behind them, and it was cooler than before and they could tell that the elevation had changed as it was more difficult to breathe.

The rain came from nowhere, a hard rain which soaked them as there was no shelter. It pelted them with a relentless ferocity, and then, without transition, it simply stopped.

Jack walked north in the dark to the road that led to the border. From the bushes he watched a constant train of trucks headed toward Cameroon. Many of them were empty, but Jack knew they would be returning in a few weeks' time and that they would be full of everything the land-locked nation might use. The only trucks that were not empty were those that were laden with burlap sacks of coffee, each sack eighty bulging kilos, and the cotton trucks that were fluffs of white snow contained by mesh netting. As he watched, it began to rain again.

Faith and Mari were sitting by the fire with blankets pulled over their heads and it was going to be a long, wet night before morning.

"How long has he been gone?" Faith asked.

"A few hours. He'll be back soon."

"It's so cold. When we get to Cameroon, I am going to take a long, hot bath. I'm going to soak in the tub for a week and order room service."

"What will you order?"

"Croissants and jam and eggs and ham and coffee, lots and lots of hot coffee. And fresh orange juice. And you, Mari?"

Mari smiled. Water dripped off her forehead into her eyes and she wiped them with the back of her hand. She reached out to the fire and warmed her hands, and then crossed her arms and pulled the blanket around her neck, but the blanket was too wet to do much good. "First, I too would take a bath. A bubble bath."

"Good."

"And then I would dress in clean clothes."

"A new sari."

"Yes."

"And I would braid your hair."

"Thank you. And then I would order the coldest beer in Africa and a plate of fresh fish, *Capitaine* broiled over a fire, and a bucket full of *pommes frittes*."

"You're making me hungry."

"And for dessert a large piece of chocolate cake."

"Oh, and ice cream. Vanilla ice cream."

"Yes. And then coffee."

"Mari, I can't wait to get there."

"Me either. It sounds to me like you're going to be okay."

"Yes. It was just a moment of weakness. I don't have those often, but this afternoon I was so tired of walking."

"And now here we sit in the pouring rain and you are having a moment of strength?" Mari laughed.

"Yes, I guess I am. I'm sorry about today. Not only for just being so weak, but for being inconsiderate of you. For that I am sorry, Mari. Do you forgive me?"

Mari was no longer smiling. "Of course."

When Jack returned from his reconnaissance, he found the two women dripping wet with wet blankets wrapped around themselves, and he felt bad that he could do nothing to make things more comfortable.

They reached the border before noon, but the mountains were steep and there was no place to cross except for the road that cut through the pass where the border station was situated. They rested in the broken shade of an acacia tree and discussed the alternatives. Jack said he did not know how far it might be to walk south in search of a traversable pass through the mountains and that the alternative was to go up to the border town at night and sneak into the bed of a cotton truck and bury themselves with cotton and cross that way.

Neither Faith nor Mari much cared for that plan, but as it was the only alternative and as they were both so tired of walking, and knowing that if they chose to walk south looking for a pass it could be days before they found one, they agreed with Jack to hike to the road that night and climb into the bed of one of the cotton trucks that Jack had seen the night before.

They spent the day napping in the small shade of some boulders. They ate what remained of the canned fish, and they discarded anything that they would not need and took only some jerky that had been O'Malley's and the two guns Jack kept in his belt. That night, well after sunset, they began the walk to the village by the border.

This was as far north on the African continent that either Mari, Faith or Jack had ever been, and the terrain was rockier than it had been in the south; there was little foliage except for occasional copses of acacia. Faith was worried about lions and so was Mari, but Jack told them there weren't any here and as they didn't come across any, he thought he may have been right.

At the border, the trucks were lined up for a kilometer and those that came from Cameroon were released in sporadic spurts so that where Jack, Faith and Mari were huddled in the darkness in a ditch behind a wrecked truck that was a rusted-out vestige of some freak accident from years before, they could see the traffic pass. The trucks came in bunches, first two and then three, all of them heading east from Cameroon, and then for twenty or thirty minutes there was nothing and Jack guessed that the lack of traffic was evidence of a stubborn driver who refused to pay the requisite bribes to get into the Republic. Then a truck came rumbling past them laden with goods from Cameroon, and then two and then three, and all the while the trucks heading into Cameroon, a rich, fertile country on the sea that because of the ocean was more developed than the Republic, moved slowly and steadily one at a time in a symphonic lull orchestrated by the Cameroonian border guards who spit in the dirt when they talked about the Central Africans entering their country.

It was dark and the trucks in line to the west showed only their parking lights. When there was no movement, the drivers climbed down from their rigs and stood and smoked and talked, and then a truck would move forward ten or fifteen meters and the other drivers climbed back up and drove forward and stopped, and then climbed back down and gathered in groups, smoking and talking in hushed voices.

Jack walked well off the side of the road in the shadows of truck lights and he crept as close to the border as he could as Faith and Mari waited for him behind the junked truck in the ditch on the side of the road.

Jack could see the Central African border guards standing by the barrier blocking the road into the country and he watched as a driver passed down his papers. The guard looked through them, took them to the hut to be stamped, and called to the driver who got out of his truck and went into the hut where money was passed. The driver returned to his truck and drove through and the barrier came back down in the glow of tail lights and another truck took its place, its headlights shining into the Republic.

This was a ravine in the mountains where the road crossed the border and a generator hummed and everything smelled of diesel and the lights were on poles five meters high bathing the ground in watery yellow light. Beyond where the flag of Central Africa flew, Jack could see the Cameroonian flag and the Cameroonian guards who worked more quickly than the Central Africans. The trucks pulled up to the barrier into Cameroon and the guard stamped the papers and Jack saw soldiers look under the chassis of each truck that passed and they searched the beds of the trucks as well. Jack wondered if this were normal procedure or if they were searching for two Americans and an African. When a cotton truck pulled up, Jack watched closely.

It was a ten-ton truck and the bed was two meters high fluffed with cotton contained by the wooden side rails of the truck, and the hemp mesh over the top kept the cotton from floating away into the darkness. The guard looked at the driver's papers, stamped them and handed them back to the driver through the window as two soldiers climbed on the back bumper of the truck and pulled back the hemp mesh covering the load of cotton. They stood on the side rails and with pitchforks they jabbed into the cotton as they carefully moved forward toward the cab and then they jumped down and the guard waved the driver on after the mesh covering was pulled back.

Jack crouched in the shadows on the side of the road and watched for thirty more minutes and each cotton truck was searched in the same fashion. Jack tried to think of an alternative method of crossing the border, but save hiking south looking for a pass in the mountains, he could not think of one as viable as crossing in the bed of a cotton truck where they would be buried beneath an avalanche of white snow.

Jack made his way back to the wreck where Faith and Mari awaited him. He took his time and was careful and stayed well away from the road; it took him twenty minutes.

"Well?" Faith whispered when he came up behind them and sat down on the ground.

"A cotton truck is our best bet," Jack said.

"We are ready when you are," Mari said.

It was dark behind the truck and Jack could not see either of their faces.

"It would be better to wait for it to rain," Jack said.

"Why?" Faith said.

Jack didn't say anything and Mari asked him what was wrong.

"It is the guards. They must have been informed about us. They are searching the trucks very carefully."

"Why would it be better to wait for the rain?" Faith said.

"Because they will be less careful, that's all."

153

"They won't find us in the cotton." Mari was confident.

Jack didn't say anything and he thought about their chances if they were deep enough in the cotton, but he didn't like the idea of being buried in the back of a truck, either. "They are even checking the cotton," he said.

"How can they do that without removing it all?" Faith said.

"With pitchforks."

Mari and Faith were silent. Jack said, "I think if we climb down deep enough and stay in the middle, we will be okay. See, there are only two soldiers with the pitchforks and there is one on each side of the truck and they can't reach the middle. If we get up by the cab of the truck and stay in the middle, we'll be alright. Besides, they start at the rear of the truck and work forward and by the time they get to the front they are bored and know there is no one in the truck and they don't poke so deep."

"I can't believe this is how they search for fugitives," Faith said and she hadn't thought of the word but now that she said it, she fully realized that she was a fugitive and that they were indeed in grave trouble. She was on the run and the police were looking for her and her parents had no idea where she was, and she was more frightened than she had ever been. "Isn't there some other way?" she asked. Although she did not say so, she wished she were back home in Boda eating dinner with her mother and father.

"This is our best chance, Faith," Jack said.

Faith thought about the very word *chance* in English and she thought that it was not really a cognate in French for in the latter it meant *luck*, and now, she thought, they were certainly taking a chance and if they were to succeed they would need lots of luck. Prayer, though, was how she could help them succeed, and she did pray, she prayed that they would make it through to Cameroon, and then to some safe haven where she could be reunited with her parents, where she could have them see that Jack Burke was not the man they thought he was, that he was, in fact, a very good man. Soon, she thought, all of this would be over and she could return to a life of normalcy where one ate three meals a day and did good work for the Lord.

It was just after midnight and still the rain came down. The drivers waiting in line stayed in the cabs of their trucks. Jack led the way through the brush to the end of the line and it took them fifteen minutes to walk to the last truck which was loaded with coffee. They crossed to the north side of the road and hid themselves behind some rocks, huddling in the rain as they waited for a cotton truck. Except for the red glow of tail lights, it was dark and they were wet and cold. When a truck pulled to a stop, Jack tapped each woman's shoulder and they ran up to the side of the truck. Jack tossed up the two small bundles of clothing, and then helped first Mari and then Faith climb up the wooden railings on the passenger side of the truck. Then he climbed up and pulled back the mesh so that the two women could climb into the bed and they fell on the cotton and as Jack was climbing over the rail, a truck came up from behind with its headlights on and they shined on the truck and Jack dove on top of Faith and Mari, reaching up and pulling the mesh back in place. They clawed their way forward to the back of the cab and dug themselves down to the bottom of the cotton, and Faith and Mari lay belly to belly and Jack was to their side, and they couldn't breathe well so Jack pushed himself up against the cab and made a kind of tunnel between the cotton and the cab where their heads were and then they could breathe and feel the rain dripping down off the back of the cab and onto their faces.

The truck started and then moved forward and then the truck stopped again, and the driver cut the engine, and soon he started it and then killed it again. This went on and on for over an hour. The rain finally stopped and then, when it did, they could hear the drivers talking outside and when they weren't talking the engines would start and the trucks would move forward and then they would be talking outside again in voices that seemed low and solitary on the night.

The feeling of confinement overcame Jack and he perspired and he told himself that he could get up and leave the truck any time he wished and that he was not locked in as he had been locked in the closet when he was a little boy, that now he was actually free despite the confinement in the bed of the truck under the piles of cotton because freedom was only a matter of choice. He felt he was being smothered and it was difficult to breathe. He closed his eyes and created visions of open spaces and that helped some, but still he was frightened and he only wanted to get out of the truck so he pretended that time had stopped and that he would actually be getting out of the truck in one second but that now

155

because time was stopped he was frozen in an instant and soon he would be in the next time frame when he would again be free. He only hoped that when he was once again free, he would not have to kill anyone else. He lay there thinking of the men he had killed and he could not believe he had killed anyone except for the Frenchman who had raped Mari. The others, they had been accidents. Then he thought of his friend O'Malley; he wished that O'Malley had refused to drive them north to Bouar because somehow they would have made it without him and now he would be alive.

He forced his thoughts to go outside of the truck into the open air, but still he felt powerless to escape the bed of the truck, buried alive beneath all this cotton, smothered now, something more powerful than himself holding him down. It was time itself he needed to control, to push himself ahead into a future when he would be walking through open fields, but still the fields were of cotton. No matter what he thought, he was penned in and his heart beat fast, he could feel its pulse, he could hear the throb of coursing blood in his head, he was finally going to die, and he wanted to yell to be let out, to be freed, would no one help him?

The drivers spoke in Sango and Jack could not understand what they were saying. He didn't concern himself with their talk because he figured it was about the border or about driving in general or maybe about women. But Faith and Mari could both understand and they listened to the two drivers talk about the murder of a policeman and a truck driver and an American.

The unembodied voices of two men came from beside the truck. They floated through the cotton, muffled by its weight that pressed down upon them, a weight made heavier with the rain that had fallen throughout the night.

"His name is Jack Burke, a crazy American," one driver said.

"I heard he kidnaped a missionary's daughter," said the other.

"And a whore from Bangui and he has them at gun point."

"They are probably dead now."

"They might be."

"He killed a policeman in M'Baiki, too."

"Have you ever been to M'Baiki?"

156

"No. I don't like those people. They are the same tribe as Bokassa."

"Well, he killed the policeman there and also one near here in Bouar."

"I know. Did you hear about the young gendarme in Berberati?"

"No, what?"

"He said this man was called The Rabbit."

"I heard that he was called The Rabbit, but I didn't know why."

"He is CIA."

"Really?"

"Yes, or so the gendarme said who was promised a secret job. The code was "the sun was high in Berberati.""

"What does that mean?"

"I don't know, but the radio said that this CIA man was trying to stop Mobutu from overthrowing our government, so it must be a secret code about the invasion."

"That's crazy."

"I agree."

"But why has The Rabbit killed all these people?"

"They say he is crazy. It might be syphilis. Like Idi Amin."

"No."

"Yes. It might be that he enjoys the killing."

"But why does he take the whore and the missionary?"

"Sex. He has an insatiable appetite for sex."

"But think about it, what a pair."

They laughed.

"I know. But maybe he likes it dirty with the whore and clean with the missionary."

"Or the other way around."

"Yes, that could be."

"But still, what a pair of women."

"Do you think he will kill them?"

"I am sure of it."

"How can you be sure?"

"Because he is a cold blooded killer. Look, he does not kill for money. He has not robbed anyone."

"True. But he may be CIA."

"I don't believe that. The gendarme was young and had stars in his eyes. Besides, the CIA has no interest in this country."

"They say we have uranium."

"That is a rumor."

"So you think he is just a crazy bandit?"

"I know that he is. The police will kill him. They say he has vowed not to be taken alive."

"Why would an American bandit come to Africa?"

"He may be on the run from authorities in that country."

"What did he do there?"

"Probably the same."

"He's a dangerous man."

"A killer."

"He uses a knife."

"No, I heard it was a gun."

"Well, both then. He killed a Frenchman in Bangui. Stabbed him three-hundred times in the belly with a butcher knife."

"He is sick, then, if he stabbed him so many times."

"That is what I have been saying all along."

As Faith listened, she wondered about Jack and she wondered how the drivers could be so misinformed. She again wondered about Jack and who he really was and she asked herself questions that she could not answer, questions about herself and she had never really had to do that before because she had always had faith, and she wondered if her parents had named her so that she would never be bereft.

It was hot under the cotton and it tickled their noses and it was difficult to breathe. The headlights from the truck behind them were barely discernible, a filtered yellow that reached them in the dark. For Jack, time and freedom were inexorably affixed to the movement of the truck so that now as the truck was stationary, so was time and Jack felt permanently enclosed, locked in, shackled with no will of his own. If the wheels were to roll forward, so would time begin to move, and it would be soon that he would be free, but never soon enough.

A truck started and then several engines turned over. "The line is moving," one driver said.

"Will you be going to Yaounde?"

"Yes. You?"

"Douala," he shouted, and the truck door slammed shut. Both Mari and Faith were thinking of the drivers' conversation and each wondered about Jack and the public perception of what he had done. Each woman wondered how everything was going to end and if it would end soon or if they would ever make it to Douala and the sea. If it ended here at the border, Faith thought, did that mean that it would all be over? Would she visit Jack in prison as had Jack visited Mari? She thought that if Jack were arrested he would never be free for the authorities might well believe the first man had been killed in self-defense, but what about the others? How could you seriously tell a judge that you had killed a succession of men in self-defense? Thinking of this, Faith analyzed each killing and when she wondered if she really knew Jack, she quelled the thought for how could you be in love with someone you did not know? Then she thought of her father and mother and she wondered if that was the way it was, that a couple could be in love and yet be strangers.

They could hear the engine start, they felt the rumble through the chassis, and with the first movement forward, Jack sighed.

After two hours, the truck pulled under the lights. The light filtered through the cotton and everything looked white underneath the billowy fluff. The truck pulled forward and the Cameroonian spoke in French to the driver and as he spoke they could feel the rear of the truck dip down under the weight of the two men climbing on the side rails, and then they could hear the susurrus of the steel through the cotton. The steel did not hit the wooden floor of the truck bed or they would have heard it.

Along with the soft sound of steel swishing through cotton, they could hear the interrogation of the driver.

"Where are you coming from?"

Shsh-shsh, shsh-shsh.

"Bozoum."

Shsh-shsh, shsh-shsh.

"And your destination?"

Shsh-shsh, shsh-shsh.

"Douala."

Shsh-shsh, shsh-shsh.

"Have you seen two Americans, a man and a woman, and an African woman?"

Shsh-shsh, shsh-shsh.

"No, but I have heard. The Rabbit."

Shsh-shsh, shsh-shsh.

"Yes. You have seen nothing?"

Shsh-shsh, shsh-shsh.

"Nothing at all."

Shsh-shsh, shsh-shsh.

"Okay, you may go on when the men are done with their search."

Shsh-shsh, shsh-shsh.

"Thank you."

SHSH-SHSH, SHSH-SHSH.

The steel tines of the pitchforks swished through the cotton cutting up and down on either side of them like pistons and when they were done, Jack turned over and then he could hear the steel and at the same time feel its sting in left his hand, in and out as quick as the dip of the needle of a sewing machine, and the guard shouted to the men, "Anything?" and the men shouted, "No." Jack could feel the relief of the men's weight as they jumped down to the ground, the truck bed springing back up, and the truck started and they were moving again and the light went dark and Jack whispered, "I've been cut."

An hour later, after a succession of coffee trucks, the soldiers were jabbing their pitchforks in the bed of the next cotton truck to pass, and one soldier retrieved his pitchfork and in the light he noticed the tuft of cotton sticking to it. Standing on the side of the cotton truck, he held the pitchfork up to the light and touched the tines with his fingers and he saw the blood. He shouted to the other soldier and then to the border guard on the ground by the driver and he blew a whistle and the soldiers came running out of the building that served as a barracks and the driver was held at gun point as the guard yelled for the occupants to get out of the back of the truck. But no one was there to hear the order, and it took

160

the guards three hours to unload two tons of cotton. The border guard was angry and he shouted at the soldier that it must have been one of the trucks that had already passed, and then, looking at the log, he saw that there had not been a cotton truck in the last hour.

It was morning when the truck pulled into Yaounde. Jack's hand throbbed under the bandanna he had used to tie off the bleeding. They sat at the side of the truck still under the cotton, but they pushed away some of the cotton so they could look out between the railings and the noise of the traffic told them that this city was far larger than Bangui.

"We need to get out here," Jack said as the truck drove slowly through the morning congestion.

"Why?" Faith said. "The driver said he was going all the way to Douala."

"It doesn't feel right," Jack said.

"Your hand?" Mari asked.

"No. Everything."

"Can I fly out of Yaounde?" Mari asked.

"Yes. They'll have flights to Kinshasa."

Faith looked at Mari. "You're going back to Zaire?"

"Yes. Jack said he would send me back."

"What about your sister in Bangui?"

"He will wire her money."

"Jack, how are we going to get to Douala?" Faith whispered.

"I don't know yet, but we need to get off this truck. It just doesn't feel right."

"I think since we're on a truck to Doaula, we should stay on it. No one knows we're here," Faith said.

"I think Faith's right," Mari said.

"She may well be—it's just that something doesn't feel right, and right now I'm going with my feeling."

"Okay, okay, Jack. We'll go with your *feeling*," Faith said.

The truck turned off the main road and pulled into a dirt yard where there were a dozen trucks lined up. They pulled up at the end of the line of trucks, and the driver got out and slammed the door and they could not see where he went.

161

"Let's go," Jack said and there was no one about on their side of the truck. Jack pulled back the mesh and they climbed down the railing. Jack felt an immediate wave of relief standing in the open air, a palpable liberation that itself was a sigh. They brushed the cotton from each other's backs, pulled it from each other's hair simian style, and hurried out of the yard still brushing cotton off of their clothes as they went. It was morning and the sun was rising and with the growing heat of the day came the humidity, as thick and heavy as a wool shawl soaked in hot water. The streets pulsed with every kind of traffic, cars and buses honking and coughing exhaust, Africans in brightly colored saris crowding the sidewalks on each side of the street that was lined with white stucco buildings, and children darting between the cars. Faith and Mari led the way off the main street and down a narrow alley as Jack followed some thirty meters behind, the crowd a wave moving to the central market that was lined with stalls. In the market, Jack joined the two women, feeling it was safe as there were so many foreigners out shopping for souvenirs among the stalls where Africans sold ebony masks and ivory carvings of lions and elephants and monkeys. Faith and Jack were accosted by many of the Africans selling such souvenirs and they ignored them all. Mari asked a vegetable vendor about hotels, but he knew nothing about hotels, and then she asked a man who sold watches and he told them of the big hotels downtown, and Mari asked about smaller hotels, and he told her of the hotel on the hill above the market.

They climbed the hill, again Jack following them from a distance he felt safe. Faith told Jack that they should check in separately, and Jack agreed that Mari should check in alone. The man at the reception desk was French and he said yes, he had a nice room. Jack said that would be fine, and then he asked about their luggage, if the cloth bundle that Faith carried was all they had, and Jack said that they would fetch the rest of their luggage later.

"And how long will the Monsieur and Madame be staying?"

"*Je ne sais pas encore*," Jack said.

"Fine. Please, though, inform me the day before you plan to check out."

The man showed them up the stairs to their room.

162

Mari entered the lobby carrying a cloth bag. She approached the desk behind which the same man who had helped Jack and Faith was now going through the register.

"Excuse me," Mari said. "I would like a room."

The man looked up over his glasses. "Yes?"

"A room please."

"We do not allow prostitutes in this hotel."

"I am sorry. I am not a prostitute," Mari said. "I would like only a room for the night."

"*D'accord.* But no men in your room or you will be asked to leave. Five thousand francs."

Mari paid him and then he called a bellboy to show her to her room.

As Faith sat in the bath, Jack drank beer and smoked with the window overlooking the hill behind the hotel open to the morning breeze. This was the safest he felt in a long time, but his hand still throbbed and he tried not to think about the pain.

Faith came out of the bath with a towel wrapped around her. She dressed, and Jack poured her coffee and then he took a shower and after he dried off he looked at his left hand in the mirror and it was red and swollen where the pitchfork had cut him and it throbbed. Faith came in behind him.

"Let me see your hand."

She looked at it and then looked at Jack in the mirror. "You're going to have to see a doctor."

"I know. It's not good. It hurts like hell."

"We'd better go right away, Jack. Before it gets worse. It looks infected."

"Let's eat first. Go get Mari, will you?"

"I don't know what room she is in."

"It's one of the rooms across the hall. I heard them come up a moment ago when you were in the bath."

Faith went across the hall and Jack dressed in his dirty jeans still stained with blood. Mari came in looking clean in her green sari. They sat and ate the croissants and cheese Jack had ordered and Mari had a glass of beer with Jack, and Faith drank coffee.

"How was the bubble bath?" Faith asked Mari.

"*Magnifique.*"

"Good. Later we will have that meal we spoke of, Mari. Now, though, I must get this stubborn man to a doctor or I will have to cut off his hand and then what good would he be?"

Mari smiled and said she would wait for their return.

Faith went down and asked the proprietor where there was a doctor. He gave her directions and Faith and Jack went out and Mari stayed in the hotel to rest.

It was not far to the doctor's office. It was across the street from the Peace Corps headquarters and there were many young Americans walking in and out of the building, and Faith and Jack did not look out of place because most of the Americans were poorly dressed.

They went into the building and the nurse told them to wait and then she called Jack. Faith waited in the reception area where there was a television. She had not seen television since she had last been in the United States the summer before. She watched the newscaster and listened to the newscast in French.

The doctor was young and well groomed with a thin moustache. He did not look like he had been out of school long, and despite that his English was worse than Jack's French, he insisted on speaking English. "What problem with hand?" he asked.

"I cut it."

"How?"

"What do you mean, how?" Jack asked. He was irritated by the doctor's arrogance and showed little patience with him. "Just tell me if it is infected and if it is, then give me some antibiotics, will you?"

The doctor sat on a stool and Jack sat on the table before him. The doctor examined the hand and he squeezed it and white, frothy pus surfaced to the skin. Jack winced. The doctor looked up at Jack.

"It would help to know where the cut was from, if you please?" He swabbed his hand with iodine and Jack winced with the sting.

"It was from a pitchfork."

"And what is this pitchfork?"

"A fucking farm implement."

164

"I see. But I do not understand."

"It is a big fork for picking up hay. You use it on farms. Would it be too much to know if the hand is infected?"

"Oh, yes, it is eenfected, and it is probably because of the manure of a farm."

"Fucking great."

"What is that you say?"

"Can you give me some antibiotics for it?"

"Yes."

"Thank you."

"But they might not help." The doctor sighed.

"Why?"

"The infection is spreading. How long has it been?"

"Only a day."

"Then it must have been dirty, very dirty, what did you call it?"

"A pitchfork."

"A very dirty peechfork, then."

"So what's the prognosis?"

"I will give you inoculation of penicillin and some pills and in two days' time you return, and we shall see if the drugs are working or if we must cut off the hand."

"You're joking."

The doctor frowned. "No. I never joke to a patient."

"What are the chances of having to cut off the hand?"

"About seexty-forty, I would say."

"Which way?"

"The way you would not want to gamble unless you are one who likes the shots that are far away."

"Long shots. Give me the shot then, will you?"

The doctor called the nurse and she gave him the shot and bandaged his hand. She filled a bottle with pills and told him to take two after each meal, and she told him to return in two days.

At the desk in the reception area, Jack asked how much he owed. "Nothing today," the nurse said. "You can pay when you return in two days."

"Thank you."

Jack turned and saw Faith intent on the television. "Come on, Faith, let's go."

Outside she asked him how his hand was, and he told her everything was fine and that he had some medicine. They walked back to the hotel and went up to their room and it was not yet noon and Faith suggested that Jack shave. He went downstairs and bought a razor and shaving cream and after he had shaved they lay down to sleep. The rains did not come until late in the afternoon and Jack got up before dusk and Faith was still sleeping when he went across the hall and knocked on Mari's door. Mari had been sleeping. The rain came down in torrents so that the room was a wash of noise from the rattling roof above them.

As she dressed, she told Jack that she had had a dream about the two of them adrift in a small boat as the rain beat down upon them as it did now for as Jack sat on the edge of her bed, he could hear the rain on the roof above them, an incessant rattle that reminded him of Bangui when the two of them would take siestas beneath the corrugated iron roof of her home.

"What happened?" Jack asked.

"What do you mean?" She said as she pulled on her bra.

"At the end of the dream."

"I don't know. You woke me up."

They went downstairs to the bar and ordered beers, and they sat and talked about her future in Kisangani, but they did not speak of his. It was almost like old times until Faith came in and joined them well after dark.

"Have you eaten yet?" Faith said.

"No, we were waiting for you," Jack said, and Mari said nothing.

They ordered roast chicken and potatoes and salade Nicoise and Jack and Mari drank beer and Faith had Coca-Cola for the first time in a year. It was the first decent meal they had had in some time, and the first food Jack had been able to enjoy since finishing the medicine for the dysentary.

"Mari is flying back the day after tomorrow."

"What time?"

"Three o'clock."

Faith looked at Mari and Mari smiled.

"I've got to go the bank tomorrow, Faith, and see about a wire transfer.

166

But I don't want to do it until as late as possible in case they are tracing my account."

"That makes sense."

"And then we'll fly to Douala. There's a flight at six the same day."

"Good."

"We should celebrate tonight. We should go out dancing," Mari said, and Jack looked at Faith and she smiled because she was thinking of a joke that Jack had told her one night that seemed so long ago when everything was different, when innocence was a clean slate on which nothing dirty or dangerous was ever written.

"Yes, that would be nice, Mari," Faith said.

"I don't know if that's a good idea, Faith," Jack said.

"We'll be careful. Besides, it is dark in a *boite*. No one will see us," Mari said. "It is our last night together."

"Anyway, you don't look like Jack Burke without the beard," Faith added. "At least not the Jack Burke the gendarme near Bouar will remember."

Jack was about to say there was only one gendarme who could remember anything, and then he stopped himself and said, "Okay, then. I'd like to see if a Baptist can really dance, anyway."

Mari looked at both of them, but did not understand.

When they finished eating, they asked the proprietor where there was a *boite de nuite* and then they went up to their rooms. Mari changed into clothes she had bought that afternoon, and she waited for Jack and Faith in the lobby.

When they were clean and no longer looked like they had been on the run for eight nights, they took a taxi to *centre ville* in the falling rain.

The disco was dark and the parquet dance floor was in the center of the room. Above it was a spinning globe that emitted dashes and dots of light so that it looked like the room was spinning in a visual morse code. They took a table in the back corner of the room, and Jack went to the bar and came back holding two *trente-trois* beers by the necks with his right hand and an orange soda tucked under his left arm, his left hand bandaged in white that looked blue in the light of the night club.

The tables were almost all occupied with young African women and there were the government functionaries in their leisure suits and some Frenchmen and some Americans and most of the women were prostitutes and they were young and beautiful; many of these young women were from the small villages of the country and they were having the time of their lives dancing. Some women danced alone and others danced with other women, and they were sleek in short dresses and their dancing was fluid. The music was so loud that people trying to converse had to lean over tables toward each other and still they had to shout.

Faith wore new jeans and a blouse she had bought that afternoon and Mari wore a new sari that was orange and black and Jack wore new jeans and a denim shirt he had bought in the market. Jack and Faith were dressed much the same as the other Americans, but the Frenchmen stood out in their slacks and dress shirts and thin, leather shoes.

"Faith, you want to dance?" Jack asked.

"No, not yet. You and Mari go ahead."

Jack took Mari by the hand and led her to the dance floor. The music was slow and Jack had his right hand on Mari's back, his left hand at his hip, and Mari had her arms around his shoulders. She leaned on him and their movement was slow until the next song which was much faster and they released each other and danced with more energy and watching them dance made Faith strangely sad as if their mutual past were circling now, coming back to the present, and there she might be excluded and that frightened her as well. She wondered why she had not told Jack about the newscast she had seen in the doctor's office which reported that an American had kidnaped an African and an American and that it was believed that they had crossed the border and were now in Cameroon and that the man was armed and dangerous, that he had killed four men. They had a sketch of what Jack looked like and it was not a bad likeness at all except the man in the picture wore a full beard and now Jack did not look like him at all. Faith watched them dance and she knew why she had not told Jack and she knew she was wrong, but she was tired of running and wanted a sense of normalcy even if for only a day; just one day when they could pretend they were not criminals who had murdered and—in her mind, she had the image of Jack bent over the body of O'Malley, Jack taking the money from his pocket—robbed. Murdered and robbed was the refrain that went through her mind as she watched Jack and Mari sway to the music, *murdered and robbed*, over and over again, and she had trouble believing she was Faith Sellers sitting in a night club in Cameroon, a night club full of prostitutes and men drinking beer and whiskey, *murdered and robbed*, and again she was pulled apart by two desires for she wished to be with Jack in some safe country and she longed to be back home in Boda with her mother and father whom she loved and who must be on the very edge of coping, a place far beyond worry because they were powerless to find her and it had been over a week since she had disappeared with a strange man no one really knew.

They came back to the table and sat down and Jack was perspiring and Mari was smiling. Jack took a sip of beer and lit a cigarette, and he kept his left hand in his lap beneath the table. He asked Faith to dance.

"I don't know, Jack. I have never danced before."

"You danced with the pygmies."

"That was different."

"What?" Mari said. "You have never danced?"

"No."

"Then you had better let me show you, Faith," Mari said. "Jack is a terrible dancer, the worst I have ever seen."

"You never told me that," Jack said. "You always said I was a good dancer."

"Only because that is what you wanted to hear. If I had told you the truth of how you really dance, you would have never danced again."

"And how do I dance?" Jack asked.

"Like a man with cement in his shoes." Mari laughed and stood and took Faith by the hand and at first Faith resisted but Mari was unrelenting and she pulled Faith to her feet and laughing, she led her to the dance floor.

The music was fast and loud and Mari held both of Faith's hands and she led Faith into the rhythm before letting go, and the two of them danced: Faith watched Mari's body sway to the music and she tried to mimic her movements, the roll of the shoulders and the twist of the hips and the shuffle of the feet back and forth, but she was self-conscious and she felt as if all eyes were upon her.

"Faith, let the music move you," Mari said.

"I'm trying."

"Don't try and do not think."

She tried not to think, and she let the music move her, and soon it was as if she were catching on to this dancing, and she looked up and saw the smile on Mari's face, wide open and genuine, and she smiled herself, and then laughed, and Mari couldn't hear her but she saw Faith's loss of inhibition and she felt something new had been achieved because now Faith moved as if tickled by a breeze.

When the song was over Faith came back trying to stifle her smile, but Jack could see the pleasure in her eyes, something he had not seen since one morning in Boda when they were two different people leading two different lives in a world when innocence might have been safe to enjoy.

"Very good, Faith," Jack shouted across the table. "Now my turn." He stood and they walked hand in hand to the dance floor and Mari watched them dance, and similar to Faith a short while before, Mari thought of a time that did not belong to her and it was the future when she would be in Zaire and these two, Jack and Faith, would be somewhere together where she could not be, and thinking of this made her warm with a sadness that flushed the insides of her cheeks.

When a rock and roll song came on, Jack took Faith by the hand and twisted and spun her with his one good hand, and Mari could see she was laughing and having a wonderful time. Mari went to the bar and bought two more beers and an orange soda and it was as she returned to the table that she noticed the two policemen at the door talking to the manager. She carried the bottles back to the table and set them down and filled their glasses as if nothing were out of the ordinary, and Jack and Faith danced out three songs in a row. When they came back to the table, they were both perspiring and Jack was out of breath, and still he lit a cigarette.

"She's a good dancer, isn't she, Mari?" Jack said after he had drunk from the glass of beer.

"Yes, very."

"No, you are exaggerating," Faith said with an effervescent pride she could not conceal. She looked at Jack. "How is your hand?"

"Not bad."

Mari leaned across the table. "Jack, there are two policemen talking to the manager by the door."

Jack looked up and the two men wore blue uniforms and they were led to the bar by the manager who poured them each a glass of whiskey *fine*, and they stood by the bar and looked over the crowd of dancers.

"I see," Jack said. "But they couldn't possibly be looking for us."

"Jack?" Faith said.

"What?"

"At the doctor's office I saw a newscast. They said that it was believed we made it across the border."

"Shit," Jack said in English. "Why didn't you tell me, Faith? God damn it, how come you didn't say anything?"

Mari recognized the tone and some of the words and she took Faith's hand and said, "Jack."

In French, Jack said, "Your timing is great."

"Sorry I didn't do everything the way you like, Jack, but I thought maybe we could have one day, one night where we wouldn't be running. You know? One day of peace? That's all I was thinking."

Jack looked surprised at her outburst. "She dances for the first time and it's a damn revolution. I can only guess what's next."

"Very funny," Faith said. "Very, very funny."

"I think we had better get going," Mari said. "They are showing pictures to the bartender and waitresses."

"Shit," Jack said. "How do we get out of here, Mari?"

"I will go distract the officers and Faith, you leave first. Wait outside across the street. And after you have left, Jack, I will come out and meet you."

"Okay. But be careful, Mari," Jack said.

Faith and Jack watched as Mari walked up to the bar. She stood at the bar next to the policemen and she ordered a beer and when she had paid for it she knocked it over and the beer ran over the bar and onto the laps of the policemen. Jack told Faith to go and she got up and went toward the front door and Jack watched her as she exited the disco and then he watched the policemen shout at Mari as she took a napkin and tried to wipe the legs of one of the officers who pushed her away.

Jack stood and walked through the crowd of tables and he went to the door and before he opened it, he looked back at Mari. She was standing at the bar and the policemen were talking to her and showing her a photograph, and Jack saw Mari shake her head and then he went outside and crossed the street where he found Faith at a newsstand looking at a newspaper. Jack took her by the hand and they went into the shadows between two buildings and Faith handed Jack the newspaper and on the front page was a picture of Faith and the headline read, "The Rabbit's Victim," and it took him almost a minute to realize who The Rabbit was and that it was himself.

Thirty minutes had passed before Mari came out arm in arm with one of the officers, and he took her to the police car parked a block up the street. Faith thought she was being arrested.

Jack watched as both Mari and the officer got in the back seat of the car and Faith asked Jack what they were doing and Jack knew and didn't respond.

"Jack, they've been in there for ten minutes," Faith said, and as she said it, she knew too.

"They could be waiting for the other officer," Jack said, and he hoped that was not true.

Finally, Mari came out of the car and then the policeman climbed out and he tucked in his shirt and they walked back to the disco and at the front door he said something to Mari, and she shook her head and he went inside. Mari came across the street and found them in the alley.

"It was a good plan, Mari," Faith said, and then she wished she had not said it as Mari looked at her and frowned. They hailed a taxi and when it stopped before their hotel, Jack told the driver he had changed his mind and could he please take them back downtown.

"What are you doing, Jack?" Faith asked in English, and Jack pointed to Mari's second story window where the lights were on and through the curtains they could see the silhouettes of two men. As they drove away from the hotel, they passed three police cars parked in a vacant lot across the alley from the hotel, and Jack knew they had been discovered.

Jack sat behind the driver and he leaned forward and tapped him on the shoulder. "How much would it cost to take us to Douala?" he asked in French.

172

"What? To Douala? But that is very far. Maybe three hundred kilometers." The driver looked at Jack in the rear-view mirror. "You could fly and it would be much faster."

"How much?"

"I cannot drive you to Douala. It is too far."

"You can do it. How much?"

He continued to drive and the yellow street lights shined through the window and although it had stopped raining, the streets were still wet and the tires hissed in the water. Downtown the traffic was heavy and the drivers honked their horns at the most minimal of delays.

"I might be able to drive you to Douala for twenty-five thousand francs, but I would rather leave in the morning when it is light. The road is not so good and it is three hundred kilometers," he said as looked up into the mirror.

"No, now, tonight. Thirty-thousand francs. Agreed?"

The driver was silent a moment, and then he looked in the mirror and said, "*D'accord*. But you must pay me half in advance."

Jack took out his wallet with his right hand and he counted five ten-thousand franc notes. He reached over the seat and handed the man two.

"Thank you. When we get to Douala you pay me ten thousand more," the driver said.

"Yes."

The road to Douala was heavily pot-holed tarmac and the Peugeot 504 hit the bumps hard. The driver swore whenever he hit one so that he was almost always swearing. Mari leaned on the door and slept. Faith, sitting between her and Jack, leaned her head on Jack's shoulder.

"I'm sorry I didn't tell you about the newscast."

"It's too late now. Don't worry about it."

"I just thought, I just wanted one day when we weren't running."

"It's okay."

"We're in a lot of trouble, aren't we?"

Jack turned and looked at her in the faint green light from the dash. "Yes, you could say that."

"What are we going to do?"

"Get Mari to the airport."

"What about us?"

"The port."

"You think we can get on a ship?"

"We have to. Maybe to France."

"I've always wanted to go to France."

"This won't be a first class voyage."

"I don't care. We need to get somewhere safe. Somewhere no one is chasing us."

"It's not going to be easy."

"I know. Nothing's been easy since I met you."

Jack put his arm around her shoulders and she lay against him. "I wouldn't blame you if you were to go to the police in Douala after I leave."

She sat up and looked at him. "What are you talking about? I won't do that, Jack. You know I won't."

"Okay, I just wanted to say that I wouldn't blame you. You could say you were kidnaped. That way you wouldn't be in any trouble."

"No, Jack. I'm already in trouble."

"But if you were to go to the police, you could say, I don't know, that you'd been kidnaped, and then you could go back to Boda and everything would be okay."

"I can't do that, Jack. Don't you know that?"

"But your parents."

"When we were at the mission in Berberati, Jack, I thought, I felt like running, like going to the Baptist mission and telling them what had happened, so I could get home to my parents, I mean."

"I understand, Faith."

"No, wait. I was so afraid. I was lonely for my parents. Worried about them worrying about me. They have no idea where I am, Jack."

"I know."

"But I thought if I did that, if I went back to Boda then, I would never see you again. And I couldn't do that, Jack." She started to cry. "I couldn't not ever see you again."

"Faith."

"I couldn't do it."

"Faith, easy, Faith, easy now. Don't cry. I love you."

"Do you, Jack? Do you really love me?"

"Yes, I really love you."

"And we'll be happy and finally safe?"

"Yes, we'll be happy. And safe."

"Promise?"

"I promise. We'll be happy and safe and someday your parents will visit us and their grandchildren will play in the yard as we sit on the porch and drink coffee. Yes, we'll be happy." As Jack said these words, he wondered about them, wondered about his own ability to fool others and even himself, and he wondered if he could really recognize when he himself was duped. But he had to think things would be fine in the future because when he didn't, he thought of everything that had transpired in the last week and when he thought of that he became afraid of his own violence, afraid of whom he may have become, and he wondered how he could become such a man as he now was without a palpable transition. It seemed that he had gone to bed one night as Jack Burke, a man who worked at the United Nations building schools out of concrete block, and he woke up the next morning as Jack Burke, a man who butchered a Frenchman with a knife and then shot his way through the Central African Republic on a narrow road through the jungle, a new man who was in love with two women, a prostitute and a missionary, each woman with him on this road to the sea.

She leaned back against him and Jack cracked the window and lit a cigarette and the driver looked in the mirror at him, and Jack handed him a cigarette and he lit it with the lighter from the dash.

"You think I'm awfully naive, don't you?"

"No, I never said that."

"But you do, don't you?"

"A little. There's nothing wrong with being naive."

"Yes there is."

"Don't worry about it, Faith. You hang around me and you'll be less naive by the minute."

"You're a good man, Jack. Mari said that, too. You just won't admit it."

"I'm okay. Not good or bad, I think. I just do what I have to do. And recently, everything I've done is bad."

"I know what Mari was doing in the car, Jack."

"Don't let's talk about it."

"I know, though. She did it for you, you know."

"Let's not talk about it, okay, Faith? I just don't want to talk about it."

"Okay. But I used to think that prostitutes were such terrible people."

"They're just people, Faith. No different than you or me. No different than your parents. She makes a living the only way she can. Those girls in the disco? Many of them came from the villages where there were no schools where there was little food where there was no money where their days were spent grubbing in the dirt for manioc roots. Where the future was yesterday's hunger. Where their sisters and brothers died in their arms. Malaria and every disease you can imagine. The only hope was the city. And you get to the city with no skills and no education, there's just not a hell of a lot you can do. But I suppose you see enough Merecedes drive by, you figure out what the only thing you can do is." He looked at Mari where she slept against the window. "It's not some terrible crime. It's a living."

"I know. But I used to think they were such terrible people. And Mari is so sweet."

"She is."

"I'll miss her."

"So will I."

"I know. You still love her, don't you?"

"In a way, yes. In a way I'll always love her."

"I hope she always has something to remember you by."

Jack flicked the cigarette out the window and rolled it back up. He thought about what Faith said for a moment. "What do you mean by that?"

"Nothing, Jack. I'm tired. Let's sleep a while."

She lay against him and Jack rested his head against the window and he thought about what Faith said. As Jack lay awake, both Faith and Mari slept, and it was early in the morning when Jack could see the lights of Douala in the distance. He wondered if things were going to work out because after all they had been through, they had to or none of it would have been worth the journey.

It was still dark when they drove into the city and Jack could smell the

176

salt in the air. When they stopped at a traffic signal, Mari awoke, and the driver asked Jack where he would like to go.

"Are there any hotels at the port?"

"Of course. But the nicer hotels are downtown."

"Take us to the port then."

It was before dawn and there was very little traffic, but there was a steady stream of pedestrians walking in one direction and Jack thought they were going to the market. Faith woke up as they drove and they were all sleepy as they drove through downtown and then the buildings steadily deteriorated as they approached the port.

"The hotels are not so nice by the port," the driver said as he looked at Jack in the mirror. "Mostly sailors."

"That's fine," Jack said. "Just get us to a hotel by the port and I'll pay you."

Fifteen minutes later the driver turned down a narrow street that was lined with gray concrete warehouses and then he turned again and there were men walking about, and Jack rolled down his window and they could hear the ship horns blast the morning air and the sea smelled of salt and diesel.

They stopped in front of a gray building with iron grates over the windows and the only word on the sign above the door was *hotel*. Jack told the driver that would be fine and paid him the balance and they got out of the taxi and the driver turned around and honked his horn twice and drove on.

They walked down the street for several blocks before they came to another hotel and they checked in and took two rooms and Jack and Faith's room was musty from the wet air of the sea and the season. Jack opened the shutters and the view was of corrugated iron roof tops and beyond that the port. In the false dawn they could see the lights of the ships yellow on the water, and Jack felt that they might make it out of Africa after all because they had traveled all this way and now they were on the very edge of the continent and it seemed that they only had to step off it to be safe.

Faith sat on the bed and looked out the window as Jack washed in the sink in the bathroom. "How's your hand?"

"It's okay." Jack washed it carefully because it hurt to touch it and it was swollen and he thought about the pills that he had left in the hotel in Yaounde. "I think it's getting better."

"Good."

They slept until noon and then Jack went to Mari's room and the three of them went to the coffee shop in the lobby, but it was closed so they went outside and up the street to a small restaurant that was alive with the scurry of roaches. They ate breakfast and they were all three very hungry and Jack had three *Croque Madames* before he was satisfied. They drank coffee and then they went out into the heat of the day and Mari asked about the smell again, and Jack explained about the salt in the ocean and Mari said she had never seen the ocean before.

"It smells so fresh," she said as they walked back to the hotel.

In the lobby, Jack called the airlines and reserved a ticket in Mari's name, and then he went up to his room where he found Faith and Mari looking out the window at the port. He told them that the plane departed at six that evening and that he had to go out to the bank and run some errands, but that he would be back for them at four and that they would take a taxi to the airport. Before he left, Faith asked him about his hand again, and it pulsed with the pain and Jack told her it was fine, that he thought it was getting better.

He waited in line at the *Banque Central* and it was a much more orderly line than in the banks in Bangui where the customers mobbed the windows of the tellers, pushing and shoving to get service first before the money ran out. He had to explain to the manager what he wanted to do because the teller did not know how to make a wire transfer. He was able to withdraw the balance and close the account, but the manager tried to convince him to keep it open and Jack was impatient and told him that if he wanted to keep the account open, that is just what he would do. He left with over two hundred ten-thousand franc notes which was only about ten thousand dollars, but combined with the fifty thousand francs he took from O'Malley, it was all the money that he had after the wire transfer to Francoise and it would have to see them through to France and then what, Jack did not know.

Jack went to the port. He asked the seamen he met about ships to France, and some shook their head, and others told him of bars he should inquire at, and finally he was invited on *The Emerald Sea* where he met the captain, an Algerian with a smile devoid of joy, but one that increased in scope once money was exchanged.

While Jack was at the port, Mari convinced Faith that they should take a taxi to the beach because she had never been on a beach before and she had never set foot in an ocean, and Mari said she wanted to do this because it would be like touching the rest of the world, and she might never get the chance again. Mari wrapped a turban around her head with cloth she cut out of a sari, and the two women giggled as they made their disguises. Faith put her hair back and covered it with a scarf and she wore sunglasses and looked like a tourist at a windy coastal resort in England, and then she wrote a note to Jack telling him of their destination.

The taxi took them north along the port and it was only about ten kilometers to the beach and Faith asked the driver to wait for them because they wouldn't be long.

They took off their shoes and walked through the sand. There were few people on the beach, but there were fishermen thigh deep in the surf, and some children were swimming. They walked up the beach until they came to an arm of rock that rose above the beach beneath which was a cove they could not pass. They turned around and walked back the way they had come, each silent with her own thoughts. Above them, the afternoon clouds were beginning to gather, but it was still warm and they sat in the sand and looked out at the ocean, a blue expanse with crests of white waves.

"It's so big," Mari said.

"If you cross the ocean you would come to the United States," Faith said.

"How long would that take?"

"By airplane? I don't know. Ten hours, I think."

"No. By boat."

"Two or three weeks maybe."

"And that's what you'll do?"

"I think we are going to France."

"And then?"

"I don't know. Maybe the United States. I really don't know."

Mari drew a circle in the sand with her finger. "I'll miss you. But you will write, won't you?"

"Of course."

"Maybe someday you will come to Zaire, to Kisangani?"

"Maybe. I would like that."

They were quiet and they could see the fishing boats on the ocean bobbing up and down as if they were playing peek-a-boo with each other. The seagulls cried as they soared on cupped wings.

"What will you do in Kisangani?" Faith said.

Mari had her elbows on her knees and her chin in her hands and she did not avert her eyes from the ocean, from the waves that gently flopped onto the shore before retreating—it was as if she were transfixed by the movement of the water. "I don't know what I will do," she said. "It's been a long time since I've seen my mother. I would like to see her again before she is dead."

Faith did not say anything. She stared out at the sea and there were tears in her eyes. "Faith, it will be okay. You'll be able to write your parents now. Their worries will be eased."

"I know. I'm just afraid, Mari. Afraid of everything."

"It's fine to be afraid. When our life changes, we are afraid of losing what was before the change. And what will come after it. To be afraid is a good thing, isn't it? To have no fear is to not be human."

"Mari, I just don't know what I'm doing here."

"You love Jack."

"Yes, but how can life be so different now from what it was just ten days ago when I was teaching at the school, helping my mother at the house? Talking to my mother each night."

"All this will be over soon."

"I hope you are right. Now, I feel I am between everything. In limbo. And I wonder if I have made the right decision."

"I, too, am in limbo. But that we have arrived here in between is a matter of fact. Now we must go on."

"And you'll go back to Zaire."

"Yes."

"And your sister and her children will come after you."

"Yes."

"And what else?"

"What else? I don't know. What else will take care of itself."

"Maybe you will meet someone nice and get married?"

"I've met someone nice before and we didn't get married."

"I'm sorry, Mari. I'm stupid. I shouldn't have said that."

"Don't worry. I'm fine. And I may meet someone, as you say, nice."

"You will live with your sister and her children?"

"Yes. We will see if my parents are still alive."

"Will you miss Bangui?"

"No, not really. My friends, yes, I will miss them. But not the city itself. It is just a city like all cities and Kisangani is a nicer city than Bangui. At least they're my people there."

A man carrying a burlap sack over his shoulder walked down the beach toward them and when he arrived before them, he greeted them and set the sack down on the sand by their feet. He carefully emptied it and spread out ebony and ivory carvings and jewelry on the sand. Faith waved him away and said she was not interested, but Mari looked at the souvenirs he had laid on the sand, and the man could not be dissuaded by Faith when he saw the keen interest in Mari's eyes.

Mari reached out and picked up an ivory necklace that was of a dozen small elephants that lay on her chest when she held it around her neck, and then she turned and held it to Faith's neck and said, "It looks nice on you."

She reached under her sari and took out the purse that hung from her neck and she asked the man how much it cost. He told her five thousand francs and she laughed, and he told her for her, three thousand francs, and she laughed again and finally she paid him two thousand francs and handed the necklace to Faith.

"This is for you to remember me by," Mari said.

Faith put it on. Tears came to her eyes and she thanked Mari, and Mari said it was nothing but something to recall their journey together.

"I will never forget you, Mari." Faith reached out and picked up a wide bracelet of silver studded with jade stones, and she asked Mari to try it on and she slid it on her thin wrist and the jade itself contrasted well with her

181

black skin. Faith paid the man what he asked, five thousand francs, and Mari protested but the man put his wares back in his sack and hurried down the beach.

"Thank you, Faith. I will always think of you when I wear this."

"Do you like the jade?"

"Yes, it is beautiful."

"I'm glad."

Mari stood. "Before we go, I would like to put my feet in the ocean," she said, and they walked to the end of the beach and Mari pulled the sari up to her knees and she stepped into the edge of the water and the waves rolled in and swept past her ankles and she laughed at the cold water. Faith watched her and smiled and was sad to see her so child-like standing on the edge of Africa with the water rolling by her feet. "Faith," Mari said. "I have touched the whole world now."

It began to rain and they walked back up the beach to the road and put on their shoes. The driver was sleeping with the radio on and they woke him and he drove them back to the hotel by the port. Jack was still out so they went to the coffee shop that was now open in the lobby of the hotel and they had pastries and coffee, and it was almost four o'clock when they went back to Faith's room and still Jack had not returned.

They were sitting by the window when Jack came in the room.

"Sorry I'm late. It took longer than I thought."

"Is everything okay?" Faith said.

"Yes, fine. I made the wire transfer to Francoise. You will have to write her from Zaire and tell her what it is for."

"Thank you, Jack. I will," Mari said.

"Did you find a ship that would take us?"

Jack sat down on the edge of the bed. "Yes, finally. But without an exit visa they are charging a lot."

"Did you have enough money?" Faith asked.

"Yes, enough. Don't worry."

Jack took out a roll of bills from his front pocket and he counted off twenty of them and handed them to Mari. "This will help you get back to Kisangani from Kinshasa." He stood. "We've got to go now. The plane leaves in less than two hours."

Mari stood.

"Faith, I think you should stay here," Jack said.

"But I want to see Mari off."

"Say goodbye here. Your photo was in the paper. It would be safer this way."

"But Jack, I would like to say goodbye to Mari at the airport."

"Faith, he is right. We will say goodbye here."

"Hurry up then," Jack said. "I'll go down and call a taxi. Don't be long, Mari."

Jack left the room and the two women were standing at the foot of the bed.

"I will never forget you, Mari."

"Nor I you."

"Does Jack have your parents' address in Kisangani?"

"Yes."

"Then we will write you and sometime we will see you again."

Mari said nothing.

"Maybe we will have the money to send you a ticket to come to visit us in the states."

Mari had tears running down her face and she did not say anything, and then Faith began to cry as well. Mari looked up at Faith, and behind Faith the window was open to the sea and she could see the ships in the port and the rain was falling down and the sky was gray and looked the color of the sea. Mari walked up to Faith and hugged her and kissed her on both cheeks and she could taste the salt on her tongue from Faith's tears and Faith squeezed her with both arms, hugged her and cried on her shoulder. Mari kissed her once more on the forehead and gently freed herself from Faith's grip and turned around and with her back to Faith she walked to the door and opened it and then she turned around. She looked past Faith at the sea one more time and then at Faith and she said, "I will never forget you and I will pray for your safety, but remember that when things become difficult, you always have to watch out for yourself." She closed the door behind her.

Jack sat in the back of the taxi next to Mari and the rain continued to fall. He was quiet and Mari was as well. At the airport, they went to the Air

Afrique counter and Jack paid for her ticket and the woman asked about Mari's luggage and she said she did not have any and she was given the boarding pass. It was a little after five and they had almost an hour before the plane would depart. They went upstairs to the bar and ordered beer and sat at a table by the window where they could see airplanes taxiing through the rain. They were quiet, each waiting for the other to say something, each thinking of what might be safe to say, but goodbyes between people who had once been in love were anything but safe, and leaving one behind in Africa was saying goodbye forever.

Jack was tapping his pack of cigarettes lightly on the table as he looked out the window and Mari put her hand on his and he looked down at it and the jade bracelet she wore on her wrist. "Jack?" He did not say anything and it may have been that he did not trust his voice, but he looked in her brown eyes and he could see a whole history they had shared, the moments of joy and laughter like when he had tried to teach her to ride a motorcycle and she had sat on the seat with her hand on the throttle and before he could explain about the clutch she had stepped on the gear shift and the bike had lurched forward and her hand had twisted the throttle and there she went with the front wheel in the air until she crashed into the fence at the end of the street. She had not been badly hurt, but she had been hurt enough to yell at Jack, and when she was done yelling they had laughed together. And he remembered how one night the thieves had come and blown smoke through the window to drug them, and how they woke up as the thieves were pushing the motorcycle out the living room door, and how Mari had jumped up and with a high-heel shoe she pummeled the thief in the back of the head as he pushed the bike until finally he dropped it and ran away.

As Jack looked in her eyes, he saw memories like these and others: how he had slapped her when he thought she had aborted the baby. He had not wanted a child, true, but still, to make such a decision on her own without consulting him. And then he found out that he had been wrong about that, wrong about so much. Now he wished everything were different, wished that he had never hurt her so bad as he was hurting her now, as he was hurting himself in trying to say goodbye. He remembered too saying that someday maybe they could live in America, and that lie made him sadder than all the others.

"Jack? Faith is a good woman." Still Jack said nothing. "Did you hear me, Jack? Faith, she's good for you."

"I know. But you were good for me, too, and I ruined that. I'm sorry."

"No, Jack. There are no sorries today. We did what we did and as you say, there is no going back."

"Okay."

"But I wanted to tell you that I will always love you."

"Mari."

"No, I'm not done. Everything that has happened is over and there is no use talking about it. Instead, I want you to think about the future and if you ever think of me, think of me happy in Kisangani. And I will think of you that way, too."

"How?"

"Happy with Faith wherever you are."

"I will write you once we get settled somewhere. And I will send you some money."

"Jack, you don't need to send me any money. But, yes, write me with your address and when I have a family I will send you a photo."

"Would you like to come to the United States sometime?"

"Don't."

"We could send you the money."

"Don't, Jack. This is goodbye. Let's not pretend that it is anything but that. This is our last time together so let's not pretend there will be others."

He wiped his eyes with the back of his hand.

"How is your hand, Jack?"

"I think it is getting better. The medicine is working, I think."

"You should see a doctor again."

"I will."

"And Faith, she knows about us. Tell her I love her, too."

"What?"

"Nothing. But there is nothing to feel guilty about. Just be good to Faith."

They heard the boarding call for Mari's flight and she stood up and Jack stood. "I don't want you walking to the gate with me, Jack. We will say goodbye here."

She walked up to him and hugged him with both arms and he wrapped his arms around her with his face on top of her head, and she could feel his chest move up and down as he cried. She pushed him away and looked at his face and she leaned forward and kissed him on the lips and his eyes were red and tears covered his cheeks, and she said, "Good-bye, Jack. I love you." She turned and walked away and Jack watched her and when she went out the door of the bar, he said, "I love you, too." He wondered if Mari felt as much pain as he felt when Karen had left him, and now, causing that pain, he hurt as much as he ever had, and he cried and did not try to hide his tears as he walked back out of the airport to the line of taxis.

Jack took a taxi back to the port. It was raining when he stepped out in front of the hotel and he was still thinking about Mari and he did not want to see Faith when he was sad from Mari, so he walked up the street, looked in the window of a doctor's office, and then went into a bar that was full of seamen. He ordered a *trente-trois* beer and it came in a liter bottle and he sat by the window and drank the cold beer, and as he drank he thought of all his days with Mari and he was deep with melancholy and he remembered O'Malley and how he once said that the Irish were special because they knew how to embrace melancholy and enjoy its warmth and that it was a good feeling if you knew how to secure it and keep it for yourself, but Jack didn't have an Irish bone in his body and all that this melancholy did for him was make him sad and he wished that things were different.

The bar was smokey and despite the ten or fifteen sailors who were drinking, it was quiet and Jack wondered if each of the sailors had a story like his own and he wondered if any of them were capable of enjoying melancholy the way O'Malley had said was possible. He looked at the sailors and the name of the bar was a lie, he thought, the *Sans Souci*, because everyone seemed under the weight of some great burden. The bartender came to Jack's table and she smiled at him but it was almost a smile of pity, Jack thought, and she asked if he would like another beer. He said yes, and a pint of whiskey and a glass, and she looked in his eyes before turning to the bar and when she came back she asked him if he was all right, and he said sure, he was fine, just thirsty.

He poured himself a shot of whiskey and he swallowed it whole and then he drank the beer and the beer tasted sweet after the whiskey. It grew dark outside and the rain continued to fall on the edge of the continent, and it was three more days before the ship would sail and he wondered if he could stay in the bar and drink for three days; he smiled to himself at the thought because he knew Faith was waiting for him at the hotel. He didn't want to see her now because how could he love her so quickly after so much of his love had left on a plane for Zaire? It was as if he had been cut in half. If he could do everything over, he thought, he would have listened to Dieudonne in Boda. He could have weathered the incarceration, he knew he could have done that. If he could do what he had done these past ten days, he could handle being locked up for a week or two, maybe longer. And if he had been convicted of killing the Frenchman, well, he would have contacted the American embassy in Bangui, and someone would have helped him, Smitty or Davidson or someone. And then, everything would be different. He would be back working at the United Nations, playing poker on Friday nights, and no one would be dead, and Faith, well, Faith—Faith, she would be teaching at that little school in Boda, living with her parents as any seventeen year old American girl should be doing, and he wouldn't be in love with her because you couldn't be in love with someone you had never met.

He ran everything through his mind chronologically as he had done before, but still everything turned out the same way. Still, he felt no remorse for having killed the Frenchman and he then wondered if he should regret having stabbed him, but there was no way, he thought, no way I would do anything differently than I had done that evening in Bangui. I would kill him again, the bastard.

But he thought of the gendarmes in Bangui, the young men in uniform, and for them he felt sadness for they were innocent men who probably had families and for them the funeral drums were still beating in small, smoky villages where mourners writhed and wailed before thatched huts, fire burning in their eyes. And Pierre who was simply after the reward, he felt bad for having killed him, too, and the other gendarme who had climbed in the truck and pulled back the tarp, and now, sitting in the bar by the window as the rain came down through the yellow wash of the street lights, he could see the fear in the man's eyes, the recognition of death just before Jack pulled the trigger, and then, then all that blood. There had been so much blood. The blood, it was everywhere. There was no way you could ever wash away all the blood. It was still in his beard, he felt his cheek now and realized, remembered, that he had shaved, but the blood was still there, it would always be there, in his hair, under his fingernails, everywhere there would always be the blood, puddles of blood in his wake.

And O'Malley. God, O'Malley. That night in the Catholic mission O'Malley had known—he must have known—the danger in helping Jack, Faith and Mari. He must have known. And now he was dead because Jack had asked him to drive them to Bouar, O'Malley was fucking dead because Jack had asked him for help, and O'Malley had hesitated as if he had known that to help them, to help *Jack*, would be the end of everything. He surely must have known.

The street lights outside the window shined dully and the rain on the street took on a somber hue, yellow like sadness itself. Jack drank another shot of whiskey and when he finished his beer he ordered another. When a little wisp of a man came up and asked him in English if he wanted a girl for the night, Jack told him no and the man could see that Jack was in no mood for a woman, and he went back across the bar and sat down with two other men.

The bartender brought Jack some peanuts and he said he was not hungry and she said that it was not good to drink without eating and she set the peanuts on the table. Jack lit a cigarette and looked at his own reflection in the window, and he did not like what he saw. He saw himself and in himself he saw a man who had made so many mistakes and he didn't have the religion to forgive himself and he didn't have the lack of a belief in a God to forget it, and he was quite drunk when the little man came back to his table and asked him if he had changed his mind about a girl, and Jack just shook his head and did not say anything in reply.

Mari had told him that you couldn't look back and examine the causes of where you now were, and he thought about that but he thought she was wrong because when he looked back everything led to him sitting in this bar, Mari on an airplane to Zaire; everything, even the miscarriage, seemed

188

preordained, but still he wasn't a whole fatalist—he was a half a fatalist and he thought everyone was dealt a hand and it depended on how you played it and he had played it wrong one card at a time and had discarded Mari, and it was his fault that things were the way things were. He smiled in the window thinking that he at least always took responsibility for everything he had done and in that there was something good, or at least something respectable. He never blamed others for his own problems and he was proud of that. He asked the bartender for another pint of whiskey and she said yes, but she looked sad at this business, and when she brought the bottle she asked him what was wrong. He looked up at her and she was still pretty at thirty or forty and she had sea-shells braided in her black hair in the fashion that Mari had once followed, and her skin was the color of brown toast, and he told her nothing was wrong. She said he drank too much and he smiled and looked back out the window and she stood there for a moment before going back to the bar. He took on a rueful smile when he thought of the irony of a bartender telling him he drank too much. He took another shot of the whiskey and it helped dull the throb of his hand, and he chased it with beer. He thought the hand hurt like hell but that maybe the pain was part of the healing process and he hoped it was getting better, but now he did not really care one way or the other because he was drinking and getting drunk and that was enough. Then he thought of Faith in the hotel waiting for him and how she would worry because he had gone to the airport and had not returned. He thought she must be worrying about him the way her parents were worrying about her, and the only one who might not be worried now was Mari on the airplane to Zaire, but then, he thought, she was probably worried about her sister and who in this life, Jack wondered, was not worried about something out of their own control? It was a futile exercise in which most everyone partook.

He was drunk and time took on a more circular quality and there was nothing linear about it now. He thought that he could sit and drink some more and he would still be on time for he hadn't told Faith when he would return, and Faith, he thought, was young and pretty and he loved her, but what did he have that she could love him? She was so young and had been living the life of an only-child at a Baptist mission in Africa and maybe it was just that she was in love with the notion of being in love and that it would be better for her if he left her. Then she could go back to whatever she had before and spend some more time growing up before she really fell in love, and he smiled now when he remembered that she had said a young Baptist missionary in Georgia or Alabama had proposed to her and she had never given him an answer. Then he wondered what it would be like if it were he who was the Baptist missionary in Alabama or Georgia, and he laughed at the thought. If he were a missionary, he would tell everyone to go to hell and be done with it.

He decided he loved her and he took another shot and ordered another beer, and he was sure that she loved him and he hoped that they would make it out of Africa okay, but he wasn't sure they would and if they didn't, well, he just knew that they would never be together. He stood and walked to the bar and he walked with stiff legs to keep from weaving. He paid the woman who sat behind the bar and again she asked him if he was all right, and he said he had never been better. He walked to the door, and then he turned and asked her if the doctor's office he had passed earlier would be open so late, and she said no, it was probably closed and that he would have to return in the morning. He thanked her and walked out into the rain.

He walked up the street to the doctor's office and he banged on the door with his right hand, but there was no answer, and he banged again and he saw lights through the window upstairs, and he shouted that he needed a doctor, and a woman looked out the window and said just a minute. She came down and opened the door.

"What is wrong?" she asked. She was an older woman and she wore a white robe that came down to her ankles.

"Are you the doctor?"

"No, my husband is the doctor. The office is closed."

Jack put his right hand on the door frame to steady himself but still his knees were like those of a man who has been on the deck of a ship in high seas when he first steps on the land. "I need to see the doctor now, *s'il vous plait*. It is my hand."

He stuck his left hand out before him and pulled off the bandage with his right hand, and he could smell the flesh rotting. It was swollen and dark. She invited him in.

He sat in a chair and he was tired and drunk and he sat back with his head on the back of the chair and a middle-aged African came in wearing a robe and he introduced himself.

"I am Dr. Youseff Bonaga. My wife says you are injured."

"Yes. An accident. Could you look at my hand?"

"Yes. Come with me."

The doctor stood by the door to the examination room and waited for Jack to pass through, and then he followed and told Jack to sit on the examination table.

The doctor looked at Jack's hand and he squeezed it, and Jack said, "Fuck," and then the doctor's fingers played up his arm to the elbow and the hand was bad with gangrene and the forearm was swollen, and he told Jack that it was too late and that the arm would have to be removed from the elbow and they would have to go to the hospital. Jack said no, he would like it done here, and the doctor laughed.

"You are very drunk, Monsieur. We do not perform amputations here in the clinic."

"You are a surgeon?"

"Yes. But I perform surgery at the hospital and we can do it there."

"No, I don't have time. We'll do it here."

"Really, I cannot cut off an arm in my office."

"Why not?"

"It is just not how I work."

"Well, this will be the first time for you to work like that."

"I cannot."

The doctor stood and went to the telephone on the desk and picked up the receiver.

"What are you doing?"

"Calling the hospital to make a reservation for surgery tonight."

Jack stood and walked across the room and took the phone from his hand and replaced it in the cradle. "No, we need to do it now. We'll do it here."

"I only have local anaesthesia."

"That's fine. I'm quite drunk."

"I can see that. It's not safe."

Jack took out a roll of cash and he took ten bills and set them on the desk. "One hundred thousand francs to do it now."

"Well, I don't know."

"That's a lot of money. Let's do it."

"The hospital would be safer."

"Do you have what you need to do it here?"

"Yes, but as I said, I only have the local."

"Let's get started. I don't have much time. My wife is waiting for me," and when Jack said this he laughed and the doctor looked at him with concern.

"You're very drunk."

"I am."

"I only have the local."

"Fine. Let's go."

Jack was not sure if he were sleeping or awake as the doctor worked, but he felt nothing in the arm until it was gone and when it was gone he could feel his arm where it had once been: The entire arm was a dull ache. He lay on the table and when he tried to prop himself up to a sitting position, he fell to his left side as his right arm pushed and his left arm— the one he felt he had, the one he felt push himself up in concert with his right arm—only worked in his mind. He felt out of balance but that may have been the booze. The white sheet blanketing the operation table was red with blood and Jack used his right hand to grab the edge of the table and pull himself upright. He saw his arm in a pan and he stood and walked to the table in a slanted weave as he was out of balance without the left arm, yet his brain told him it was still there.

The arm, cut from the elbow and bearing his hand, lay in the pan. He reached down and was surprised to note that only right hand was able to touch the wrist watch wrapped around the amputated wrist of his left hand, surprised and confused because he felt both his hands work at the leather watchband, the watch itself strapped just above what seemed now to be a third hand.

As he struggled to take the watch from its wrist, the doctor came back in.

"How are you?"

"My arm hurts."

"Sit down. I'll get the watch for you."

Jack sat down in the chair and watched as the doctor picked up Jack's forearm and removed the watch from its wrist. He then strapped the watch to Jack's right wrist and asked how he felt.

"The pain is here." He used his right hand to motion below his left elbow. "But my arm is there in the pan." The doctor raised his eyes and he was sure that this American was crazy and he would have to report him in the morning. From his hip pocket, Jack extracted his wallet, thumbed it open, and then handed it to the doctor. "Here, you take out ten bills."

The doctor did as instructed and handed the wallet back to Jack.

"You will need to change the bandages tomorrow."

"Can you give me some?"

"It would be better if you came in and I did it so I can examine for infection."

"No, I'll be out of town. I'm on my way to Yaounde."

"I see. Well, in that case, I can give you some bandages, but be sure to have a doctor check it in two or three days."

"I will. Thank you."

Jack went outside and it was midnight and the clouds had passed and the stars shimmered. He walked up the street and a mangy dog with exposed ribs barked and it came up behind him and growled and Jack turned and kicked at it and it retreated. Jack turned to walk and it followed him to the hotel and Jack thought the dog could smell his blood.

He went into the hotel and the clerk was asleep behind the desk. He slowly climbed up the stairs to the third floor and when he opened the door to the room, Faith was sitting by the window and she had tears running down her face. She stood and hurried to him and she started to put her arms around him when she noticed he was missing an arm. She backed away. "Jack, what happened?"

"They had to cut off my arm, Faith. It was infected."

"Sit down."

He sat on the bed and she took off his shoes and his pants and he lay down and was thirsty and drowsy from the drinking.

193

"You smell like you've been drinking."

"I have. Anesthetic."

"Does it hurt?"

"It does. The whole arm aches. And the arm is not even there."

"Can I get you something?"

"Water, please."

She poured him a glass of water from the pitcher on the table, and he drank it down and she poured him another. She sat down next to where Jack lay and she started to cry, and he put his one arm around her. "You're not sad that you're living with a one-armed bandit?"

She looked at his face as he lay with his head on the pillow and the tears came down her cheeks. "Of course not."

"You can still love me?"

"Of course."

"I'll be okay."

"I know."

"Really. Don't worry. After a good night's sleep, I'll be fine. I promise."

"The medicine didn't work?"

"No. I left it in the hotel in Yaounde."

She touched his cheek. "Are you okay?"

"I'm fine. Really, it doesn't hurt much. Just a dull ache. But my balance is upset." He closed his eyes. "You should go back to the Republic now."

"What?"

"I have only one arm now."

"That is not important."

"It will be more difficult to escape."

"Maybe. I'll help."

He laughed. "Yes, you'll help. But I only have one fucking arm. I'm no good."

"You're drunk."

"Yes, I'm drunk as ten sailors. But I have only one arm."

"Jack, go to sleep now. Everything will be better in the morning."

"Except my arm. How could you love a man with just one arm?"

"It is not your arm I love, Jack. I love *you*."

"I know. But I have only one arm. Just one arm."

"Go to sleep now."

"I will. You said everything will be better in the morning."

"Yes, it will."

"I hope you're right."

"I am. Did Mari make it okay?"

"Yeah, she did. She made it out fine. She's in Kinshasa now and then she will go to Kisangani. And they cut off my arm."

"And we will make it out okay, too."

"Of course. In three days we'll be on the high seas to Marseilles and we'll be fine, and I'll always have just one arm."

"Jack."

"It will be okay, Faith."

"I know, Jack. I know. I will take good care of you. God bless you."

Jack fell asleep on his back and Faith checked the bandage and then she turned off the light and got in bed beside him. She lay next to him with one arm over his chest and she was afraid for Jack more than for herself because he seemed to be deteriorating and losing his strength and they still had so far to go if they were ever to be happy together. She didn't sleep that night, but instead she thought about all that had happened and she worried and thought of her parents and how they must be worried about her. She decided that she would send them a letter the day they left the port and she would explain all that had happened and how she was in love. But she knew that would hurt them even more that she had left of her own volition, and she was sad at how hurt they would be, but it could not be helped because she loved Jack and she would not let him go no matter what it was he did or would do from now on.

As she lay there, she prayed for Jack and she prayed for herself and for her parents and for Mari, and it seemed to her that she was asking for quite a lot. She apologized to God for the amount of her request, but she said that it was necessary and that there would be less to ask for in the future.

Jack slept through the morning and Faith sat at the table writing a letter to her parents as he snored. When he finally awoke, he felt that his left arm was still asleep, as if he had slept on it and in so doing had stifled the circulation. He tried to shake it awake, and the fingers of his left hand felt the high voltage of electricity. Then he reached with his right hand and tried to rub the left arm that was not there.

He could smell coffee and the sea breeze came through the open window. He watched Faith with her back bent over the desk as she wrote. He had forgotten that he had had his arm amputated and with both hands he tried to push himself up to a sitting position and he fell to his left side, moaned, and remembered the arm. Faith turned and came to the side of the bed and sat down.

"Are you okay?"

Jack laughed but it was not a real laugh; it was stoic and feigned. "I forgot my arm."

"Does it hurt?"

"I hope not. It probably misses me, though."

"Don't be sarcastic. I'm serious."

"Sorry. No, it's okay. Is there any more of that coffee?"

"No, I'll go down and get some more."

While she went down to the cafe, Jack gave himself a sponge bath at the sink and his head hurt more than his arm. He found himself trying to wash his left arm with the washcloth he held in his right hand, and he shook his head in disappointment. How could the arm still be there when he knew he had left it in the pan in the doctor's office, and if he washed it now, would the arm become clean at such a grave distance?

With difficulty, he dressed and sat back down on the bed and waited for her to return.

She brought a tray with coffee and croissants and sat down in a chair by the side of the bed. He sat up with his back against the headboard, and the crumbs spilled on his lap, but he didn't care and after he had eaten, he shook a cigarette out from the pack and he put it between his lips and Faith lit it. They drank coffee and it was early afternoon and the clouds gathered once again as they always did now that it was the rainy season and as it rained they left the window opened and the air was fresh. She took off her clothes and she undressed Jack and she was on top of him and he felt both of his hands on her shoulders as they made love, and as he came, he felt a tingling sensation in his left arm. Outside, the rain came down, and then they fell asleep and napped until evening.

They went downstairs to the cafe and Jack was hungry. He wore clean jeans and his long sleeved shirt was tied off at the arm. Faith wore jeans, too, and she had washed her hair and she looked fresh and much younger than Jack. They took a table in the corner, and the cafe was full of French ex-patriates drinking and talking in loud voices.

The young Cameroonian waiter who had served them before came up to the table and he stared at where Jack's arm should have hung and Jack ignored him and asked for menus and a beer and an orange soda.

"What happened?" the waiter said in French and he kept staring at Jack's shoulder.

"I lost my arm," Jack said.

"I see that, but how?"

"*Je ne sais pas.* I went to bed with two arms and I woke up this morning and there was just the one. I probably misplaced it and it is probably under the bed."

The waiter went wide eyed and turned and went back toward the kitchen.

"You shouldn't tease him," Faith said.

"I know. But it is my arm and I should at least be able to have some fun with it."

The waiter came back and he stood on Faith's side of the table and he set down the drinks and gave them menus as he stared at Jack's elbow and Jack could see he wanted to ask him something.

"Well, what is it?" Jack said.

"How could you lose an arm?"

"The same way you lose anything else, I suppose."

"But you had the arm yesterday."

"Yes, and it confounds me that it is gone today."

"It could have been a sorcerer," the waiter said.

"Yes, I think it was. Maybe he will return the arm at a later date."

The waiter went back to the kitchen and through the window in the swinging door Jack could see the face of the cook and behind him the waiter.

197

"That's enough, Jack. It's not very funny," Faith said and then she forced a smile that was one of such sorrow she seemed on the verge of tears.

"Sorry. No more dark humor."

The waiter came back and again he stood by Faith and Jack ordered *steak au poivre* and *pommes frites* and Faith ordered fish and rice and Jack asked for a bottle of Portuguese red wine.

"We'll be on the ocean in two days at this time," Jack said. He picked up his glass of beer. "*Salute* to a pleasant voyage." They clinked their glasses and then the waiter came back with the wine and two glasses and he filled them both. He looked at Jack again and then at the elbow and he hurried back to the kitchen.

"He probably thinks you are a sorcerer."

"Maybe."

"You really shouldn't tease him."

"I know."

Jack finished his beer and tasted his wine and it was sour but not so bad as to be returned, and he didn't really care.

"Where would you like to live?" Faith said. She had her elbows on the table and she cradled her chin in both hands and her blue eyes were far off in some distant dream.

"What?"

"Where would you like to live when we are out of Africa?"

"I don't know. I like the northwest."

"What's it like?"

"Mountains and trees and rivers and lakes and everything is green and it's wet a lot in the winter."

"It sounds pretty."

"It is."

"What will we do?"

"I don't know. It's kind of hard for me to get back into construction with just one arm. We'll think of something."

"Do you think I would be able to go to school?"

Jack smiled. "Of course. We'll need a doctor in the house."

"I would like that. I really would." Faith took a sip of wine and made a face. "It's sour."

"Do you want me to send it back?"

"Can you?"

"Sure. If you don't like it."

"No, it's fine." She took the smallest of sips and set the glass down.

Jack lit a cigarette. "You could go to the University of Oregon in Eugene and then to the med school in Portland."

"Would we be able to afford it?"

"We'll work it out. There are student loans. Don't worry about the details so much. They always work out."

"It's exciting."

"Good. There will be a lot to look forward to."

"And you can find a job?"

"Yes. I know some people in Eugene who own a chain of lumber yards. I could probably work in the office, anyway."

"Jack?"

"What?"

She shook her head and leaned back in her chair. "Nothing."

"What is it?"

"Nothing, I was just thinking."

Jack rubbed his cigarette out in the ashtray. "Faith, it is something, not nothing. What?"

"Oh, I was just thinking about if we would ever get, you know, married."

Jack felt bad because he realized that she had been waiting for him to broach this subject and now it was too late for him to ever do so because she had spoken first. He reached across the table with his hands and when he took her hand in his, he saw that it was only his right hand that held hers, yet he could feel her hand being clutched by both of his. He looked up in her eyes and she smiled, but he could see she was somehow sad.

"Faith, of course I want to marry you. I was just waiting until we got to France."

"I'm sorry."

"There's nothing to be sorry about."

"Okay, but I shouldn't have said anything. I was just wondering about it, that's all."

"Faith?"

"Yes?"

"Will you marry me?"

She started to cry as he held her hand and with her left hand she wiped away the tears and smiled and said, "Yes, Jack. I will marry you. I love you."

"Good. I love you, too. You don't mind marrying a one-armed bandit?"

"Jack."

"I'm just kidding."

"I know."

The waiter came and he stood behind Faith and he set down the plate of fish before her and from behind her he reached across the table and set down the pepper steak and Jack asked him for a bottle of champagne. "And before you bring that, I want to tell you what really happened to my arm."

"Yes?"

"I was hunting up north near the Chadian border and a crazed lion broke through the brush and my gun jammed and the son of a bitch came at me." Jack reached to his belt and took up his knife and held it out in front of him. "I grabbed my knife but before I could cut him he bit my entire arm off and then he ran away with it. That, Monsieur, is how I lost my arm."

The waiter stood behind Faith and he looked at Jack with a kind of amazement in his eyes and he turned and hurried to the kitchen and the cook was looking through the window at Jack again.

"You think you are so funny."

"I guess I do."

Faith took a bite of her fish and then she looked at Jack who was looking at his steak. "Let me cut it for you," she said, and Jack said no, that he was going to have to get used to dealing with one arm and he might as well start now. He picked up the knife in his right hand and he tried to slice the steak but it moved on the plate so he put the fork in his mouth and leaned over the plate and with the fork in his mouth he held the steak in place and sliced it into pieces with the knife and there were stares from the other customers.

"See, not bad?"

Jack took a bite.

"How is it?"

Jack chewed and swallowed and said excellent, and he asked her how the fish was and she said it was fine, and the young waiter came with the champagne and the other customers watched as he wrestled with the cork and it was apparent he had not done this often for he did not have the bottle covered with a towel and he held the bottle straight up toward the ceiling. The cork shot to the ceiling and bounced on the floor and the champagne overflowed from the bottle. He hurriedly poured it into the two glasses he had set on the table.

He picked up a glass and set it next to Jack and no longer did he stand behind Faith as if he were afraid of Jack, and then he handed Faith her glass. The waiter looked at Jack and said, "Monsieur, may I ask you one question?"

"Yes."

"I saw you with two arms yesterday so how is it that you were lion hunting by the border today?"

"We flew up in a helicopter."

"I see. And one more question?"

"Yes?"

"Is it true what they say about losing a limb and still being able to feel it where it once was?"

"Yes, it is. But I can now feel it in the stomach of the lion and it is being eaten away by the juices in the lion's stomach that are like acid and I can feel the skin being burned away."

The waiter hurried back to the kitchen and Jack picked up his champagne glass. "To you and a long and happy marriage, Faith," and she picked up hers and they clinked glasses again and they drank and Faith put her glass down quickly and wiped her nose and mouth with a napkin.

"What is it?"

"It tickles my nose."

"I forgot. You've never had champagne before."

"No."

"Do you like it?"

"Yes, it's nice, I think. I see why they call it bubbly."

201

They ate and between bites Faith said, "I never knew you were such a comedian."

"I never had a chance."

"What do you mean?"

"Well, if you remember, ever since we have been together we have been running and it hasn't been all that pleasant."

"True."

"I like to have fun as much as the next guy."

"I can see that." Faith took a bite of the fish and Jack bent over the plate to cut more meat, slicing the rest of it into bite-sized pieces, and they ate and drank the champagne.

"Were you an only child, Jack?"

Jack looked up from his plate and he took a mouthful of champagne before answering. "As far as I know."

"You don't know then?"

"No. I only know that I was an orphan and was in foster homes until I was six and then Mrs. Peterson adopted me and she had two children of her own so after that, no, I wasn't an only child."

"She was good to you?"

"Yes." Jack leaned back in his chair. "Yes, she was very good and so was her husband. They're good people. Her parents had a wheat farm in eastern Oregon and in the fall we went pheasant and chukar hunting there."

"What's a chukar?"

"A small bird like a partridge."

"Good to eat?"

"Yes."

"And the brothers and sisters?"

"No, just sisters. Both a lot older than me. When they adopted me, the girls were in college. They are more like aunts than sisters, I guess."

"I am an only child."

"I know."

"I was thinking about children."

"Yes?"

"I would like to have at least two."

Jack didn't say anything but drank more of the champagne and he lit a cigarette. He didn't want to talk about the future this way, but then he knew it was only playing and it was a game that Faith needed now, to know that the future would be golden. Jack only knew that there would be no future unless they were able to board that ship safely and sail away from Africa.

"Being an only child is kind of lonely even if you have good parents," Faith said.

"I suppose so."

"You are the only one and there's no one to talk to about kid things."

"Like what?"

"Like why your parents are the way they are, for one thing."

"I see."

"Do you think we could have two children?"

Jack thought about it for a moment and then smiled and his eyes took on a distant quality and he said sure, they could have as many children as she wanted. "It would be a pleasure to help you produce them," he said.

"Jack."

"You know what I mean."

"I do, exactly. Remember, I am a Baptist."

"And here you are sitting with a heathen drinking champagne and talking about sex. Not only that, you have been dancing."

She smiled. "At least you're a heathen with good intentions."

"Not a heathen. Well, maybe in the eyes of some. An atheist, though."

"Not an agnostic? You don't allow for the possibility of God."

He thought for a moment. "No. Impossible. And why should there be, anyway?"

"Why should there be a God?"

"Yes. I guess it is just human weakness. Unable to admit that they don't know why we are here, or how we evolved into who we are. Every culture makes up a religion. It's just that some get very big, and then they must compete with the other big ones."

"Other big ones?"

"Well, Christianity, Islam, Judaism. Those are all pretty big. No one wants to admit they don't know why we are here on earth. But the question should never be asked because we do not know why and we never will. In fact, there is no why. We just are."

"Just are?"

"As in to be. We are. Simply and only that. So we should quit making up religions, though it is a good way to get rich."

"I'll need to pray for you."

"Yes, you will."

They finished the meal and Jack left the waiter a good tip. At the counter, Jack asked for another bottle of champagne and two glasses and they went up to the room and opened the window and sat looking out at the sea. It was a clear night and the stars were out and the night was quiet except for the occasional blast from a ship's horn that sounded dolorous on the night. They sat side by side sipping champagne and talking about the future as they looked out on the sea that was oiled by the black sheet of night.

They left the window open when they went to bed and the clouds moved across the sky from the other side of the continent and the lightning broke out in long, yellow streaks and the thunder that followed reverberated and shook the hotel. Not long after, the rains came down hard and hit the pavement under the street lights and the rain drops bounced back up from the ground and the wind blew the rain to the sea. The shutters banged against the side of the hotel and the wind whistled through cracks in the building and the rain pounded on the corrugated iron roof above their bed. It was a violent storm of huge power and it blew through much of the night and the waves in the sea kicked up and rocked the ships tied off at the docks, and the sea crashed wave after wave on the shore. It became like the sky itself so that above and below was a maelstrom of violence that kept on until it was seduced and then quieted by the first light of dawn.

It was still in the morning and the sea gulls' mournful cries woke Jack. Faith slept on her side, and he pushed himself up, again almost falling, and careful not to wake her, he went into the bathroom and cupped water in his right hand and washed his face as best he could. Still, the arm that was not there pulsed with a constant ache. He went downstairs to the coffee shop and at the glass door he looked in and could see the young waiter talking to a policeman at the counter and the waiter looked up and saw him and waved. Jack walked in and sat down at a table because the policeman had turned to look at him and maybe he was just here for breakfast, but Jack did not want to arouse any suspicion by turning away.

The waiter came up to his table. "Good morning," he said. "Is Madame joining you?"

"No, she is still sleeping."

"Would you like coffee?"

"Please."

"I was just telling the officer of how you lost your arm to the jaws of a lion."

"I see."

"He was greatly impressed."

Jack did not say anything and the waiter went back to the kitchen and as he did the policeman came to his table.

"Good morning. May I sit down?"

"Please."

The man was neatly dressed in a blue uniform and it was starched and had no wrinkles. He took off his cap and he placed it in his lap.

"You are a hunter?"

"Yes, a guide in the Republic."

"But what are you doing here in Cameroon?"

"I am on vacation with my wife."

"I see. The waiter must have been mistaken. He said you had been hunting lions yesterday."

"Yes, he is mistaken. It has been a week since the accident."

"It is bad that you lost the arm."

"Yes."

"You won't be able to hunt anymore, I imagine."

"Possibly not."

"What will you do?"

"I haven't decided yet."

The waiter came back with the coffee and he asked the officer if he would like some. "No, no thank you. I must go to work." The waiter went to clear the table beside the one where Jack sat with the officer and Jack could tell he was listening to their conversation.

Jack took a sip of the coffee and took out a cigarette and the officer reached across the table and lit it. "Have you seen any other Americans recently?"

"No. At least not that I know of. Last night there were many whites eating here but I think they were French."

"How do you know?"

"The way they dressed."

The policeman laughed. "Yes, the French dress differently than the Americans." And he looked at Jack's shirt and his jeans. "Anyway, we are looking for an American. He has kidnaped two women and he is believed to be in Douala."

"What does he look like?"

"He has a black beard."

"What did he do?"

"As I said, he kidnaped two women. An American and an African." He took out a picture and showed it to Jack. "This is the woman, a missionary." Jack looked at the picture of Faith and although it was a couple of years old, it resembled Faith in a younger time.

"I see. No, I have never seen her."

The policemen put the photo back in his breast pocket. "Very well, then." He stood. "Enjoy your stay in Cameroon."

"Thank you, I am sure we will."

The officer left, and the waiter came over to Jack's table and sat down across from him. "That picture, it is your fiancee, I believe?"

Jack didn't say anything.

"He showed me the picture and told me she had been kidnaped, but last night she did not look like she was kidnaped."

"No."

"I believe that you proposed marriage last evening?"

"How do you know that?"

"The champagne and the look on her face, and besides," he smiled, "my English is not so bad."

"I see. What are you going to do? With the police, I mean."

"Nothing, I think."

"Thank you."

"Did you really lose your arm to a lion?" He asked and Jack could see the awe in the young man's eyes and he didn't want to lie to him, but everything seemed to depend on the waiter believing he was a lion hunter.

"Yes, I did. But please do not tell anyone else because we were hunting in Cameroon and I did not have the proper license so I told the officer that it had been a week ago in the Republic."

"Don't worry. You can trust me."

And Jack thought he could. He ordered a pot of coffee and the waiter carried the tray and followed Jack up to the room and Faith was still sleeping when he sat down at the table. As the waiter turned to leave, Jack said, "Here," and handed him a five-hundred franc note.

He poured two cups and he took one and set it on the bedside table and he sat next to her and stroked her hair until she opened her eyes and could smell the coffee.

They stayed in the room through the morning and at noon they dressed and went downstairs to the cafe to eat. The young waiter whose name, they learned, was Gilbert, waited on them as though they were a king and a queen. After they finished eating, they took a taxi to the beach and Faith had her hair tied back and she wore sunglasses. Jack felt they were safe because Faith didn't look so much as she did before with the glasses and the hair pulled back now, and with one arm and no beard, he didn't look much like Jack Burke and he didn't even feel much like him now because he thought of Mari often and Jack had always been a man to ignore regret, but now he was full of that emptiness of wishing he could go backwards in time and undo all that he had done, and all that had been done to him.

They walked up the beach hand in hand past the fishermen who waded out and cast their nets into the sea. The sand was white and hot on their bare feet so they walked where the sand was wet and the water would sneak up past their ankles before retreating and giving way to new water that took its place.

"Tomorrow we leave," Jack said.

"I'm tired of the waiting."

"Me too."

"Do you think we'll get out okay?"

"The captain seemed honest enough."

Faith laughed and Jack looked at her.

"What's so funny?"

"Honest enough to smuggle us out of Africa."

"I meant we could trust him."

"Did you pay him?"

"Half."

Faith bent down and picked up a rock and tried to skip it on the surface of the water, but it only skipped once.

"I forgot how good the ocean smells," Faith said.

"It reminds me of something," Jack said and he closed his eyes for a moment.

"What?"

"I'm not sure. It's like it's there in my head and I know what it is but my brain can't quite reach it, can't find the words. It's the same with my arm. I can feel it but it isn't there. It's just a longing."

"Nostalgia."

"Kind of, except that I don't know what it is that I'm nostalgic for."

"You'll think of it," Faith said.

"No, I don't think I will. And that's the funny thing. I'm not sure I even want to know."

"Is it bad?"

"No, it's good."

"Mari?"

"No, not her. But it's some kind of longing."

"I wish I could share it."

Jack looked at her and bent down and kissed her on the forehead and then they walked on through the water just off the beach. The water was cold on their toes and each of them felt as though they were almost free, but not quite, and they each anticipated leaving all of Africa the following day.

Two children came down the beach toward them. They were small and wore only shorts. One boy carried a papaya and the other child followed the bigger boy. They stopped at the water and asked in French if they would like to buy a papaya.

"How much?" Faith asked.

"Fifty francs," the older boy said. Jack was ready to walk on, but Faith walked up to the boy and gave him one hundred francs and he gave her the papaya and she told him it was all right, he could keep the change. The boys ran back up the beach.

"An expensive papaya," Jack said.

"Come on, let's sit down and eat it."

They walked up the beach and sat down in the sand in the small circle of shade of a palm tree. Jack unsheathed his knife and handed it to Faith. She cut the papaya and the meat was orange and it was stringy and sweet.

After they had eaten, Jack lay down on his back and Faith lay her head on his chest and she could feel him breathe.

"Faith?"

"What?"

"I was just thinking, if we have children, I don't want to raise them in any religion."

"Why not?"

"Just because."

"Why? They don't have to be devout or anything."

"I know. Like you."

"Just because I'm the daughter of a missionary doesn't mean that I am devout. I believe, but I can let others believe what they want and I'm not at all self-righteous." She rolled over to her side and propped her head in her hand. She reached out and stroked Jack's cheek where a black stubble now grew like a bristled brush.

"I know."

"I'm different from my parents."

"I know. It's just that there are too many people like your parents. I don't mean your parents are bad, it's just the idea of being a Christian, I don't know, the Christians feel that everyone has to be a Christian or they'll go to hell."

"Let's not talk about religion now, Jack. You believe what you believe and I'll believe what I believe."

"That's what I mean. The same for the children. Let them grow up and figure it out for themselves. I just don't want to brainwash them early on by taking them to church."

"You have to set an example, Jack."

"You can set an example without going to church."

"Like how?"

"Well, you give them love and teach them about what's right and wrong and respecting other people and their beliefs, and I figure that's enough to get them started."

"Maybe."

They were silent for a while. They could hear the ocean lapping at the shore and the sea gulls' cries and the sound of the waves. Although it was peaceful, both Jack and Faith were still on edge and would be until they set sail for France.

"I'm just saying that religion is not a real tool."

"What's that supposed to mean?"

"Do you think O'Malley and the others are in heaven now?"

"I don't know. Probably."

On their backs, they both looked up at the palm fronds as the breeze came up and the fronds waggled and the trunk was metronomic, first swaying with the breeze and then bending back against it, back and forth, back and forth, and both Jack and Faith were drowsy and the breeze off the sea felt cool and good.

"Do you really think there is a God, just one, Faith?"

Faith thought about that for a moment before replying. "Yes, but all religions are the same and God looks at them as all being equal."

"But why does there have to be a God at all?"

"What do you mean?"

"I just wondered why people have to explain everything with a God."

"Sounds like the theory of evolution."

"Well, kind of, but that's not what I mean. For one thing, if there is a God, why should we have to worship him?"

"Come on, Jack."

"Why would you want to worship a God, anyway?"

"That's just natural."

"I don't think so."

"Well, it is."

"No. We just created God so we could explain our existence is all, and we put him on a pedestal and decided that we should worship him so that we could rationalize everything as being his will."

"That's funny."

"I'm not trying to be funny."

"Well, still, you are."

"Okay, how about this: If there were a God, then why couldn't we hate him?"

"Now what are you talking about? That's crazy."

"I'm serious. With all this happening, we could say that God seriously messed up and that he was not worthy of our respect."

"That's really crazy, Jack. Really crazy."

"Maybe it is. I was just thinking about it. The bottom line, though, is there is no God, at least to my way of thinking."

"That's fine. I still love you."

Jack lifted his head and kissed her cheek and Faith rolled over and kissed him. She sat up and Jack did as well.

"So Faith, you believe in God?"

"Of course."

"Tell me this. Who created God?"

"That's a lousy question, Jack. It's all about faith."

"That's pretty egocentric."

"What?"

"Just a joke, Faith, just a joke. It's all about you."

Jack stood and helped Faith up, and she brushed the sand off his back and he did the same for her with his right hand, and they walked back up to the road. "Well, tell me this, Faith," Jack said as he took her hand in his.

"What?"

"Will your God forgive me for everything I've done?"

Faith was silent a moment before saying, "Yes, I believe He will," and then she wondered about that.

"Then that's some God you've got, Faith. If he can do that, then

211

maybe he's not so bad because sometimes I'm not even sure I can forgive myself."

There was a knock on their door, and Jack got up carefully and asked who it was.

"Gilbert."

Jack opened the door and told him to come in, and Gilbert looked around the room as Jack shut the door behind him. Faith was sitting at the desk writing a letter, turning when Gilbert came in. Jack stood by the door next to him.

"What is it, Gilbert?"

"The police were here asking for you."

"When?"

"Just after you ate lunch. They asked me about you."

"What did you tell them?"

"That you were a lion hunter."

"What did they say?"

"That you were no such thing."

"What?"

"You told me you were a lion hunter."

"I am."

"That is not what the policeman said. He told me that a doctor cut your arm off because of an infection."

Jack looked over at Faith and then looked back at Gilbert.

"They think you are the man they call The Rabbit and they said you kidnaped the girl."

"Faith, did I kidnap you?"

She smiled. "No."

"I know you did not kidnap her. I can see that."

"I'm sorry I lied to you Gilbert. I am not a lion hunter."

"I know."

"I work for the United Nations and Faith and I are leaving for France."

"The police will be back again soon, I think. You might want to leave before they come."

"Thank you for telling me, Gilbert."

"It is nothing. You do not seem like a bad man."

"Thanks."

"But you shouldn't have lied about the lion hunting. You made me look like a fool before the policemen."

"I'm sorry."

From his pocket, Jack took out two bills, and Gilbert backed away from him with his hands pointed up and he waved them and said no, he did not want any money. Jack put it back in his pocket.

"Thank you, Gilbert. We will be leaving soon."

Faith stood up and came and shook his hand. "Are you the missionary from the Republic?" Gilbert asked.

"Yes."

"And you are not kidnaped?"

"No. We are getting married."

"Congratulations then." Gilbert reached out and shook her hand again. "Good luck to both of you." Jack opened the door and Gilbert left the room.

"We better get going, Faith. Pack your stuff."

"Where will we go? To the ship?"

"The captain said we could not come aboard until the last minute because of customs."

"Then where will we go?"

"I don't know."

"Another hotel?"

"I don't think so. They'll be checking all the hotels after they find out we've been staying here."

"We could go back up to the beach. At the end of the beach there is a cove Mari and I found."

"Okay. Get packed. I'm going to go downstairs and pay for the room. I'll be back in a minute."

Jack walked down the stairs and he went to the front desk and the clerk was again sleeping behind the desk and Jack was about to wake him up when through the window of the cafe he saw two policemen talking to Gilbert. Jack hurried back up the stairs.

213

"Faith, we've got to get out of here. There are two cops downstairs."

"How do we leave?"

"The fire escape."

"Is there one?"

"Hell, I don't know. There's another door down at the end of the hall. Maybe another set of stairs."

Faith stuffed some clothes in her bag, and Jack told her to hurry. They went out and turned down the hall, and the door at the end of the hall was locked and Jack kicked it and it opened and it was only a closet. They went back to their room and Jack opened the window.

"It's only about ten feet to the balcony."

Faith looked out the window. "Still, it's a long way."

"We'll tie the sheets together."

"They won't be strong enough."

"Sure they will."

"And what do we do when we get to the balcony?"

"Jump down to the ground. Help me push this armoire in front of the door."

Together they pushed the armoire, Jack pushing with his right shoulder, until it stood before the door. "Now the sheets."

Jack pulled the top sheet off the bed and handed it to Faith and then he pulled off the bottom sheet. "Do you know a square knot?"

"Yes."

"Then tie these together with one."

Faith tied the sheets together and pulled the knot tight. "Now what?"

Jack walked to the window.

"You ever shinny down a rope?"

"A short one from a tree-fort in Alabama."

"Just keep it between your legs like this." Jack stepped one ankle over the other. "Cross your ankles. And hold on with both hands. You'll be fine."

"Okay. But how will you be able to climb down with just one hand?"

"Don't worry about that. Now help me slide the bed over to the window and we'll tie the sheet to the leg." Jack pulled the bed to the window with one hand as Faith pushed. When the bed was next to the window, Faith bent down and tied the end of the sheet to the leg of the bed. She stood and dropped the sheet out of the window.

"It doesn't reach all the way."

"Still, it's better than jumping from here. When you get to the end of the sheet, let go. It'll only be a couple of feet."

"Okay."

Faith climbed to the window ledge and stuck her feet out and took the sheet in her hands. "What about my bag?"

"I'll toss it down."

Faith pushed herself to the edge of the ledge. "I'm scared, Jack."

"Hurry up. I'll hold it."

She had the sheet between her legs and she gripped it tightly with her hands and Jack watched her and told her to go slowly. She pushed off from the ledge and rubbed her back on the side of the building and she slid down little by little until her feet were dangling in the air with no sheet between them and she held on with her hands. "Let go," Jack said as loudly as he felt safe.

She did and she dropped the four feet to the concrete balcony and fell down. Jack climbed over the ledge and there was a knock on the door and a voice in French said to open the door and Jack tossed the bag down to Faith and then he slid down the sheet and with one arm it was difficult, but he managed and he let go and dropped down to the balcony. From the balcony they could hear the pounding on the door above.

The balcony did not appear to be used as there were no tables or chairs, and the curtains to the windows were closed and Jack tried the door, but it was locked, and he ran to the side of the balcony where a mango tree grew and he looked over the wall and Faith came up behind him.

"We'll have to climb down through the tree," Jack said.

"You first, Jack. I'll hold the branch for you."

"No, you go ahead, Faith."

"Jack, quit being so stubborn. Now go."

"Okay."

Faith held a branch for Jack and he climbed atop the wall of the balcony and reached out and grabbed the branch with his one hand and pulled himself into the tree. Faith tossed her bag down to the ground as

Jack climbed to the trunk and made his way down and Faith followed with much less difficulty.

Once on the ground, they ran around the building to the front of the hotel and climbed in a taxi. Jack told the driver to go to the central market, and Faith looked at him but didn't say anything.

It was twenty minutes before they arrived at the market. They paid the driver of the taxi and went through the crowded square and bought some bread and fruit and Jack bought a bottle of whiskey and a bottle of water, and they exited on the opposite side of the market where they found another taxi. Jack told the driver to take them to the beach. The streets were crowded with traffic and with the windows opened they could smell the exhaust, and the horns blared and it was thirty minutes before they got to the beach.

"*Voulez-vous que Je vous attend?*" the driver asked.

"No, thank you," Jack said and paid him.

"But it is going to rain soon. I can wait."

"No, we are meeting some friends."

"Very well."

They walked up the beach to where they had sat that afternoon and Faith led him on up the beach to where a rib of rock jutted out to sea. It was at the base of the rock where the cove was located. As the tide was in, they had to walk next to the rock to get to a small cave at the back of the cove where the water had eroded the rock, and they sat down in the sand that now with the high tide was only a meter in width between the cave and the water. Jack could see that the sand of the cave was dry and it would be a good place to wait. They sat in the sand and Jack opened the whiskey and took a sip and offered it to Faith, but she just shook her head and leaned against the rock wall that rose straight up twenty meters. She watched the water of the cove and saw little fish swimming, darting to and fro.

"That was close," Faith said.

"Too close. But we made it. Tomorrow at this time we'll be on the ship."

"I hope so, Jack."

"We will. We got away today and tomorrow we'll get away for good." He took another sip of whiskey and he leaned against the wall next to Faith. Where his arm should have been there was nothing and if he had the arm he would have put it over her shoulders and he actually tried before remembering the arm was gone and he smiled. The muscles in the missing arm felt tight. He wondered when he would finally be able to let the arm go, to forget it as if it had never been.

"What now?"

"Nothing. I just tried to put my arm around you."

She didn't say anything to that, but after a moment she said, "I hope Gilbert is not in trouble."

"He'll be okay. Remember, he believed I was a lion hunter and not a kidnapper."

"Yes."

"It seems that what is important is what other people believe of you."

"It doesn't matter, Jack. It doesn't."

"No, I think it must."

"You know who you are." She touched his cheek with her hand.

"I thought I did, but now, I don't know. Everyone else thinks I'm a cold blooded killer, a kidnapper."

"You're not."

"I don't know, Faith. I just wish everything were different. I wish I could go back to Boda for the first time and do everything different."

"You can't."

"I know that, Faith. I know that. But still, I just wish I could start over now. I keep thinking about the men I killed, the gendarme crawling over me in the truck, pulling back the tarp. When he saw me his eyes went big, white. He knew he was going to die. I didn't want to kill him, but he only knew he was going to die. What if I didn't shoot him? What if I didn't?"

"Jack."

"I know, Faith, but see, now I have to live with this and I don't know if I'll ever really be able to."

"You will. First, we get to France. Then you can start living with it. I'll help you."

"I hope you can."

With their backs to the rock wall, they looked out at the sea as the sun was dropping down to the water's edge, inextricably pulled by the weight of the day. It was orange and then purple and then it was gone. It was dusk, and the first star of the evening could be seen. It was quiet and warm and the tide pulled away from them and the stretch of beach to the water was longer and the water from the top of the cove had been swept back so that the edge of the cove was now ten meters away. They sat quietly and listened to the sound of the water as small waves folded in before pulling back the water that was before them. The ocean was retreating. They both were thinking that the next evening they would be on a ship bound for Marseilles and once the ship pulled out of the harbor they could look back in its frothy wake and feel safe, truly safe for the first time since they had first met at the mission in Boda almost two weeks before.

Jack hoped that a new life could wash away the old, erase it from existence so that it would never have been, but then he thought that there were surely parts of the past he would like to keep, moments like the day he tried to teach Mari how to swim in the Ubangui River, and how she had clung to his arms so that her nails cut through the skin leaving ten half-moon crescents, four on each tricep and one on each bicep, marks that lasted a week. Then of course he thought back to the lost arm that was not so lost as he could still feel it where it had always been. He thought of it as a memory that rode side by side with the present so that past and present merged into one.

The stars began to appear one by one and then the sky was a blanket of twinkling stars and the clouds with the rain had not come this far west yet, but they knew the clouds would come in the night because they always came during the six months of rain, every day they came fueled by the wind, and now, in the far distance they could hear thunder. Faith opened her bag and took out a sari and went to the cave and spread it on the sand, and then she came back out and sat next to Jack. She had a *baguette* which she broke in half. She handed him a piece and they ate the dried bread and Jack drank whiskey and Faith drank water from a plastic bottle they had bought in the market. They could hear the wind blow over the crest of the rocks above them, but they were protected and were warm.

"I left the letter on the table," Faith said.

"What?"

"The letter to my parents."

"Oh. You can write another on the ship and we'll mail it from Marseilles."

"No, you don't understand."

"What?"

"In the letter I wrote that we would be leaving Douala by ship."

Jack was quiet for a moment before he realized what she meant. "Shit."

"I know. I'm sorry."

"There'll be police all over the fucking port."

Faith sighed.

"You didn't mention what day we were leaving?"

"No, I just said we were leaving by ship. That's all."

"Maybe we'll be lucky and they won't see the letter or maybe they'll not understand the English." But Jack did not really believe that.

"Yes, maybe."

"At any rate, we'll have to be careful in the port."

It began to rain and they crawled into the cave as it was only high enough to crawl, but it was wide and deep enough for them to keep their heads out of the rain, and they lay on the thin sari and looked out at the lightning as it exploded into the sea, the thunder reverberating off the rocks around them.

Faith kissed Jack and said she was sorry about the letter and he told her not to worry about it because it was already done. He put his one arm around her and held her and then he kissed her and unbuttoned her shirt. She was careful with his shirt and asked him about his arm, but he told her not to worry about it because it was gone. She smiled and in the dark he could not see her, but he could feel her and their bodies came together and their skin was warm despite the rain that fell outside of the cave, and again his left arm felt a buzzing tingle.

"Jack?"

"Yes?"

"Remember when you first came to the mission and I was mean to you?"

"You weren't mean." Jack stroked her hair.

"Yes, I was. I know. I was mean to everyone then."

"Well, okay, you weren't the most hospitable person in the world."

"And I told you about the Frenchman, the journalist?"

"Yes, I remember."

"I didn't tell you. I thought I was in love with him."

"It's okay, Faith. Everyone has a history. You've met some of mine."

"But you should know. I didn't really love him. I only thought I loved him. I only knew him three weeks."

Jack laughed quietly.

"What?"

"I was just thinking that we've only known each other less than two."

"I know, but Jack, I wanted you to know that I realize I didn't love him. I was just silly. It was just infatuation."

"Don't worry about that, Faith. Don't worry. You sleep well now."

"You, too, Jack. It's just that I wanted to tell you. I feel better now."

"Good."

Jack fell asleep, and Faith lay awake thinking about the edge she was on, knowing that she would step forward, but wondering if she should step back. She worried about this decision and hoped Jack was as strong as he seemed. He would have to be, she thought, because if he weren't, they would never get out. Somehow she would have to find the strength to help him.

When Faith woke, Jack was sitting in the shadows by the cove and the tide had come in and Jack's hair was wet. The sun had yet to rise high enough to crest the rocks behind them and reach the sand that stretched out to the water that would be their future, the water that would carry them away.

Faith crawled out of the cave and sat next to him. "You didn't go swimming with that arm, did you?"

"What arm?"

"Very funny."

She bent over the water and cupped her hands and rinsed her face with the water.

"I just washed the sand out of my hair," Jack said.

"Remember how we went swimming in Boda?"

"Yes."

"And those boys?"

Jack laughed. "Yes, I remember."

"Boys will be boys, you said."

"And so did you."

"I was thinking last night that I would like to have a boy and a girl. That would be perfect."

"Yes, it would."

"You could teach the boy to play baseball."

"With one arm?"

"Sure you could."

"Yeah, I guess I could at that. I was pretty good. I played third base in high school."

"And he'll look just like you with your dimples."

"I don't have dimples."

"Yes, you do. When was the last time you looked in a mirror?"

"Small ones then."

Faith was silent for a moment. Jack watched her, saw her smile as she said, "I would like to live in the country."

"That would be good. We could have a garden. When I was a kid, I used to grow pumpkins, huge ones."

"And animals. I would like to have a cow and goats and a pig and chickens for eggs."

"Why a pig?"

"Because they're cute."

"They're ugly and mean."

"No, they're not. Well, they can be mean, but they're cute. We had pigs at the mission. The big one was named Mr. Ham Bones. We could name ours Sir Francis Bacon."

"Ha, ha. We could get a few acres outside of Portland."

"What's Portland like?"

"It's a nice city. Pretty clean. Green. We could get a few acres up the Clackamas River outside of Portland and then if we wanted to go to the city we could, and if we didn't want to, we'd be in the country."

"It sounds perfect."

"It is pretty, Faith. It's nice."

"It would be good for the children to grow up in the country."

"Yes."

"But no religion, right?"

Jack turned and looked at her and he saw her smile.

"Forget about that for now, Faith. We'll work out some kind of compromise."

"Okay. Jack, do you really think any of this will come true?"

He looked in her eyes and he could see the fear in them, and it didn't matter what he really thought; it was what they needed to believe that was important. "Sure I do. All's you have to do is believe and it will come true."

"You're sure?"

"Yes. As sure as I can be. What good does doubt do?"

"We'll be married and live on a farm and have children and we'll be happy?"

"Yes."

"Good." She lay down and put her head in his lap and he stroked her hair.

"But you will still miss Mari?" she said after a while.

He thought about that and said, "Yes, I will. But I love you."

"I know. But you're right. It is better not to forget Mari or pretend to forget her."

"Yes."

"I hope she's happy as we will be."

"I'm sure she is. She's pretty much always happy because she doesn't have all of our expectations."

"Are you saying it's bad to expect so much? Like the farm and the children?"

"No. I'm not saying that. It's just that when you don't expect so much you don't fall so far when you don't get what you want. Right now, I'm only hoping we get on the ship okay."

"I'm sorry about the letter."

"It's not that, Faith. Forget it. I'm just hoping is all. I guess you have to have hope."

"And you have to have faith."

"Well, I do. I have you."

She smiled and stroked his hair. He leaned forward and kissed her on the forehead.

"It'll be okay. How long will it take to get to France?"

"A week. Maybe two."

"And then?"

"We'll fly to the states."

"What about passports?"

"We'll go to the embassy and tell them we lost them. Something like that. Or the black market. It'll work out."

"I hope so."

"It will."

"You're always so confident."

"I don't know about that. But it's no use being negative."

"I love you, Jack."

"I know. I love you, too, even if you are a Baptist."

"At least I can dance."

"Yeah, you can dance all right."

"It might lead to fucking standing up. We haven't tried that yet."

"Faith."

"What? Are you a prude?"

"No, I just can't believe you said that."

She laughed. "Either can I."

Jack looked down at her face cradled in his lap and she was smiling. He thought about how different he had thought she was when he first met her from how she really was, and her boldness frightened him in a way because he didn't want to disappoint her as he had disappointed Mari. They would have to get out on that ship and live on a farm and have children because the least he could do was see her happy and that would be enough for him, he thought. If Faith were happy, then he thought it might be possible for him to be that as well. At least he could do some good if he could make her happy. That might be enough.

There were no clouds in the morning nor in the afternoon. The sun was warm and it was peaceful by the cove. They ate bread and napped in the cave and they sat up and talked about the future. Faith talked about the color of the house, a white farm house she said, and then she talked about going to school. They painted a bright future together, and the rains did not come. They watched the sun set into the ocean again and the sky went purple and the stars sparkled white and there were so many stars that the black sky was almost filled in. They walked around the cove and then back down the beach the way they had come the day before and they walked on the beach for as far as they could until they came to the rocks and then they went up to the road. They had to walk for thirty minutes before a taxi passed them and Jack waved it down. He asked the driver to take them to the port.

The streets were puddled from the last rain and the air was pregnant with the mosquitoes that hatched in the stagnant water. The rats, some as big as footballs, darted in and out of the warehouses, and children and adults set traps for the rats and Jack said the only health concern for doing so was the one of hunger.

The taxi stopped in an alley between two large warehouses and if the driver wondered about this destination, he did not ask. When Jack opened the door and they were no longer protected by the taxi's air-conditioning, a waft of fish and garbage rushed in and Faith held her hand to her nose until they were out on the street and the smell of decay was alive.

They stood in the dark alley until the red tail lights of the taxi were gone around the corner. They walked down the alley to an intersection and they turned left on a wider street that was crowded with sailors and seamen of all sorts, men who had the secret lives mothers would never hear of. Faith became an immediate anachronism in that crowd of rough men who were in port to drink and screw women. She felt the eyes on her as if they were hands groping for the buttons of her shirt, the focus of the eyes as tangible as dirty fingernails scratching her back and neck, so that to be raped was just to have been looked at.

They crossed the street and turned right down another, this one lined with the shops of palm readers and dingy bars where the shelves of bottles had never been dusted. In those bars were women who looked like they had run the gamut of disease so that now penicillin was as much a part of their system as the blood that ran through their veins. Jack held Faith's hand as she carried her bag and they walked quickly but not too quickly as to arouse suspicion; they only walked fast enough to avoid being accosted.

Men sat in doorways passing bottles and the smell of urine was thick in the air, like some massive sewer without ventilation. There were men who slept on the pavement and some slept on their bellies with their faces in the vomit of their last drink. Jack and Faith stepped around these men and breathed through their mouths as the retched odor made them both nauseous; the sea salt in the air was only just negligible even though they were now on the street where the ships were tied off with hemp ropes as thick as a man's arm.

"Which ship is it?" Faith asked as they walked past ships that were as big as stadiums. Many of the ships rode high in the water and some were so low that they looked like they were sinking under the weight still in their bowels.

"It's *The Emerald Sea*. It's still a ways."

They walked on the sidewalk on the far side of the street from the ships and stayed close to the buildings in the shadows and out of the yellow wash of street light as best they could. There was very little traffic on the street and there were only men walking from the ships to bars and from the bars to ships and many of them were quite drunk and they stumbled more than walked, legs sometimes working out of synch with each other, lurching one way before another, all the while continuing on in the general direction of some destination they had in mind. They saw men who could walk no farther who were sitting on the curb waiting for their legs to come back.

"That's it there," Faith said and Jack nodded as they both read the faded letters on the stern of the ship. The ship was low in the water and it either had not unloaded its cargo or it had taken on coffee and lumber for France, and Jack hoped it was the latter because the ship was supposed to set sail that night.

They were parallel with the ship and they kept walking until they came to a bar that had no sign on the door. The windows looked like they had not been washed in a long time. Jack told Faith that they were to meet a man in the bar at nine o'clock and it was now eight o'clock so they had an hour to wait. They went into the bar and took a table in the back away from the door and windows. The place stank of beer and the concrete floor was dirty with spilled drinks of all kinds, and broken glass and cigarettes, some of which still smoldered. A large man stood behind the bar and did not come to serve them so that Jack went to the bar and ordered a beer and an orange soda. He went back to the table where Faith waited and the men at the other tables watched him and they looked at Faith with a certain hunger that Jack was embarrassed to recognize, a feral and atavistic desire that civilized men kept under wraps but that here was as out in the open as the bottles on the tables, the cigarettes in their mouths. Jack felt bad that they had to wait in this bar and that Faith had to sit and be stared at. He wished he had two arms.

"It won't be long now," Jack said. "An hour at the most."

"You think he'll come?"

"Yes."

"How can you be sure?"

"He wants the rest of his money."

Faith began to pour soda in the glass when she saw the smudges around the rim and she drank out of the bottle after wiping the neck with her shirt sleeve. Jack drank out of the bottle, too, and the beer was cold and tasted good on the back of his throat.

They watched the door from where they sat and men came in and went out of the bar and each time the door opened, both Jack's and Faith's expectations rose commensurate with the rise of their fears.

It was five minutes after nine when a man came into the bar and his cotton shirt stuck to his back from the rain. He went to the bar and ordered a beer and then he leaned on the bar and surveyed the patrons until he saw Jack and Faith in the back. He walked to their table and sat down. It wasn't the captain of the ship, but another Algerian who was the first mate, he said, and he had come to take them to the ship.

"But we have to be careful," he said in French. "The police are searching the ships."

"How will we board?" Faith asked.

He ignored her and looked at Jack. "Are you ready to go?"

"Yes, we are ready."

The Algerian led the way. Jack and Faith held hands and it was raining hard and the rain could be seen in the street lights and it came down at an angle from the east. The Algerian walked quickly and he had his hand in his pocket and Jack watched him carefully from behind because when Jack had asked the captain who would come to meet them at the bar, the captain had said he would send Pierre and then he laughed and now Jack was thinking about the captain's laugh as they walked across the street to the pier where *The Emerald Sea* was docked.

The flood lights were on and men worked on the ship decks in the rain. The Algerian led them up the gang plank. Faith followed and Jack walked behind her. Aboard the ship, the sailors looked up from their work at Faith. The Algerian took them up a flight of metal stairs and then down a hall and up another flight of stairs, and the halls echoed as they walked.

At the end of the hall, the Algerian knocked on a door. They heard a voice tell them to enter, and they went inside where the captain was sitting behind a desk writing in a log book. He was a heavy-set man with the jowls of a bull dog and his skin looked like leather dried in the sun. He smiled, and Faith saw that he was missing his top front teeth.

The captain stood and looked where Jack's arm should have been. "What happened to you?"

"An infection. The doctor had to remove it."

"Bad luck."

They shook hands and the captain asked them to sit down and he told the first mate to wait outside. The captain sat down behind the desk that was littered with papers.

"You have rest of money?" he asked Jack in broken English garbed in the accent he used for his French.

"Yes."

He held out his hand palm upward.

"You'll get it when we get to Marseilles."

"But how I know you have it?"

Jack took out a wad of bills and held it up and then he put it back in his pocket.

"Okay. You pay me in Marseilles, then."

He stood up. "Pierre will show you cabin. It is nothing so nice, but then you too occupied with, what, the police, to be concerned about accommodations." He laughed. "Pierre," he shouted, and Pierre came in and in French the captain told him to take the Americans to their cabin.

Pierre led them down four flights of metal stairs that echoed as they descended into the guts of the ship. They walked down a narrow hall and at the end of the hall Pierre opened a door to a small cabin with a bunk bed and no window. It was hot and the air was stale. Jack thanked him and Pierre told them to stay in the room until they set sail because the customs people could always come back before they left port, and he left and closed the door behind him. Faith sat down on the bottom bunk and Jack opened a small door and saw the roaches in the bathroom that was only a sink and a toilet with no seat, and he closed the door because the room stank of sewage, but Faith could smell it before he closed the door.

"It's not the Queen Elizabeth, but it's a ship," Faith said, and Jack sat down next to her as there were no chairs. He shook a cigarette from the package, and he handed Faith the boxes of matches. She struck the match, and she lit the cigarette as Jack inhaled.

"We made it, Jack."

"Almost."

"We're on the ship."

"Yes. I'll feel better when we're out at sea."

"It won't be long now."

"It can't be soon enough."

"Are you all right?"

"I'm okay. I don't much like being down here in the bottom of the ship in this little room, though."

"We'll be able to go up on deck once we're at sea, won't we?"

"I think so."

"It won't be so long now."

"I know."

Jack stubbed out the cigarette on the floor and lay back on the bed and there were no sheets, just a cotton blanket and a pillow, and he lay down and Faith stood.

"Where are you going?"

"This bed's too small for the two of us."

She climbed to the top bunk and lay down.

228

"I'll sleep up there," Jack said.

"No, your arm. It's easier for me."

They were quiet and they could hear nothing except for the occasional clank of metal from someone working somewhere on the ship, and then they could feel the vibration of the engines as the rpms increased and cool air came in through the vent above the door.

"I think we're moving," Faith said.

"It feels like it."

"Jack?"

"What?"

"Nothing."

"What, Faith?"

"Do you think we will really go to Australia someday?"

On the bottom bunk, Jack smiled to himself, but it was not an altogether happy smile because Australia was very far away. "Yes, Faith. We'll go to Australia someday. And you'll see your kangaroos."

"Do you think that's so silly?"

"No, I don't. I think it's a dream as worthwhile as any other."

"Then don't laugh."

"I'm not laughing, Faith. Believe me, I am not laughing. I just think you're cute."

Faith lay on her back and prayed that they would make it to France and that they would have a life together. Jack thought about Mari and everything in Africa that he had just broken away from with the movement of the ship from the dock and everything that was now in his wake was really only Mari and an arm, and five dead men including O'Malley who had only been trying to help. There was nothing more because everything for him had been connected with Mari. It now seemed right to him the way he was leaving: he was sneaking off the continent at night in the rain on an Algerian ship, being smuggled out of Africa for two hundred thousand francs with an American Baptist missionary and that was the only twist in the entire affair because everything else just seemed to have been inevitable, one mistake at a time. It was almost as if there were something to be balanced and all the mistakes he had made allowed him to leave Africa with Faith, good for the bad. Three years in Africa had left him empty and sad, yet he now sailed with a future but he would think about that later when he was done digesting Africa and the life he had led there. He didn't think it had been a bad life except for the last few weeks and he thought about Mari and her sister and how he had set up a sense of normalcy in the middle of the continent with Mari and her sister and her two children and how they had sat on the porch and cooked over charcoal and listened to the radio and gone dancing in the *boites*. Now, though, he wondered if he had been fooling himself with Mari to think as he did at the time that they would always be together and that they would have that same life somewhere else forever, and he thought maybe he had been blind, or maybe it was just that he had been young, but now, only three years since he had come to Africa, he was leaving and he was leaving much older than he thought he should now be.

He was young when he arrived on this continent. Africa was escape and adventure and that is what he had found, but the price was higher than he could have imagined. He left a woman he loved and an arm and in his wake there were men dead and he thought about O'Malley and he thought he now knew what O'Malley had meant about embracing melancholy and allowing it to soothe because it really was an elixir if the dose was heavy enough; Jack thought that there had never been a dose as heavy this.

He felt in-between now lying on the bunk, between everything, between continents to be sure, but more than that he felt between the past and the future as if these moments on the ship were merely a long pause and that the future would come soon, but not yet because the past was too close; this was the melancholy working on him and he didn't fight it but instead did as O'Malley had said: he pulled it around himself and was wrapped by it so that there really was no past or future, but merely a present where time was melded together in a stage in-between, a place where he now felt he would always be, this liminal place of great sadness.

He thought about love and of how he loved Karen so long ago and then Mari and Faith and how there was nothing hypocritical or contradictory or at least wrong about loving two women at the same time, loving each with identical measure, and he felt that Faith could probably understand this and that Mari could as well, and he knew there was something in love

230

that all fools could not see and that in part it was being loved that made you love and it was that simple.

Faith loved him as Mari had loved him and he had never had that before and he loved each woman, he felt, because they loved him and he had not ever really known he was worthy of being loved by a woman other than by his adoptive mother because no one had told him that he was worthy of being loved except Karen, but with her it had been a trick or a lie because she had left him for some other man. It had taken Mari to make him see what love was and that it could be differentiated from sex as sex was the animal instinct that was bereft of emotion and that love was something far greater; you could always have sex, but not necessarily love and he had been lucky enough to have both with two women who were so much the same. Now the melancholy helped him realize how much he loved each woman still and to have known love like this was rare and he had been lucky enough to have known it twice. That, at least, was something.

When these thoughts evaporated, he opened his eyes and saw where he was, and then he closed them quickly and pretended that he was not there in the small cabin at the bottom of a ship. But it was no use. He was afraid and closed in. It was as if the walls of the cabin, and the floor and the ceiling, were all closing in upon him like some room in a horror novel, and soon he would be crushed.

He was more afraid than he had ever been because they were so close to escaping from Africa where everyone saw Jack Burke as an American killer, and though, for the first time in his life, he had begun to question who he really was, he knew he was more than just a killer. Certainly, he had killed and when you take a man's life, he thought, you can never be the same because with the killing is the recognition of mortality and with that comes the knowledge of the true ephemeral quality of life, that it can be taken from you and that you could take it away from someone else very easily and maybe without reason. As he lay there, he thought he knew something now of the need for religion and his need was strong because not only did he feel the need for forgiveness, he felt the need for something more. Those men were dead and for what? Was that all there was? You are born and you live and you die. Was that all there was to this? He felt the

231

need now, the need that there just had to be more. It was like he had played a game and it was over and he'd lost and now he wanted another chance, another chance to win the game because now he had more knowledge and he would play with more skill. But that was the knowledge of the aged: that if you could only take what little you know now back to a time when you acted recklessly not knowing what you didn't know but confidently thought you really knew.

Faith was excited and nervous with the prospect of such a bright future that was just before them but that was not yet sure, and as long as she thought about the future she was happy, but she kept thinking about her parents and how worried they must be. She would write them as soon as they were in Marseilles and then they would be both happy and disappointed, but happy that she was alive and disappointed that she had run off with Jack Burke, and she worried about how they would be able to come to an understanding. She prayed that they would. Her father, she thought, would never understand, but all her hope lay in her mother because she was a woman who had lived so much of her life at that lonely mission in Boda and maybe it was that her mother would remember her own dreams when she had been young, dreams left behind in the long ago.

Jack wondered if he were wrong to put Faith through all this, wondered if he were only selfish, but he placated his sense of guilt by telling himself that Faith would never have stayed behind, but the problem for him was that he would have parted with her only with a great sadness; he had done that with Mari and he could not do it again. He needed Faith now. If he were alone now, he thought, he would be too weak to go on.

Faith fell asleep and she slept for an hour and when she woke, she could feel the movement of the ship beneath her as if the ship were not moving at all, but it was the sea that was being pulled back from under them and that they would be in the same spot forever, but the world would have moved and left them stranded in the middle of time.

She sat up and saw Jack pacing back and forth from the door to the wall.

"How long has it been?" she asked.

"A little over an hour."

"Do you think we can go up on deck?"

"I think so. I need to. This room…it's just so damn small. There's no air."

Faith climbed down from the top bunk. She embraced Jack and kissed him, and then she let go and opened the door. They went out and they got lost in the circuitous hallways and it took them ten minutes to open a door to the air. They came out on a catwalk at the stern and a man greeted them in French as he passed, and then they were alone looking at the lights of Douala recede in the distance, all of Africa forever behind them, a sinewy curve of sparkling lights. It had stopped raining and the air was fresh and the night breeze cool. To Jack, the salt air had never smelled so cleansing.

"It's beautiful," Faith said, and Jack said nothing but he lit a cigarette and she could tell he was thinking about something and she guessed that something was Mari still on the continent of Africa that to them was now a mere island in their wake, an appointment they had each in their own fashion met and would now, finished, leave behind. In the light of the moon, she could see the froth of their wake spread wide into a large V, and there were yellow lights blinking on ships in the distance. She leaned on the rail as did Jack and the sea was calm, but still they had to hold the railing where they stood as the ship churned through the sea going west with the stars.

The breeze was refreshing after the stale air in the cabin and Faith breathed deep and gulped and swallowed the air as if she had a great thirst in her lungs, and Jack put his one arm around her and held her for support. Then they saw the lights of two boats approaching from the shore and they thought nothing of them until they were closer and could see how quickly the boats were moving and that the distance between the ship and the two boats was being eaten away. They saw the red lights spinning on the boats and Jack knew the boats were for him.

"It's the police, Faith," he said. "Real trouble now."

"How do you know?"

"It is."

"And how do you know they're after us?"

"They are," he said and Faith knew that, too.

"What do we do?"

Jack thought about that and there was nowhere to go but to stay on the ship. They watched as the boats approached from behind and then the lights disappeared on the other side of the ship, and Jack knew they would be boarding soon and that they had to do something, they had to find somewhere to hide, but he couldn't think of anywhere.

Then he saw the lifeboats. It was a chance they would have to take.

They hurried along the catwalk and down the stairs two decks to the deck where the lifeboats hung suspended above the water, steel boats six meters long that looked too heavy to float.

Mesh netting was draped from the boats and tied off at the railing at the edge of the ship's deck.

"We'll hide in the boat," Jack said.

Faith looked at the netting they would have to climb across like spiders and she did not say anything and Jack told her to go on and she climbed out onto the netting with her hands gripping the rope and her feet pushing off the rope and ten meters below she could see the white water being tossed up from the side of the ship. Jack climbed beside her and the netting swayed with their weight and the movement of the ship, and the lifeboat before them rocked back and forth. They climbed on their bellies and gripped the rope with their hands and it was hard for Jack with just one hand, but they managed to pull themselves into the lifeboat where they lay down on the hull side by side in a puddle of rain. It was the best place to hide, Jack told Faith, and they lay on their backs with the stars above them and the sea below and after a few minutes the boat swayed less than it had when they had started climbing the mesh.

"They won't think to look here," Faith said and Jack hoped she was right.

They didn't talk and the boat rocked gently now and the movement was peaceful and if circumstances had been different, they would have gone off to sleep. They could hear the engines of the ship cut back to a lower hum, and Jack knew the police had boarded and that it would take some luck for them to get out of this jam.

An hour passed before they heard voices and the hollow ring of boots on the metal stairs and the voices were in French but were muffled and they may not have been as close as Jack was afraid they were. After a few minutes the voices came closer as did the sound of the boots on the metal of the deck and Faith squeezed Jack's hand and he turned his head and kissed her and she kissed him back.

"I love you," she whispered, and he squeezed her hand.

Jack released his grip of her hand and Faith could feel his hand move down by her hip and she heard the snap of the button on the sheath and she knew that he had his knife in his hand now and she was afraid and was about to say something when a voice asked in French if anyone were in the lifeboat. She kept still, and then they heard another voice give an order to climb up the netting and they felt the weight of the man on the netting now and with each of his movements the boat shuddered and then swayed, and they could hear the man breathing as he climbed, but they could only see stars.

Jack rolled on his side and crawled to the front of the boat and then Faith saw two hands grip the gunwale and with the butt of the knife Jack pounded the fingers, and the man screamed, but held on. Jack hit the other hand and the man fell and Faith looked over the side and saw him tumble down the mesh netting to the deck below where two men in uniform stood in the yellow light that washed the deck. Jack pulled back on the crank that held the boat in place and it jerked suddenly, and Faith fell to her back and then she felt them falling in air. When the boat splashed in the water, Faith hit her head on the gunwale and when she sat up she saw Jack lying on his back. The ship was already pulling away into the dark distance, and she knew that it was over, that they could never get away now.

Jack kneeled and squeezed the bulb on the line between the engine and the red gas tank that was on the floor of the boat at the stern and he stood and pulled the cord to start the outboard motor, but it would not start, and the ship had passed them and they were alone in the sea and she knew it was only a matter of minutes before the police boats came and arrested them. Jack pulled and pulled but the engine would not start, and she sat up and called his name, but he either did not hear or he ignored her because he kept pulling the rope and the engine would not start, and she started to cry.

Still he pulled, and she stood and went to him and pulled him down to the floor and they sat and she held him, and they both knew it was over.

Faith kissed him and told him she loved him.

"I love you, too."

The night was dark as oil and it was difficult to see where the sky met the water. When they saw the revolving red lights on the boat that was approaching from the distance, Jack thought of everything he had done, that everything would have to be this way because he did not have a choice, not after all he had done and all that had been done to him, and he kissed Faith and she had her arms around him and he pried them loose as gently as he could and as he stood in the dark, she wrapped her arms around his legs.

"Faith, I love you."

She held him as he took off his shoes and as he unbuckled his belt, and she was holding his jeans as he stepped out of them. Then he took off his shirt and he stood above her and he looked down at her and he could see the tears on her face. He bent down and took the wad of bills from his pocket and he peeled off five and tucked them in his shorts and he handed the rest to her. He took the belt from his jeans and he said, "Faith, please, now, buckle this."

She buckled it around his waist with the sheathed knife in place. Then he threw his clothes overboard.

She held the money in her hand and he kissed her once more and he wanted to explain what he was about to do, but there was no time and besides, he wasn't sure what it was he would tell her. She grabbed both of his legs and he pulled out of her grip and stood by the side of the boat, and he said, "When they come, tell them I fell out as we hit the water," and he turned his back to her and readied to jump, but he turned back once more.

"Faith, I love you. And maybe I'll make it out okay and then I'll write and we will have the future we talked about."

"Jack, no."

"Faith, it's too late now. I'd be in jail for the rest of my life. We'd have no life together. This is the only way where there's at least a chance."

"Jack, please."

"Pray for me, Faith. Pray to your God that I make it to shore. And then pray that I make it to safety somewhere where no one is trying to get me. And if that all works out, I'll write you and we'll have that future we talked about with children. And if that happens, then maybe I'll thank that God of yours, maybe even become religious."

"Jack."

"Faith, I love you."

Faith was about to say something, but he dove in and as he dove, she said his name once more, and she watched him swim on his side until he crested a wave and then he went down the other side of the wave and she could no longer see where he swam.

Soon the police boat was alongside and everything was over for her as they took her aboard and she told them that Jack had fallen out of the boat when the boat hit the water. In the dark, they searched the water for an hour before giving up, and one policeman said to another that The Rabbit must have drowned.

Faith, however, would never believe Jack had drowned even when she was back at the mission in Boda, the town that was far away, but not so far away as she thought, Boda, not quite a town and not quite a village, her home for now as she went back to teaching at the school at the bottom of the hill below the mission, teaching and waiting for a letter from Jack Burke, a man whom she loved, a man she had last seen swimming in the sea off the coast of Africa.

The End

 Tim Schell is the winner of the 2004 Mammoth Book Award for Prose for his novel *The Drums of Africa* which was published in the fall of 2007. In 2010, Tim's novel *The Memoir of Jake Weedsong* was The Finalist in the AWP novel competition, and in 2011 it was published by Serving House Books. Tim is the co-author of *Mooring Against the Tide: Writing Fiction and Poetry* (Prentice Hall, 2nd edition, 2006) and the co-editor of the anthology *A Writer's Country* (Prentice Hall, 2001). Currently, he is the Chair of the Writing, Literature and Foreign Language Department at Columbia Gorge Community College in Hood River, Oregon.

Acknowledgment

I am in debt to journalist Miles O'Brien for his excellent article in describing his own phantom limb syndrome after having had his arm amputated, and I would like to thank Serving House Books co-publisher Walter Cummins and other readers for their perspicacious comments. Without his close reading and suggestions, this book would be much less than it now is.

Made in the USA
San Bernardino, CA
23 August 2018